ARCADIA

ARCADIA

J. D. LYONS

There is no one on the road. He is walking on a sidewalk, going north. Always heading north on the road towards Mayfield. The sun is setting to his left, and except for the orange clouds there is no color. Then he hears Bogart's loud guttural purr. He feels Bogart's paws on his chest. He reaches out to caress the soft warm fur. With his eyes still closed he murmurs, "Morning, buddy." But there is nothing there. And his hand falls back empty onto the bedcover. Then he remembers. Bogart died decades ago. That was back in the days at Thornton.

1

The Call

ON A MUGGY May day in 1972, Greg walked to the Art History office to drop off some marked papers for his students to pick up. Walking over to Chapel Street he could feel the shirt sticking to his chest, an unwelcome harbinger of the New Haven summer. As he placed the large, sealed envelopes in his mailbox, he heard Grace call from inside her office.

"Gregory Byrne, get in here. I have news!"

He had been spending lots of time with Grace, going over the last formalities for the degree. Not only the many forms, but also the rules about the number of required copies of the approved dissertation, the kind of paper to use, the regulated margins and the signatures of the chair, the director of graduate studies, and the readers on the cover page.

This time, though, Grace looked cheerfully excited. It was clearly not about another formality.

"Professor Begemann wants you to know about a new

opening. You and Tom and Irene. He got a call from Thornton College in Vermont. They need to appoint someone at the last minute for the fall term."

Except for public occasions, everyone abbreviated Egbert Haverkamp-Begemann's name one way or another. The students simply called him "Eggy." The secretaries could not permit themselves that degree of informality when speaking of the director of graduate studies. Grace explained that Begemann expected a letter from the college with more details. There would be interviews scheduled in New York before the end of the month. The college was contacting the leading art history departments around the country. However, given that candidates would need to pay their own way to New York, it was likely that the Yale Ph.D.'s would be competing only against other new art historians from New England and the Middle Atlantic. And, of course, against one another, the three of them who were completing that year.

Later that day he spotted Irene in Sterling, in the main reading room where they usually worked. They decided to walk to Hungry Charlie's for a coffee to discuss this surprise. Irene was not easy to talk with, but Greg enjoyed the challenge. She did not put up with platitudes and bullshit. He never saw her relax. He wondered if she ever smiled. She was intense and expected everyone to match her laser-like focus. Even though she and Tom and Greg were at this moment competing for the tiny number of entry-level teaching positions in art history, they had learned over the years that it was better to cooperate. They had studied for the Ph.D. orals and writtens together, and, of course, they had worked as teaching assistants in the same courses.

"Sure, Thornton's a big deal. All that old-timey aura," Irene said. "But why would I want to be a prisoner in a men's college in the middle of nowhere? Prestige, you'll say. Why freeze my ass off in a place where no one gives a shit about what interests me?" She leaned forward for his answer, pressing him to justify this waste of time.

Thornton was now admitting women, he pointed out. Just like Dartmouth. And this was only two years after Yale. She and Greg had, in fact, taught art history to the very first classes of Yale women in fall 1969.

"Sure," she said, not at all satisfied. "But New Haven is not a remote village in the mountains with *no graduate school*, probably nothing resembling an art gallery, and a library like the one in my high school in West Pomfret."

"Wouldn't it be better than what we can scrape together here?" he asked. " At Southern Connecticut or Quinnipiac? Driving up I-91 to Middletown to teach two or three times a week? Or down to Fairfield? Or cataloguing in Sterling?"

He knew that Irene and Tom, like himself, had come up dry at the College Art Association meeting. Their teaching assistantships ended once they earned a degree. At that point Greg's personal plan B was to work as a paralegal in his uncle's firm in New Bedford.

"Why are you so eager to get me to apply? Will you expect an agent's fee if I get the job? Besides," she pointed out, "we haven't even seen the job description."

She was right about that, he thought. They had not seen the details.

He went to the department office each of the following days, for no other purpose than to find out if more news had come from Vermont. Greg realized he could have telephoned, but it was only a few blocks from the house on Park Street, and the walk calmed him and made him feel as if he were doing something to nudge the process forward. About 11 on

Friday morning he stuck his head in Grace's office door, and she waved him in.

"You can make a photocopy, if you like," she said. "I think you'll like what you see."

Grace and Janice, the other secretary, kept an eye on the department Xerox machine, strictly off-limits to graduate students. So this was a sign of special favor.

Grace knew the topics of the dissertations, and she understood right away that Tom and Greg would find the position description to their liking. Thornton wanted someone who focused on early modern European art and could also teach general introductory courses. Whoever was chosen should, in short, be capable to teach the courses assigned to the late Professor Volker Baum.

"It's too bad for Irene," said Grace. Grace did not like Irene, and she did little to disguise that fact from Greg. It was true, though, that with her dissertation on surrealist sculpture, Irene would be wasting her time if she followed up with Thornton.

With the photocopy of the position description in hand, Greg walked back toward the house. Damian was heading in the other direction, going to his studio in the new art building. Deeply absorbed in his thoughts, he passed Greg without even seeing him. Of Greg's seven housemates, Brother Damian was clearly the strangest, but perhaps also the most interesting. A Benedictine monk on leave from his monastery, he was also one of the few practicing artists Greg knew.

He took a photocopy of his CV from the folder, the one he used to write for the positions listed in the CAA job list. With a small bottle of white-out he covered over the parentheses and the date, thus modifying the line that read "Ph.D. 1972 (expected)." Once the sheet was photocopied the correction would be invisible. Which chapter of his dissertation should he send for the requested writing sample? He paged through his one remaining copy. Only the week before he had taken the required archival copies to the graduate school registrar in HGS, the Hall of Graduate Studies. Finally, he settled on the chapter "Implied Narrative in Poussin." He took the CV and sample chapter to Kinko's on Broadway. Fortunately, they were not busy and copied it while he waited. He had his cover letter and a large manila envelope, so that he was able to take the packet down Elm Street to the Yale Station post office. He addressed it to the search committee for Art History at Thornton College in Mayfield, Vermont.

For several days now he had been energized by the prospect of a real job that might suddenly be within reach. Now, as he walked out of the post office and past the nearby student café, the Buttery, he felt deflated. Having done all he could, he would just have to wait. To calm his nerves he continued strolling down Elm to the Green, then further south to Wooster Square—where the aromas of Sally's Apizza and Frank Pepe, the competing Neapolitan pizzerias, reminded him that in his excitement he had skipped lunch—then back up Chapel Street to Park. Once in the house, he went to his room to get a bottle of gin. It was Friday, and Greg could smell the eggplant and tomato sauce, heavy on the garlic, that Dan liked to put on haddock. Greg would go downstairs, make himself a gin and tonic, offer one to Dan, and sit and talk while the dinner cooked.

2

Brother Damian

G REG FOUND DAN in the kitchen, as expected, and Horst and Timothy were there as well, sitting at the little table on the side. They seemed excited and amused.

"Did you hear about Damian?" asked Dan, bursting with news and surely knowing that Greg didn't have a clue.

"He got decked!" said Timothy. "Right in front of me. At the front door."

The idea of a Benedictine monk in his early forties getting attacked clearly fascinated them all. From the jocular air of his housemates, Greg was sure that Damian had not been seriously hurt. He told them that he passed Damian about 2 o'clock near the art school, his usual self, deep in thought. So what had happened?

Timothy explained that he was in the living room around three fifteen. He heard Damian come in and start up the stairs. It was easy to recognize Damian's heavy, slow footsteps.

He never seemed in a hurry. He lived at a different pace from the rest of them. As Damian reached the top of the stairs, there was a knock on the inner door of the little vestibule that fronted Park Street. Damian was nearby, and he went down to the door and opened it. Timothy had been curious to see who was there and came to the door from the living room to the hallway. He saw a tall, muscular man in a dark blue Yale t-shirt looking angry. The man barked, "You Damian?" As soon as Damian said yes, the man punched him in the jaw. Damian fell back onto the stairs behind him. The man yelled, "Lay off my girl. Stop bothering her. Or I'll be back."

Neither Dan nor Horst nor Timothy had any idea what this was about. Horst had come out of his room when he heard a loud, angry voice, and together with Timothy got Damian to his feet. They told him that they would take him to student health. Timothy had his car nearby, but Damian just rubbed his jaw, said he'd be OK, and went up to his room.

Greg got some ice cubes from the fridge and made gin and tonics for all of them except Dan, who was already nursing a whiskey as he cooked. The housemates traded a few Damian stories. He was for all of them an eccentric, yet the others appeared to have no background with which to interpret the afternoon's scene. For them, the bizarre violence appeared to come out of nowhere. Greg immediately thought four years back, to the first time he heard Damian's name.

When Greg arrived for his first fall in graduate school, he felt lucky to find a place to stay so convenient to the campus. The old white wood-frame house was just across the street from Davenport College. It was an easy ten minute walk to Sterling Library and about the same to the art gallery. The building belonged to the Catholic chapel next door, More House, which planned to demolish it in a few years to make way for an ambitious expansion. Meanwhile, More House rented it to male graduate students. There was no expressed preference for Catholics, but during Greg's time there were several monks and lay brothers who roomed there, as well as a law student from Nigeria, Dan, the musicologist, several men in the French department, and an art historian from the Netherlands. Greg's room that first year was in some respects the least desirable. It was on the ground floor, on the front, separated from the street only by a narrow tree belt and the sidewalk. He thus lived, day and night, only a couple of feet above people passing by. He could hear people talking and arguing as they walked on the sidewalk. Sometimes laughter. Sometimes a scream. Trucks with the motors running during deliveries to the Davenport kitchen. The clang of barrels filled with cooking waste being loaded onto trucks from CoRenCo, the Consolidated Rendering Company. The siren of a truck leaving from the firehouse on the corner of Elm Street.

The office manager at More House, Mrs. De Vito, did not object to renters taking the initiative to paint their rooms (she would even pay for the paint), and that front room needed a coat of paint when Greg moved in two weeks before classes started.

One hot August day, Greg was standing on a borrowed step ladder with the windows and the door open for air as he painted the walls a pale yellow. From the radio came the melancholy sound of "Sitting on the dock of a bay," as he replenished the roller. He heard a voice behind him, an elderly man's voice, ask, "Do you know where Henry is? Henry Johnson?" Greg paused, put the roller in the paint tray and looked around. The man was thin and tall and had a straw hat. Despite the heat he was wearing a light blue sports coat. There was a much younger woman holding his right arm. She said to the man, "Dad, he's not Henry any more. He calls himself Damian now, remember?" The man frowned and did not seem pleased by the reminder. Then he corrected himself. "Do you know where Damian is?" Greg explained that he himself was just moving in, and that he did not know all of the others who lived in the building. He suggested that they knock on some of the other doors.

A few days later Greg met Damian in the kitchen. Damian was slightly shorter than Greg, with a build that conveyed solidity although he was not overweight—on the contrary. He never smiled and always wore well-washed blue jeans and a blue denim shirt. He looked as if he were a maintenance man sent to do some repairs in the house. In fact, he was rarely there. He spent most of his days, including evenings, in the art building, working in his space there, where he made sculptures, mostly in clay. It took some effort on Greg's part to get him to talk. Still, Greg found the effort worthwhile. Damian seemed like an apparition from another age. None of their talks were long. However, in the course of the months and then years Greg came to know a few basic facts about the monk's life.

He came to Yale from Saint Bernard's Abbey in Alabama. The abbey at that time had a college, where Damian, who had taken vows as a lay brother (that is, not as a priest) taught art. He came to the art school to prepare himself better as a teacher. His family was Protestant, and Damian had converted—much to his father's displeasure—to Roman Catholicism in his early teenage years. It was a radical move. Adolescents often rebel against their family, particularly when the family is well-off and established, as Greg knew from hagiographical sources, and Damian had gone to an extreme, becoming a Trappist, a member of what is officially known as the Order of Cistercians of the Strict Observance. Damian's description of the life confirmed what Greg had heard. It was a life of hard labor, silence, little to eat and especially no meat, strict separation from the outside world, and celibacy. Damian described living in wooden buildings so poorly insulated that the cold wind blew through the walls at night (yes, he assured a doubtful Greg, there are cold nights even in Alabama). Damian was the youngest in the monastery and was still growing, but he did not get the nutrition he would have had at home with his family. "It ruined my health," he said. And he never recovered. After a few years as a Trappist, he petitioned to move to the milder life of a Benedictine monastery.

From Greg's first contact with Damian, he had the impression that the artist lived in a different world. At first, this was simply a figurative expression, yet as the months passed, Greg realized that it was radically and literally true. Since the age of sixteen, Damian had lived in a world without women, and, especially during his first, impressionable teenage years, in an essentially medieval world. One day, when Greg was preparing a more elaborate dinner than usual for his tablemates, Damian inquired, "What's all the fuss?" Greg explained that he had invited his Italian tutor, a fellow graduate student, to dinner and wanted the meal to be perfect for her. It was unusual to see much expression on Damian's face, but at that moment he looked outraged. He struggled to control his voice as he told Greg, angrily, "A man cooking for a woman…that's against nature! That is just not right at all!" He turned and walked away, unwilling to be anywhere near such perversion.

For the second year, Greg moved up to a quieter room on the upper floor and at the back of the house. In addition to the bedroom, there was a little alcove with a sink and room for a dresser and a similar-sized closet that had a window painted over in a green so dark it looked black. On the other side of the bedroom was a door that had once led into the adjoining bedroom. Some previous resident had covered it in burlap and installed bookshelves on aluminum brackets. Instead of hearing street noises, he heard Horst's Rolling Stones. Greg knew when Horst was about to leave the house because he always played "Jumping Jack Flash" all the way to the end before opening his door. When Horst was particularly tense—probably because of an exam or a class presentation— he played the song twice in order to propel himself into the outside world. While Horst was reclusive spatially, Damian was reclusive in a different way. He simply retreated inward. He had learned well during his time as a Trappist to direct his mind toward spiritual things and to dwell in a mental cell.

Greg would encounter him in the kitchen, and after long periods of silence, Damian would make some comment about the sculpture he was working on. Damian told Greg about making portraits (heads or busts) of women he met around Yale. His models were never, as far as Greg knew, men. Damian admitted that he could not sculpt a woman without falling in love with her. In this way, he had remained the sixteen-year-old that he had been at the moment of embracing the ascetic life, except that now, in his forties, that pent-up, pulsating adolescent desire was resurgent in the midst of the late 1960s "sexual revolution."

One morning Damian mentioned to Greg that one of his fellow students, a woman whose studio space was near his, had declared her love for him. Greg asked when she had done that, and Damian replied that she had been doing so repeatedly for weeks.

"So, she just turned to you and said, 'Damian, I'm in love with you'?"

"No, of course not. She's an artist. She made me see it more powerfully and creatively."

Greg asked how she did it. Did she make busts of him? Or of them together? Or was she a painter?

"She leaves me messages. I'll show you the ones she left me yesterday."

Greg waited for him to go up to his room to get them, thinking that Damian would have them there. Damian just said, "Come on. You'll see," and started for the front door. When they had gone down the two steps to the sidewalk, he turned to the right.

"She knows the path I always take between here and the art building. So she puts them along the way for me to discover."

They walked about ten feet, and the monk stopped.

"See that?" he asked.

Greg had no idea where to look.

"It's right in front of you. What do you see?"

They were standing next to a tree. On the uneven concrete of the sidewalk was some trash.

"There's nothing here, Damian."

"You're looking right at it, but you just don't know how to read. Think visually! Think the way an artist thinks! You're supposed to be an art historian!"

The heel of a shoe lay on the cracked cement of the sidewalk next to the tree. Plus some loose gravel.

"What is the heel made out of?" asked Damian.

Greg bent over to look closer. The heel was not plastic, as he had expected.

"Wood," Greg said.

"Right! You've got half of it. But *where* is the wood?"

"On the sidewalk. Next to the tree. Near the road."

"Which of those elements is significant? Which offers the possibility of a comparison? Imagine this as a construction in a museum."

"Well, the heel is wood and the tree is wood. So what?"

"That's it! That's the message! There's *dead* wood next to *live* wood. She's telling me that I'm dead wood and that she is live wood. She is offering herself to me to restore me to life!"

Damian seemed completely in earnest. Greg never knew Damian to have a sense of humor.

"Damian, this means nothing. This is no message."

He told Greg that he would eventually understand. It was the cumulative and repeated effect of the messages that counted. Greg needed to see the context.

They went a bit further, past the row of one-story shops. Damian stopped next to a metal trash barrel that had a couple of pages torn from the newspaper lying next to it.

"You are going to say that these are just random pages, pieces of trash, but it's hard to deny the significance when you realize which section of the paper the pages are from. What section is it?"

Damian waited for Greg's answer with the look of a poker player with a royal flush.

It was the classified section of the paper—specifically the want ads.

"You see? She *wants* me! And the ads aren't all the same size. There's one in extra-large type. It just hits you in the face when you glance at it. What does it say?"

"It says," Greg read, "'Wanted. Screw press operator. No experience necessary. Will train.'"

The usually somber and impassive Damian looked suddenly ecstatic.

"It all fits! She desires me. To screw. And she knows I have no experience!"

There was a third "message" that he showed Greg. It was in a similar vein. If this had been anyone else, Greg would have enjoyed the joke. But it wasn't a joke. He thought back to the day when Damian had told him that his adolescence with the Trappists ruined his health. He apparently meant only his physical health, yet now it appeared to be more than that. Greg wondered if other people, besides Damian, could create whole stories almost out of nothing. Could so much meaning be distilled from the random events, from the scattered trash around us?

3

The Interview

TEN DAYS LATER Greg got a call inviting him to an interview in New York on May 23, at 2:30 in the afternoon at the Biltmore Hotel on 43rd Street. The location could not have been more perfect. It was right next to Grand Central, where his train from New Haven would arrive. Tom Zachetti was also being interviewed, just ahead of Greg. It was just as well that Tom planned to take an earlier train. If they had traveled together, thought Greg, their nerves would be on edge, and they would probably whip one another into a frenzy of anxiety.

And there was plenty of anxiety in the world to go around. The news about the war kept coming with depressing regularity. The Paris Peace talks had been suspended at the beginning of the month. The US was mining all the Vietnamese harbors. Closer to home, they were all devastated to hear that the Alitalia flight that was taking Giulia Rizzuto, one of his closest friends among the graduate students, home to Trapani, crashed into a mountain as it made its approach to Palermo. Two days later, though, as he got to the office, Grace, in tears, hugged him, and only slowly regained enough composure to tell him that Giulia was alive and well. She had missed the flight and had taken a ferry to get to the island. And then, only two days before the interview with Thornton, a man named Laszlo Toth attacked Michelangelo's *Pietà*, breaking off Mary's arm and a piece of her nose. He was screaming that he was Jesus Christ.

In the Biltmore, Greg asked at the reception for the party from Thornton College. The young woman told him the room number, 4163, and pointed to the bank of elevators. From comparing Tom's interview time with his, Greg understood that the interviews were at forty-five-minute intervals, and he assumed, correctly, that this allowed a discussion break between each candidate. He had arrived early and went right up to the floor indicated. There was a bench near the elevators, but he should make sure of the location of the room first. He turned left out of the elevator and went down a beige-carpeted corridor, past trays with plates covered with food scraps, crumbs, and crumpled napkins next to cups and coffee pots. He reached the door he was looking for and was about to turn away to go back and wait, when he heard from inside the room a woman's voice shouting, "You can never keep your fucking story straight!" This did not sound like a Thornton interview as Greg had imagined it, and he began to have doubts about the room number. He walked back to the elevators and went down to the lobby. The young woman at the desk did not hide her exasperation at having to tell him once more that it was room 4163, and not 4136. He felt a sudden chill and at the same time began to sweat as he power-walked his way back to the elevators and reascended. Once he found 4163, he went back a short distance to the bench near the elevator and sat looking through his notes, which trembled in his hand. Then he stared into space for a while and couldn't help thinking that Tom had a really good shot at the job. Greg knew that Tom was more outgoing, more sociable, and would make a really good impression. They knew each other well from working as teaching assistants, grading papers and exams together.

Greg was close enough to hear a door open and a man's voice say, "Thank you. We'll be in touch within two weeks." A few seconds later Tom came around the corner, red in the face and angry, and Greg was truly alarmed. Not just for Tom but for himself. How could a Thornton interview be so bad?

"Tom, what's up?" he asked. Tom didn't even look at Greg. Staring at the beige carpet he just kept repeating "That asshole! That *asshole!*"

"Who?" asked Greg.

"Elliot! This guy named Elliot. Obviously thinks he's some hot shit. He's older than the others. A real loudmouth. The others were pretty low-key. They asked me about teaching. Saw that I'd organized a conference. And then Elliot says, 'Tell us about your dissertation…' I was real happy to have a chance to talk about that. I had my five-minute version all set to go. It went great with Wesleyan at the CAA! So I was explaining how the inclusion of animals in portraits was used to characterize the person pictured when Elliot just cut in and said, really loud, 'That's ridiculous! You must be kidding!' and he started laughing, actually laughing…"

Tom was trembling with rage. Greg had never seen Tom look anything like that. And then the door opened, and a tall, thin man in a blue blazer looked at him and said, "Mr. Byrne? Come on in. We've been looking forward to meeting you."

At that, Tom took off, and Greg entered the hotel room. Five men were sitting in chairs along the wall to his right, and the tall man in the blazer, who introduced himself as Douglas Sykes, sat down on the edge of a bed in front of Greg and slightly to his left. Sykes motioned towards an easy chair not far from the door. As Greg sat down, the thick cushions yielded, and he found himself somehow trapped in the chair, his head lower than the men inspecting him. They were seated in nice, firm chairs. Sykes then introduced his colleagues, four of whom were from Art History and one, Elliot, from Humanities and Romance Languages. Sykes called him "Dean Elliot."

"Now, Mr. Byrne, you have excellent references from your Yale teachers, Crosby, Scully, and Thompson, and already at Brown, you obviously impressed Jordy (a friend of mine…). And so we're looking forward to our conversation with you. But, first of all, what interests you in Thornton? It's a quite different setting from New Haven and Providence."

The standard job search preparation had readied him for this. Avoiding vague laudatory statements about Thornton's "prestige" and "tradition," Greg launched into his concise yet minutely documented comments about the stimulation that he expected from his future colleagues, dropping references to some of their salient publications and not failing to mention the person whose untimely demise had created the opening for which he was applying. When he mentioned Volker Baum, he saw several exchange glances as if he had touched on a sore subject. At that point, Elliot said, "Now, tell us something about your dissertation."

Before encountering Tom, Greg had had no qualms about giving an enthusiastic account of his work on narrative painting in Baroque art. People he had spoken to generally found it interesting, which was not always the case for someone discussing art scholarship. He could feel his whole body tense up as he cringed before the sting of Elliot's expected ridicule. However, after mumbling the first words of his carefully prepared statement, Greg warmed to his subject. In this he was aided by Elliot's rapt gaze. The older man looked genuinely interested and began to smile—but perhaps, thought Greg, the smile was just a prelude to a belly laugh. When Greg reached the end of his carefully timed remarks (no more than five minutes), Elliot burst out with a loud "That's *fascinating!*" He turned to the others and said, "What do you say to *that?*" Then he asked a question about placing narrative painting into the context of literary narrative and then moved towards paintings in which characters were depicted in the moment of telling a story. Although there were a few questions from some of the others, especially from a stocky man who frowned at Greg and his own Thornton colleague Elliot—Elliot and Greg were carrying on as if they were sitting in a café having a lively and personal conversation. Then Sykes interrupted to say "We'll have to leave it at that for now." They had a tight interview schedule. Greg struggled out of the chair, grabbed his folder, and followed Sykes to the door.

"We'll be in touch within two weeks. Thanks so much for meeting with us today."

And that was it.

4

Leaving

WHEN THE PHONE rang outside Greg's room, he just turned over and tried to get back to sleep. The rain beating on the windows told him this was a day to sleep in. Then Horst was knocking at his door.

"Hey, Greg. It's for you. Someone at Thornton College."

Greg opened the door and sat on the old chipped oak office chair next to the filing cabinet that generations of residents had used for the shared house telephone. His heart was pounding. Surely they would not telephone to say that they had *not* chosen him?

"Mr. Byrne," began the speaker. It was a man's voice that he did not recognize. "This is Bill Stout at Thornton. As Dean of the Faculty, I'm calling to let you know that the search committee for Art History has made it clear that you are their first choice for our assistant professor opening. I hope that this is welcome news to you."

Greg felt his whole body relax, letting go of the tautness

that had become so familiar he did not even think about it. Now, all at once, a warm softness swept through him. Then he remembered that it was his turn to say something.

"Yes—yes, I'm very happy to hear that."

"Of course," continued Stout, "you will want to see the details of the offer, which has already been mailed to you. Given that this appointment has come up unexpectedly and that we need to fill the position for the September term, we are asking for your response, one way or another, in ten days. Does that seem reasonable?"

Greg agreed. After Stout made some remarks about the committee's enthusiasm, the call was over.

The letter arrived two days later, very official looking. The seal of Thornton College was visible both in the expensive stationery's watermark and printed at the top, with the Latin motto, *Vox gaudentis in silentio.* His appointment was laid out in minute contractual detail. Greg would be appointed as assistant professor for a term of three years, at an annual salary of $10,000, provided that he complete his Ph.D. by July 1. He had already done that, so much of the rest of the letter did not apply (the part about being named instructor for two years at a salary of $9,500). In any event, Thornton would give him $500 to move to Mayfield. There was other boilerplate about the college's calendar, the "Thornton Plan," laid out in four academic quarters, including the summer. Faculty would be committed to teaching in three of those quarters. They could take the traditional summer vacation or take their vacation in any of the other quarters, depending, of course, on the approval of their department.

Greg wrote and mailed the letter that same day. Although he knew it was silly, almost paranoid, to do so (just in case the mail was somehow interrupted or the letter got lost), he telephoned Dean Stout's office to say that he had accepted and that the letter was on its way.

In the evening, Greg, Dan, and Timothy went down to the Taft Tap Room for drinks—on Greg—and then to Sally's for a celebratory meal in the pizza capital of the hemisphere. They continued onward to Jack's Bar near the waterfront where they had had many a late evening, back past the Gant New Haven shirt factory near Wooster Square and up Chapel Street to Park. Even as they walked, though, Greg could feel the melancholy begin to take hold. He had loved New Haven, the city that just about everyone pooh-poohed, the city from which people wanted to flee to New York whenever they could. But in New Haven Greg had had fun times and good friends and great teachers. He had met and loved two wonderful women. He had seen moving performances at the Yale Rep and at the Long Wharf. Picnics on East Rock. Moments of discovery in Sterling and Beinecke looking through old books and manuscripts. And his department, like many there, had cast a spell that made it seem that this place was the center of the known world.

Soon two other letters came from Mayfield and gave him a slightly queasy feeling, a little like seasickness, the feeling that New Haven was slipping out from under him or that he was being sucked away, like Dorothy in the *Wizard of Oz,* by a mighty wind taking him to a foreign, almost unimaginable place. One of the letters was from the Thornton College Bookstore, a routine form letter requesting his book orders, both titles and quantities. The other was from Jean Buxton, the department secretary, who wrote that she could put together the photocopied readings for both courses, but he must get her the documents to copy as soon as possible.

Jean's letter set his heart racing. He would need to have

the whole syllabus set up to tell her what the reading selections were. The book orders would be easier because he would still have time to indicate which pages absolutely required reading. So for the moment he could just return the order form to Jean with the titles, asking her to get the quantities from Douglas Sykes and then send them on to the bookstore. Greg felt sure that he would have a freer hand with his advanced course, but what he chose for the introductory course, Art History 1, had to correspond to the vague general description in the catalog: "Study of fundamental visual principles and historical problems in the arts as exemplified in works from all periods in art history." This was one that several faculty members taught in rotation, and he was not sure what was expected. Was there a standard text? If so, that would save him a lot of work. He decided to call Jean. He went out to the communal phone just outside his door in the hallway. He got her right away, and she did not hesitate about the answer.

"I run off all the syllabi, and I know that just about everyone uses something different. There's no standard textbook. If you wait a minute, I can pull the folder from the spring."

Greg waited for a minute, hearing a classical music station playing in the background.

"OK, Greg. Here it is. There's one called *Introduction to the Visual Arts* by Baqué and Sauboa. Emily uses it. I know that Douglas used it the year before but didn't like it. He switched to *Art and its Objects* by someone named Wollheim. Tony Jones used *The Visual Dialogue* by Knobler, and I see he's reordering it for the next time he teaches. So you see, Greg, you can decide. You could go with any one of these, but if you have something else you like, go with it. But be sure that we have the order before the end of July. Earlier is better. Anything else I can help with? No? But get me the readings soon, OK? It's quiet here now, but the closer we get to September, the crazier it will be here in the office."

Greg recognized two of the titles. He had a copy of the Wollheim and used it to prepare some of his discussion sections for "Topics in Art History." Yet, why not go with the book that was most inspiring for him as a freshman? So he went with Bates Lowry's *The Visual Experience*. It was conceptual (line, light and dark, color, objects in space) but used examples from across all periods (limited to Europe except for a few from Amerindian art), and Greg could supplement it with the photocopied readings.

The other course would be easier since it was the "Introduction to Renaissance and Baroque Art" (AR 55). At least, he thought it would be easier, but the more Greg worked on it, the more he realized that it presented exactly the opposite challenge for him from AH 1. The problem was that there was so much to share with the students. Besides, art books were so absurdly expensive that he did not want to choose books that the students could not afford and would not buy. Even though Thornton, like Yale, enrolled many students from the wealthy, white east-coast élite, some students would not come from that group. He decided that as textbooks to purchase, he would select the Murrays' *The Art of the Renaissance* and Bazin's *Baroque and Rococo Art*, both well-illustrated and in paperback. Then, he could put the Renaissance volume of Hauser's *Social History of Art* on reserve, along with Hartt's *Italian Renaissance Art*, Sypher's *Four Stages of Renaissance Style*, and a few others.

It was strange to be sitting in the room where he had been a student these past five years, now having to think from an entirely different angle.

The house was mostly empty. It was hot. He missed Horst's daily blasts of "Jumping Jack Flash" from the room next door. The place was quiet as a tomb. It was a relief to get away for a week at his friend Bill's house on Cape Cod. Then, in the ten days before moving out, Greg made a deliberate attempt to photograph those parts of the city, especially lower Chapel Street, that he was sure would soon be destroyed as part of the aggressive urban "renewal" program. He went through twelve rolls of Ektachrome on his Pentax. He already felt the loss of a world he had glimpsed in its last moments.

5

The New Volker Baum

AS ASSISTANT PROFESSOR Gregory Byrne, he was now to take the place of Professor Volker Baum.

On a sunny and not too humid mid-August day, Greg closed the door of the house on Park Street, handed the keys to Mrs. De Vito, and with trepidation, pulled the UHaul truck out from its parking space into the stream of traffic. He turned onto the infamous Oak Street connector and merged into Interstate 91.

The route through Hartford, Springfield, and White River Junction got him to his new home in five hours, including a stop for lunch in Windsor, Vermont. As the habitual driver of a VW Beetle, Greg felt some pride in handling this big box on wheels. And he was grateful that his friend Dan had agreed to drive Greg's car to Mayfield. Greg did not want to push his luck driving the truck, and he saw Dan sail past him before they got to Springfield. Pulling into Hubbard Drive in the faculty housing development next to the Mayfield golf course, he found Dan sitting on the porch of his new neighbors, Susan and Alex Lean, enjoying a beer and nachos.

After opening the door of his new house and setting down his backpack and one suitcase, Greg changed his shirt and went over to join them. Susan, a Wellesley graduate, was staying at home with their first child, John. Alex, who, like Greg, had done his graduate studies at Yale, was writing his dissertation on classical Chinese literature and teaching the language at Thornton. These were the first Thornton people Greg had met outside the circle of people who had interviewed and hired him, and he was happy to be in such a welcoming company.

Dan and he got recommendations for places to eat, then went off to unload the boxes of books destined for his new office in Thornton Hall. Jean was on vacation, but she had sent Greg keys to Thornton Hall and to his office. Eight boxes of books, four flights of stairs (no elevator), two men. They were happy to drive, now in the VW, to the Riverside Grill for two cheeseburgers each, plus fries. They limited themselves to two beers because he wanted no dents, scratches, or worse on the rental vehicle as they drove back to the empty house to sleep.

After a night in sleeping bags and breakfast at the hospitable Leans, they unloaded the rest of the books, clothes, lamps, a rug, kitchen stuff, his portable Olivetti typewriter, a work table, and other sundries. By one in the afternoon, they were ready to drive to Montpelier, with Greg still in the truck and Dan following. They crossed the Lemon Fair River, located the service station that was also the UHaul agency, and left the truck. Greg drove Dan to his parents' house in Bernardston, Massachusetts, and then returned to Mayfield alone. When he got there, he was eager to settle into his first office and drove directly to Thornton Hall. The boxes of his books were there, but he had not paused to look around.

There was no ceremony to install him, yet that space was the most tangible manifestation of his new status. It was a place to hang the diploma. It was the place where students would come and address him as "Professor Byrne." Students are not fussy about the distinctions of assistant, associate, and full. His Yale mentor, Howard Gary, had once told him, "Greg, you're only a few years older than the students. Just be sure you always wear a tie and a jacket, and they'll think you're forty years old."

Now he was standing there, enjoying his privilege—the diploma reminded him that he was now entitled to *privilegia*—though he had no idea what these privileges were, other than to receive the alumni magazine and requests for donations.

Jean had told him that Volker Baum's widow had taken away her husband's letters, papers, and personal effects but had left his books on the shelves. Jean and Douglas thought it best to leave the books for Greg. He appreciated the good and generous gesture since it instantly gave him a scholarly library easily worth two thousand dollars at the low end. Art history books, lavishly illustrated, were unspeakably expensive. He used to envy his friends in English or French literature who could get by on small paperbacks.

There was still enough shelf space for his own books. After opening a couple of boxes, he wondered whether he should try to figure out Baum's organization and integrate his collection with Baum's or keep his own separate. Greg's system, such as it was, involved classification by historical period, subdivided by media (such as architecture and urbanism, statuary, and painting), and, in some cases, further subdivided by genre. So, for painting, he separated portraits (*ritrattistica*) from landscapes, religious art, and narrative painting. It was far from a perfect system, and Greg realized that anyone would be hard-pressed to locate a book in someone else's library. This last consideration made him decide against blending his books with Baum's since it would take much time and effort to investigate Baum's logic, and Greg needed to get the boxes emptied before classes started in less than three weeks.

After unpacking four boxes, he took a break to sit at the desk and admire the view. Amazingly, for a new assistant professor, his was a corner office on the southwest corner of the building. This meant he had two windows, one looking west over the Mayfield Green and the other towards nearby Amos Allen Hall, home of Religious Studies. His new friend Alex Lean had his office and classroom just on the other side of Amos Allen, in Fayerweather, where the language laboratory was also located.

Yet it was the view of the Green that was the prize. Anyone with this view had a good chance of knowing about everything that happened at Thornton and most of what happened in the town. The four roads bordering the Green carried all the traffic moving north and south, east and west as it passed through this center. The small white wood shingled kiosk on the east side of the Green was clearly something set up for the summer and autumn tourist season and would be taken down once the foliage vanished in November. Cars going north pulled over onto the shoulder to pick up maps, guidebooks, and postcards and to get advice before traveling further up the valley. People coming up the slope from the river on the west would pass in front of the Thornton Inn as they drove to one of the two supermarkets in town or might turn, just before the Inn, onto Main Street. Professor Baum, a long-time resident, would no doubt have been able to recognize his colleagues' cars as they drove from place to place.

Mrs. Baum had indeed cleared out the drawers. All that was left were some old college catalogs, course schedules (quaintly called "timetables of recitations"), and Thornton College letterhead with the college crest and the motto *Vox gaudentis in silentio.*

At Thornton people knew that Greg had been appointed at the last minute to take the place of Volker Baum, and people would often say things, with different tonalities, about this fact. "You're the new Volker Baum?" was a question that put a cheerful spin on the situation. "Well, we're lucky to have found someone to take poor Volker's place" was more wistful. And then some people emphasized the shock of his death: "It's so hard to understand what happened! So sudden! So sad for Ruth!" From all sides Greg gathered scraps that he tried in vain to assemble into a picture of his predecessor.

Greg felt that he had a strangely ghoulish relationship to Volker Baum. Sometimes, he even felt like a grave robber. Baum's death had made the appointment possible, and yet Greg knew virtually nothing about the man. Strange, since he was supposedly in his own field, late Renaissance and Baroque art.

After his interview at the Biltmore, he had done a diligent bibliographic search to see what Baum had published. It did not amount to much. When Greg was hired, it had been impressed upon him that to have any chance at all for a permanent, tenured, position, Greg would have to get a book published at a major academic press. And not only a book—there would also have to be several well-placed articles. And yet Volker Baum had not only held a tenured position, he had made it to full professor without a book, and his articles, appearing slowly over the years, appeared in a hodge-podge of almost perversely obscure journals in such places as Finland, Australia, the Netherlands, East Germany, the Hungarian Academy of Sciences, the Romanian Art History Institute, and several small hard to find journals.

On arrival in Mayfield, Greg found that everybody, with only a handful of exceptions, had positive and heartfelt things to say about Volker Baum and Ruth. He had been a beloved teacher, a generous and easy-going colleague, active not only in the college community but also in promoting the study of art in high schools throughout the state. He visited high schools from the south, near the Massachusetts border, to the "Northeast Kingdom" contiguous with Canada. The Baum's had had only one child, a son, Bernhard, who had died in Vietnam in 1966. This affected both parents deeply but in different ways. According to Doug Sykes, Volker dragged himself to class only with the greatest of efforts for the first two years after his son's death. Then, on the surface, he appeared to return to his cheerful former self, though some felt that it was only a performance, only a façade. Ruth had always been active in her Catholic parish, Saint Isidore, and struck her friends as courageous, resigned, and hopeful of another life.

No one knew much about Volker's death, and Greg heard the same details from the few people who touched on the subject. Volker had gone to Rome to give a paper on Bernini and was staying at the American Academy on the Janiculum. Since he was on leave for the spring quarter, he stayed on after the conference. His room at the Academy was in the back, away from the busy Via Giacomo Medici, and it had a mini-fridge. People mentioned this detail only because of the awful accident. Apparently, he had chilled a bottle of Prosecco. Was he expecting a visitor? Or did he plan to drink the wine by himself? Most people thought this unlikely. He was found by the woman who came to clean his room. He was lying on the floor in a pool of blood. The police investigation concluded that he had fallen while holding the bottle of wine and that a shard from the bottle had pierced his heart, killing him instantly. His body had been brought back to Mayfield, and he was buried there in Oakcroft cemetery.

The outcome of the investigation by the *questura* satisfied most people, but neither Charlie Woodruff nor Beatrice Matteoli thought it was an open and shut case.

"Why would Volker stumble in an ordinary room?" asked Beatrice. "What would he trip over, and if the police think that he fell, what would cause a healthy man to fall over—and to fall *forward*?"

Charlie added, "If Volker was ill, wouldn't the autopsy have shown some other cause of death or contributing cause, like a heart attack? And why would Volker have a chilled bottle of Prosecco in his hands? Was he expecting a visitor? Or was he preparing to go to someone else's room or outside the Academy to a meal at someone's dwelling?"

Beatrice further developed this objection. "They found Volker wearing a dress shirt, slacks, shoes, and no tie. Volker was always very carefully, even perhaps too formally dressed. He would have worn a blazer if he planned to go outside the Academy."

"But," said Charlie, "If Volker had expected a visitor in his room, it had to have been someone from inside the Academy compound, since it is impossible to get past the entry gate without being a resident, an employee, or someone on a list of announced and approved visitors. If Volker had invited someone, he would have been required to leave a name with the *portiere*, and there was no such name—the police at least bothered to learn that much."

Greg himself thought of another flaw in the official account. He noted that "Prosecco is a bubbly wine, like Champagne. So they make the bottle heavier and stronger than bottles for still wine because of the pressure. So I don't see how it could possibly have shattered just from being dropped on the floor, even if Volker fell on it."

"The Italian police just don't want to get involved and do work if it's in an American institution," said Beatrice. "They figure that if the Americans want to get serious, the consulate will find other investigators."

On one of the days before classes started—the students were already arriving for freshmen advising—Greg was in the department mailroom to photocopy some handouts for his AH 1 class. He had seen that photocopier use was much more permissible here at Thornton, and then, of course, he was a faculty member and no longer simply a graduate student. He had only done a few copies before the paper ran out. Usually there were reams of copy paper next to the Xerox, but the supply was all gone. He went to the main office next door, where Jean would know what to do. She said, "No problem. I'll bring some more paper." Greg went back to the machine. Only a few seconds later, Jean walked into the room carrying with ease a fifty-pound box of paper.

He couldn't help staring as she effortlessly placed the box beside the machine. Jean glanced at him and said simply, "Lacrosse." What did that mean? Was it a brand of paper?

Jean laughed, "Lots of people think I swim or play basketball, but I was on the lacrosse team."

It made sense. She was tall, slim, and strong. She could run the office efficiently while taking time to chat. It occurred to him that she would be a good person to ask about Volker Baum. She told him that Volker was a great guy to work with. Not demanding, always polite. Came in early most days and got some coffee from the office machine—in fact, sometimes he even brewed it himself.

"I was really shaken up when I heard what happened to him. The Mag did a beautiful obituary, though. If you'd like to read it, I have it in my desk." The Mag, as Greg now knew, was what people called the *Mayfield American-Gazette*.

Volker T. Baum, 57, professor of Art History at Thornton College, died in a tragic accident while at a conference in Rome. Professor Baum was born in Königsberg, East Prussia, Germany (now Kaliningrad, Russia), in 1915 to Torsten Manfred Baum and Elsie Rosenfeld Baum. He had completed most of the requirements for the Ph.D. in Art History at the University of Königsberg when the Second World War broke out. Although he had been baptized as a Catholic, because his mother was Jewish Baum risked death if he were to be conscripted and then discovered to have "non-Aryan blood," so he was kept hidden. His family let it be believed that he was away for his military service. Baum fled with his parents in 1945 during the Battle of Königsberg, and in the chaotic flight from the advancing Red Army, Baum was separated from his parents, whom he never saw again. He was befriended by a GI from Wisconsin who succeeded in getting Baum to the U.S., where he was legally adopted. A quick learner, he soon had enough English to qualify for a scholarship at the University of Wisconsin at Madison, where he obtained his doctorate in only two further years of study. In 1949, he was appointed assistant professor at Thornton College and was promoted to associate professor in 1956. In that year, he married Ruth Whelan, who had been his student in Wisconsin. They had one child, Bernhard, who died in 1966. Professor Baum is survived by his wife, Ruth.

6

Fall Quarter 1972

AFTER THE EUPHORIA of settling in, having his own private office, being able to structure the discussions, to determine the emphasis of a course (within the broad parameters of the approved course description), to give instructions for the students' essays, and to set the questions for the midterm and final exams—after those first moments Greg began to have a sobering sense of his changed status. Now, many little things—the brusqueness of his senior colleagues, the lack of guidance and orientation about how things were done, the always implied view of the people around him that it was up to him to stop asking so many stupid questions and just figure it out like an adult—these things told him plainly that Thornton was *not about him*. He was no longer a coddled graduate student. He had switched sides. Suppose he was having a bad day; that was his problem. He could ask for guidance, but no one had much time to give him. He was an adult professional. The job that he felt so privileged to get was a probationary one. If supervising him was costing his colleagues and the administration more effort than they were getting from him, he would soon be looking for another job.

It did not help matters that he inherited a feud between several members of the senior faculty in art history. One of them, Frank Kellenberger, did not want Baum to be replaced by someone in the same field and would have preferred the appointment of someone in museology. Greg did not disagree, of course, that the systematic study of museums, collections, and all forms of institutional framing of "art" was necessary. On the other hand, he was not the one who had decided against that appointment. Another full professor, Tony Jones, just hated the guts of Bill Farrington, who also had a degree from Yale. And then there was Kenman, a slick and surprisingly crude individual. Greg could not figure him out but suspected that under the bonhomie, Kenman was not to be trusted.

In the bigger picture, the department had been lucky to get him—not specifically *him*, but someone in a tenure-tracked line. As Greg had heard, the position (the "slot") would be swept back into the pool of faculty lines with Baum's death. Departments circled like sharks whenever they sensed that a tenured member of the college faculty was seriously ill, about to retire, or thinking of taking a job elsewhere. There were a few "anchored" positions or endowed chairs belonging to disciplines, but most were fungible. They could be given to the department that made the most noise, could point to rising trends in enrollment, happened to be in fashion in any given year, was on the cutting edge, etc. The department chairs who played tennis or skied together one day could deploy the most vicious tactics to snatch a faculty line from one another the next day.

"So why me?" he asked himself. Why a twenty-five-year-old with no publications, no prior ties to Thornton, and (as he saw with hindsight) no sophistication in marketing himself?

The answer came to him in one word: women. In Truffaut's film, *Day for Night*, he recalled, one of the main characters goes around asking people, *Est-ce que les femmes sont magiques?* For Greg, they were magic enough to land him a job. In planning for the arrival of the first women freshmen at Thornton, the task force preparing for this controversial and momentous change—a task force actually called "WD-72" (for women day 1972)—wrangled for months to figure out what women would want to study. Art history was at the top of the list, followed by English, French, and Drama. This was why Douglas Sykes, the chairman of Art History, was way out in front when it came to snagging a line.

It did not hurt that Greg was cheap. Douglas was smart enough not to push for a big name, someone already tenured elsewhere, with several books and maybe even a Guggenheim Fellowship. After all, Greg's salary was $10,000 a year. And, of course, in keeping with solid Thornton tradition, the deans and the trustees must have noted with approval that he was, as they used to say, "pale, male, and Yale."

Douglas had made a good bet, as Greg soon realized. For not much money, Greg gave the department enrollment a big boost. At his first class, "Introduction to Visual Arts" (AH 1), in the Hunter House building, one-third of the students were incoming women. Class size was 42% higher than in the previous fall. Not only did many freshmen women enroll, but some of the more alert male students who had never come near an art history course saw a terrific opportunity to meet women. By the second fall, fully half of the class consisted of women, some newly arrived and some in their sophomore year.

Some nights, as he lay awake worrying about everything, he would try to calculate the return that Thornton made by hiring him. Taking $10,000 and dividing by the number of women students, or by the total number of students, or by his hourly contact with students….And he always fell asleep before he could come to any solution.

He found it both wonderful and terrifying to be a teacher. There he was at the lectern, in AH 1, signaling the student assistant to change the slides on the two screens in the proper sequence while trying to speak conversationally without completely losing his place in his written text. He was more relaxed in the advanced class. It was a seminar-style course on Baroque art. The students arranged their movable seats in two concentric rows while he sat at a small table. For this course, there was no assistant to run the slides, and Greg had to do it himself with a single Carrousel projector, listening to the circular slide holder click clunkily back and forth to locate another photo to make comparisons. He knew the material here and did not have as much work to prepare. Nonetheless, the class session required self-control. He needed to stick to the highlights, even if it meant making generalizations and simplifications that sounded unbearable to him when the students repeated them. Still, he knew that it was what they needed to know at that point in their learning.

"Basically," Tony Jones said to him, "we teach them a lot of largely false things in the hope that they will take a further course so that we can help them unlearn those embarrass-ing approximations."

Then, there were things about dealing with students that no one had warned him about. In graduate school, they do not teach how to set up an office. Greg learned that his initial impulse had been wrong. His idea was to make the student feel relaxed and at home. A conversation was the ideal. So he placed a chair for a visitor next to his own chair, stressing equality. They could put a book or a student paper on the desk and look at it together. He remembered sitting that way at Brown in Professor Downing's office in one of the little wood-frame houses on Thayer Street that Brown used as office space.

But one day, something happened to give him a different perspective. Edith de Murga, one of the freshmen, came to talk about her paper in AH 1. Not that it was a bad paper by any means. He had encouraged her to see him to talk about how to make a B+ paper even better. He read her a couple of sentences and pointed out that the references were unclear in context. She was leaning towards him but then stood up, put her left hand on the back of his chair and then nonchalantly leaned over him. Her blue-jeaned knee was on the armrest, rubbing slightly against the tweed of his jacket, and her long brown hair fell against the right side of his face. All at once, he scented floral shampoo, the damp wool of her sweater, and the Vermont woods. She pointed to the paragraph they were discussing and said something to explain what she meant. He was so flustered by the situation he needed to invent an awkward question, rather than simply asking her to repeat, because in truth he had no idea what she had said.

She was certainly unaware of her effect on him. She would have done the same, leaning over her dad to look at a story in the newspaper. Yet, suppose someone had poked a head into his office just then. Or suppose Edith and he suddenly thought of how cozy it felt. Or suppose he had been less full of the zeal of the new teacher that he was…

By the next week, the office furniture had been rearranged. Jean and he took care of it in less than fifteen minutes.

Even though he must now squeeze around the right-hand side of the desk to get to his chair, the desk separated him from all visitors, just like the bank counter separated the teller from the client. They were henceforth face-to-face, and whatever was on the desk could be rotated, if necessary, for the student to see.

And then there was marking papers. It was new, that sensation of having a power that could bring pain or elation with a few words or even with one. It was true that as a teaching assistant, he commented on passages and wrote a summary comment. He would put a suggested grade next to the student's name to hand over with the papers to the professor who was the instructor of record. It reassured him that the final determination would be made by someone else, someone more experienced. Now, however, Greg constantly reminded himself that any remark he made about what he was reading had an entirely different valence from the same comment made to a student in his discussion section in New Haven. On one hand, this made him feel important and powerful. On the other hand, it worried him that something he tossed off in the heat of discussion could become lodged in a student's memory as dogma. So, in this way, he felt more inhibited than before.

7

Hidden Hostilities

GREG HAD BEEN around universities long enough to know that departments incubate tensions. He could remember, back at Yale, two senior members of his department, sitting alone at separate tables in the original George and Harry's on York Street, drinking their beer and pretending not to see the other one a few feet away. Yet, as a newcomer to Thornton, his perception only gradually adapted to detecting what was not being said. There were smiles, and then there were other smiles. Each type manifested something different, and to initiates this was clear, often stingingly clear—or reassuringly, depending on the case. During that first September, he thought everyone was glad he was there.

Yet by late October, he realized that Frank Kellenberger's friendly greetings told him that he was a piece of shit, Emily Latouraine's conveyed dismissive tolerance, and Lorna Wilder's reassured him of her compassion for a fellow sufferer, while Bill Farrington's were utterly opaque. Since he did not know these people during those first months, Greg's smiles were courteous expressions of his earnest desire to fit in. He must have appeared obsequious and idiotically naïve, and that was precisely what he was. Yet that was not *all* he was because day after day, he felt the joy of sharing what he loved with students, exploring the slides for illustrating lectures, and reading. The Chandler Library was generally not bad, and several departed faculty members, like Francis Crowley, Owen Daniels, Richard Cote, and Volker, had worked with the acquisitions librarians to grow the collection in the fields that interested them. This was one form of creativity that had not occurred to him as a graduate student. Like the glacial ice that had carved and polished the Vermont hills, the tiny increments of their shared scholarly activity were shaping Thornton. There was a museum, Hunter House, that Jay Curran worked tirelessly to expand. In the long, tense, wordy, and boring department committee meetings, they gave form to their discipline by deciding what the students saw, read, discussed, and wrote. But like the glaciers grinding against the granite, this shaping was quiet, hidden, and violent.

For Greg, the most vivid example of the deceptive nature of the human interactions around him took place in front of the department office. A young man better dressed than students usually were, with a blue blazer and dressy slacks—presumably a recent graduate returning to campus—came up the stairs. Seeing Justin Kenman, whose back was to him, the young man walked in Kenman's direction and called out, "Justin!" (Kenman made sure that all his students called him by his first name.) Kenman turned around with a look of ecstasy, opened his arms, threw himself on the visitor, and roared, "You're back! How wonderful to see you again! I was just wondering how you were doing since I last saw you! My man! We had such great times together!"

The former student was beaming that Kenman had recognized and remembered him so clearly. And the performance continued. "How is that great job going?"

"Well, most of us don't think of the Marines as a job."

"But it *is!*" said Kenman. "It's the very best job! I knew that you had what it takes. One look at you and I *knew*. I said to myself, 'There's a Marine.'"

Greg wondered if Kenman had any idea who the young man was but was inclined to give him the benefit of the doubt—at that first performance. Yet after the first half dozen times, he realized that Kenman had a way (as politicians do) of generating a cloud of uncertainty around any interaction, allowing the interlocutor to interpret whatever Kenman said in the most personal, even intimate, way.

A couple of weeks later, in Perkins Center, where Greg sometimes went to get a quick lunch, he overheard a couple of male students with hockey team shirts talking about Kenman's course "Kenosis." One was enrolled in that course and said to the other "Man, I mean you really gotta take it. Kenny's a blast! It's like not a real course. Sometimes it hurts, I laugh so loud. And it's a guaranteed A. No sweat." The other one asked what it was about. It had, he pointed out, a weird name. "Yeah, it's like 'no, sis!' and 'Ken oasis'" the first one said. "It's Greek, but I think he put his own name into the title with the 'Ken' part. But you don't really have to understand. There's no reading or homework. He explains what you do, and it's sort of like..., like that party game where you act out a word and people have to guess, except it's in reverse, because you know the answer first."

As the fall quarter neared its end, Greg found a

photocopied sheet in his mailbox reminding him that all members of the department were invited to "help out" with the training of the STAR team for the winter quarter. "We all know this is a **true breakthrough**, and it will mean a *lot* to Thornton's best!" It was signed by Justin Kenman. Greg tossed the note about the STAR training into the trash bin because whatever it was, it was obviously unrelated to him. Similar sheets were in all the mailboxes, so whoever was involved in this project would understand and respond. Yet on the following Saturday morning, his friend Wanda telephoned him to ask why he wasn't at the workshop. Greg was immediately flooded with a guilty feeling of having screwed up. There was great urgency and concern in her voice.

"Lorna, what workshop? Whatever it is, I completely missed it!"

"It's the Kenman thing. They really expect you to be here. We all have to attend—it's a big, big deal!"

"No one told me," he protested.

"Yes! We all got the notice in our mail to come to the STAR thing. Maybe you didn't get told at your interview, but Kenman is a big media guy, and the trustees eat out of his hand. It's not written down anywhere, but he'll consider you an enemy if you don't show up. You already have one mark against you, so you don't need any more trouble."

"What's the mark against me?"

"You're from Yale. And Sykes is from Yale, and Kenman *hates* Sykes. We're on coffee break right now. It's in Franklin. Try to get yourself here ASAP and say you overslept."

The VW would not start. There was a cold snap, and the battery did not make it. Friends had told him that he needed to put a block heater in the motor and plug it in at night, but he put that on a list of things to do after the final exams. So there he was, making his way as fast as possible on sidewalks slippery with leaves until he got to Franklin Hall. When he arrived, sweaty and red-faced from the cold and the effort, the last stragglers were returning from the coffee break to the medium-sized auditorium. There were a couple of dozen students and about a dozen junior faculty members. The only tenured members of the department present were Emily Latouraine and Kenman himself. The great man, creator of the STAR method, was up on the stage with three students. Greg had just entered and hoped no one saw him hovering near the door.

Projected on a screen above them was a photo of Caravaggio's "Flagellation of Christ." The student in the middle was holding his hands behind him, as if they were tied, and he was leaning to his left. Greg realized this was some weird pantomime, some parlor game, where the students tried replicating the posture of the three figures in the painting. What was the point?

Kenman was tugging on the arms of the student on the right side of the stage, who seemed to be pretending to secure the "Christ" student to an imaginary pilar.

"Use real muscle! Go on! You're not trying to be nice to this guy you hate! After all, you are planning to kill him later. Think of how you feel!"

So Kenman was trying to teach some form of method acting, but what did it have to do with Caravaggio? While Kenman was busy rearranging the students into the configuration he found most like the painting—a jumble of male bodies all somewhat unstable—Greg moved down the side aisle and slipped into a seat next to Wanda.

"What's going on?" he asked in a whisper.

"Just watch. It's the method."

Kenman turned to the audience and asked the seated students, "How does that make you feel?"

No one really wanted to answer, so Kenman pointed to a woman student with long blonde hair. "You, Nancy, how does this make *you* feel?"

"Um…I'm Alison," she said.

"*Of course!* Alison, my love! How could I forget! So what does this make you feel?"

After a moment, Alison volunteered, "I feel as if Caravaggio was really into…you know, bondage and stuff, and naked guys."

There were guffaws all around, and Kenman beamed. Yet he did not relent.

"But how would it make you feel, Alison, honey?"

"Pretty yucky! I would want to get the fuck outta there!"

"So you're identifying with the Christ. And they're getting to beat the…the dickens out of him, right? Now you can see how we'll get everyone at Thornton hooked on art! It's not just a picture! It's an *experience!*"

Kenman then explained to the students in the audience that by the end of the workshop, they would be ready to run art "experience sessions" for all of the AH courses. This was the heart of the STAR program, "Student Teachers as Art Resource."

Greg could see his colleagues' sheer boredom. As far as he could tell, they had absolutely no role in this except to admire Kenman and applaud occasionally. As the afternoon dragged on, other students got up to pose in imitation of different paintings. Finally, mercifully, it was over, and he, Wanda, and a few others headed to the taproom in the basement of the Mayfield Inn for drinks.

"That is so unbelievably bogus!" said someone, and there was a chorus of "bogus, bogus, bogus!"

"Why do people put up with it?" asked Greg. "We're art historians! We're not here to play charades and other party games with the students."

"It's obvious that you're new here," someone said. "No one wants to be on Kenman's bad side. Even though he has only one vote on personnel decisions, he can lean on some of the other senior faculty. And he's not above bad-mouthing people right in front of students."

"But who is Kenman, really?" asked Greg. "I know he's a full professor in our department, but he doesn't seem to attend Art History meetings."

"He's got a joint appointment with Education, but from what I've heard, he doesn't go to any meetings unless he's got some particular proposal to push or somebody's tenure decision is coming up. He presents himself to all the world like a loveable buffoon, but he's a viper," said Lorna. "You'd better watch out."

8

Thornton Night

I N DAYLIGHT, THE Mayfield Green was the epitome of a New England tradition of simple, practical organization, avoiding excessive ornamentation in favor of rational, practical planning. The pattern was familiar. As an undergraduate at Brown, during his frequent trips to Boston, if the weather was good, he enjoyed reading on the Common or strolling around to watch children playing and families taking rides in the swan boats. During his years in graduate school, Greg had crossed the New Haven Green several times a week and enjoyed the space as a meeting ground between town and gown. These places reminded him of the layout of the *bastides* in southern France. Even though churches were sometimes located on one edge of a green, this central place resisted the pull of the mystical. It was a clear, tranquil, and reassuring place.

But, as Greg discovered during his first fall there, on one night a year, at least, the Mayfield Green was something quite other than rational.

"On this sacred night that you will forever remember, we are gathered in the place towards which the thoughts of multitudes are turned. Yes, present with us in spirit are Thorntonites from all over the globe. Thorntonites in Brisbane, in Berlin, in Buenos Aires, in Dublin, Dubai, and Rome, in Nairobi, Hong Kong, and Cape Town."

The words of the small man at the podium on the slope in front of Thornton Hall reverberated from the buildings across the Green. The words seemed to come *through* him. It was not only an effect of the PA system. It was as if the body of this compact and ordinary man had been invaded by a spook, by something scary and unhuman that had taken possession of the figure dressed in a black business suit, a white shirt, and a white tie. The body belonged to Edward Constable Adams, the Librarian of the College. Somehow, for a reason unknown to Greg, he was also the chief custodian of the sacred flame. Yes, the *sacred* flame. This was not a metaphor. Next to Adams, shielded from the breeze in a glass receptacle on a long pole, was the "Undying Flame." It was kept in a tiny but important granite building, the "Involucrum," located between Roberts Chapel and Elias Moss Hall, and there were a substantial number of legends about students who had flunked out of college or met horrible ends because they had joked about the flame or showed disrespect to the Involucrum, such as vomiting on its wall after a night of carousing.

"… who does not wish to be here in this most sacred of places? A place chosen by higher powers to nurture the leaders of the world? At Thornton, at our home, in our bastion…" Adams continued in this vein, seeming at times to be on the verge of tears, moved by the hypnotic urgency of his own voice.

This was Greg's first time seeing this event, but he had

read much about it. For weeks, *Thornton Today* had been running articles about the origin and history of what had once been called "the night of the bonfire." According to legend, the founder of the college, the Reverend Wellman Thornton, had been saved from starvation by charitable Native Americans (called Indians) when the small plot of land planted by the Reverend and his thirty students failed to produce adequate sustenance. Although the strict Calvinist was troubled by what appeared to him a pagan ritual, he did not have the heart to discourage his friendly neighbors when they urged upon him a large fire of rejoicing and gratitude to the "Great Spirit."

The large pile of wood—mostly old railroad ties—stacked in a hexagonal tower had not yet been lit. Floodlights illuminated the officiant and the base of the pile. Thornton Hall itself was always illuminated from dusk to midnight. Now, the light was reflected from the faces, almost all white, of the many hundreds of people gathered on either side of the pile as they faced the orator, who was reading a series of messages.

"...now from the Thornton Club of Greater London: 'Old Thornton will always be in our hearts....'" I'm sorry that I cannot read the message in full, because it suggests doing something quite distasteful to our colleagues over in Hanover."

The crowd roared with approval, and some even came out with "Fuck Dartmouth!"

"And from our faithful brothers in Oslo, 'The Viking spirit and the Thornton spirit are one! Long live the College on the Hill! Skol!'"

Applause filled the night.

"And from Paris, from *le Club Thornton*, this Gallic blessing, '*Que nos années magiques à Thornton vivent pour toujours dans nos cœurs. Vos frères de Lutèce.*'"

Adams's French pronunciation sounded convincing.

This litany continued for a long while, and the crowd was getting impatient. They were also stone cold. Greg himself was probably the coldest of them because he did not yet know to buy boots large enough for extra layers of socks. The high priest of the cult of Thornton was in no hurry. He *wanted* them to be impatient and cold. It was not enough for them to be curious to see the bonfire—that would be too passive. They had to yearn for it. They had to need it. They had to be desperate for it. They had to see in the bonfire the sign of their salvation, just as those first starving students clustered around Wellman Thornton had *seen the light*, the light that was at the heart of Thornton.

"And from our brothers in Tokyo…"

At this point the crowd could take it no longer.

Bon*fire!* Bon*fire!* Bon*fire!* Bon*fire!* Bon*fire!* Bon*fire!* Bon*FIRE!!!*

The orator had been waiting for this. Edward Constable Adams interrupted his litany, grasping the wand with the flame at its tip. He then strode down the slope and crossed College Street. There was a sudden silence.

Greg could no longer see Adams, but he knew that he must be at the base of the stack of wood, hidden from his sight by the throng. Suddenly all the electric lights went out. It was totally black.

Then there were some muffled voices from near the stack of wood, and then Adams's voice, amazingly loud and clear, given that he no longer had the amplification of his microphone at the podium: "Thornton FOREVER! The MEN of Thornton FOREVER!"

The crowd took up the cry as the first glimmer of fire appeared over the heads of those between Greg and the wood.

"He's so full of bullshit!"

It was a woman's voice right behind Greg. She wasn't speaking loud enough for most people to hear her, and he realized that this remark was meant for him alone. Greg turned and saw a woman's face. At first, he did not know who she was, but he realized it was Clara Marsh, one of the women who worked in the interlibrary loan office in Chandler Library.

"I mean, like, it's 1972. The 'men' of Thornton. Fuck that!"

She was now so close that Greg could feel the warmth of her breath on his cheek. Clearly, she recognized him. He was already a big user of interlibrary loan. And Clara, the junior assistant, was the person who most often helped him.

"Can you imagine having to work with *him* as my boss?"

She stopped talking. The roar of the crowd was now deafening as the flames licked up the sides of the hexagon, illuminating all the faces, ruddy with cold. It was magic. It was primitive. It could have been a thousand years before in some village in Germany, France, or England. And it was scary. Only a couple of hundred years before, less than two hundred miles away, enthusiastic Calvinists had hanged "witches" caught up in a group hysteria like this. He could feel himself yielding…

"Let's get out of here, Greg. Let's go get a drink somewhere."

Clara took his arm, and they walked through the edges of the throng toward the Wellman Road side of the Green and onto the sidewalk. Within a couple of hundred steps, the streets were deserted, but the streetlamps were lit. She led Greg towards one of the few establishments not closed for Thornton Night: the Green Lantern, a bar-restaurant.

"Just so you'll know, Greg, since you're new, no one ever calls this place 'The Green Lantern.' It's universally referred to as 'the Green Latrine' or simply 'the Latrine.' But the drinks are safe."

Once they settled into a booth—the place was almost deserted, everyone was out watching the antics—Clara told him that one of the pleasures of her job was the chance to observe the faculty with an anthropologist's eye. She majored in sociology as an undergraduate before earning her master's in library science.

"I remain an amateur sociologist. I can see the patterns in the sociology of knowledge by observing what library patrons request through the interlibrary loan office. There are trends, some short-lived and others long-term, that show no signs of letting up. Some faculty members started preparing for the arrival of women students, for example, and books about women in history, art, the economy, and so forth are massively requested. The permanent collection is still far behind since Thornton didn't even seem to admit that women existed until about six years ago. I can also see the differences among individuals. Like, in your department, there's Bill Farrington, who requests *lots* of books and articles about women as patrons of art, in thematics, and as artists. And then there's Frank Kellenberger, who never, ever, tries to update himself."

"What about Kenman?"

"I've heard of him, of course, but he never enters the library. As far as I can tell, he has his autonomous operation, basically using Thornton as a reassuring backdrop for launching his brand of…whatever it is. I've seen photos of him posing in front of Chandler because the library is one of the most imposing buildings."

"And Baum?"

"Volker was really interesting. I could never tell how it all fit together. There was lots about Poussin and various books about other painters of that period. And there were books and articles about French diplomacy. Yet there were just weird things that didn't seem to relate. Like, a book by Johannes Trithemius called *Steganographia*. It sticks in my memory because the word is strange, and it was hard for us to get a microfilm of the book. I looked a bit into Trithemius, and it seemed the only thing he had in common with Volker was that they were both German. Trithemius was a fifteenth-century Benedictine monk suspected of being a magician. What did that have to do with Baroque art or with Poussin? This was just one of the strange, unrelated things that Baum asked us to get."

"Do you still have the microfilm?"

"No, we only paid for a rental. If you ever really *need* it, we can get it again. Still, remember that our interlibrary budget is not unlimited."

Greg walked Clara back to her place, and as he walked home, he thought he understood why Volker had not published much. He was a dilettante whose curiosity kept sending him down interesting paths that led nowhere.

9

The Topos

THE SMOKEY SMELL lingered in the air for several days after Thornton Night, though the magic had vanished from the Green. Front-loaders scraped up the wood ash that the Mayfield volunteer fire department had thoroughly doused.

The work of teaching shifted into overdrive just as the students' interest in learning shifted into neutral. To get everything done by the looming Christmas recess would be a challenge. Even keeping the students awake was a challenge. He sometimes thought that no one should be allowed to begin college until they had worked for ten years, but the legal system in the first years of the 1970s worked perversely to make the most reluctant male student cling to his educational deferment. As long as the Vietnam War kept male students in dread of being drafted, staying enrolled was, for many of them, a matter of life or death.

Pushing away from his desk, Greg walked down the four

flights of stairs and left Thornton Hall through one of the back doors on the side opposite the Green. It was a bright autumn day, and although most of the colorful leaves had fallen, the orange, red, and purple remnant was still worthy of a painting by Aldro Hibbard.

His steps took him toward a unique thorntonesque place, aptly named just that, but in Greek. The Topos (sometimes called *Kalos Topos*) was a forested clearing, a basin of wooded terrain with large granite outcroppings ranging from four to twenty feet tall. It was a roughly circular space, accessible only from one end by a broad sandy path. Just opposite that path, five or six hundred feet away, was a large flat boulder that offered a natural platform or stage. At the top of the slope behind this stage was a tall circular stone tower with a conical slate roof. It looked like a replica of the round towers found on the western coast of Ireland.

The place looked, except for the tower, entirely natural, a survival of the primeval forests of New England. Standing there, it seemed that roads, buildings, shops, parking lots, and all such recent human interventions must be either thousands of miles or thousands of years away. And yet, as Greg knew well, right behind these slopes lay the college power plant, a large staff parking lot, the impoundment lot for vehicles towed by the campus police, and several buildings for faculty and student housing. The Topos was maintained, to the point of obsession, by crews from Buildings and Grounds so that it would always look precisely thus. An ideal, romanticized image of "the wild."

This was the core of Thornton's identity. The northernmost outpost of learning, a place of purity, challenge, manliness, a place for the tough, the exceptional. All the students knew they would one day be the leaders of commerce, industry, and government. They would be different from those men and (as they now grudgingly admitted) women who surrounded them in the city life. The four years at Thornton would transform them. They were here as in the wilderness, to which their forebears had come at the risk of their lives. And the wilderness must remain the wilderness.

It embodied the romanticism of Longfellow, Thoreau, John Greenleaf Whittier, and—further back—even Rousseau. It emerged from the colonial myth of an empty land, a *vacuum domicilium*, a place that was theirs for the Puritans to fill and use. The Topos was kept as a relic of this imagined emptiness. It was also an exquisitely sustained artifice, a performance of the natural, an idyllic dream.

10

Ruth Baum

NOT UNTIL DECEMBER of that first autumn in Mayfield did Greg meet Volker Baum's widow, Ruth. She had been away for the summer, staying with friends in Italy, somewhere in the north. The Baums liked the region near Turin. It had become a kind of second home for them, especially because Volker's birthplace, East Prussia, had been wiped off the map.

Just as the exam period was ending, she called him to ask if he would like to come for tea. He wanted to meet her, though he feared that the reminder of the circumstances of his arrival would upset her. In the event, she seemed to find his presence a comfort.

Although the house was not a long walk from his office—that is, from Volker's former office—just three blocks uphill along Moss Street, and then, after a right into Okrent Lane, about a half mile—it was not a part of Mayfield that he knew. The houses were more stately than those along Main Street or Prospect Street near campus. It was easy to identify the Baums' beautiful, rambling, cedar-shingle bungalow with a large screened porch. He knew she painted, and a substantial addition on the back must be Ruth Baum's studio. As he approached, he saw wood smoke coming from the top of the traditional New England central chimney.

When Ruth opened the door and greeted him with a warm smile, he felt at ease—not only at ease but somehow attracted to her as a woman despite the significant difference in age. She was petite and white-haired but moved as if she were much younger. It was her face, however, that fascinated him. Her smile was authentic, mobile, and warm, and the effect was almost hypnotic.

The living room was a masterpiece of orderly disorder. Books were in bookcases, on tables, on one of the two easy chairs, and in a pile next to the passageway to the dining room. Paintings occupied almost all the wall space not taken by the bookcases. Oriental rugs were in the living room, the hallway, and the dining room.

She had him sit in the living room on the chair not covered with books, and then she went to the kitchen. He heard the sounds of plates and spoons in the background while he looked at the paintings, all signed "RB" in the bottom right corner. Mostly, these were portraits, and he even recognized some of the faces as faculty colleagues of his the way they must have looked in younger days. There were a few still lifes and only one landscape, a view of the Topos in autumn.

"My larger paintings are in my studio behind the house. I'll take you to see them later, if you like. Art was what brought Volker and me together, but we approached it from different angles, he as a scholar and me as a painter. I wouldn't have had the courage to pursue painting seriously without him. He was a marvelously encouraging teacher and a generous man."

She set the tray with the tea service on the low table and poured them each a cup.

"I didn't even think to ask you if you like Earl Grey. So thoughtless… Is it OK?"

"My favorite," he replied. "I always take Earl Grey, perhaps out of laziness, because I'm not sophisticated when it comes to tea."

"I'm sorry I wasn't here when you gave your lecture. Everyone tells me it was marvelous, new, intriguing. I've heard that from faculty members like Gino Cashman and some of the students of Volker's who are still around."

"That's very kind of you," he said. He felt it would be nice to say something about Volker, but he had found only a few of his articles and bibliographical listings of others to which he had no access. On that basis, he couldn't formulate a comment that would be concrete and even remotely convincing. The books, that was the best he could come up with.

"From the rich collection of books in his office, I can see we have so much in common."

That was undoubtedly true. They ranged widely in the northern and southern Baroque, and in the latter, more in Italy than in Iberia or its colonies.

"Volker would have loved having you as a younger colleague! He was sometimes a bit lonely here in his specialty."

They both avoided talking about Volker's accident.

So, instead, he asked if he could see more of her paintings. This was not merely a polite gesture. From the sample in the living room, it was clear that she felt a real attachment to her subjects, the fruit of an intense but playful gaze.

"There are many that I can show you, but some that I

can't because a number of my models are still at Thornton or nearby, and I feel a duty of discretion. You see, I love the challenge of painting the human form."

They walked through the kitchen, out a side door, and through a breezeway to the small board and batten studio building. They were in a large, open room with skylights on the north side of the gable roof and only one or two other windows on the north wall. A door led to something else. There were many large paintings on the walls, mainly on the windowless south side. It was like a gallery, with a long narrow table and an easel, a few cabinets and stools in cheerful disarray. The pungent smell of paint and thinner was a reminder that Ruth was still working.

The pictures were of nude or semi-clothed models. Several were of the same lovely woman at different ages. Her long brown hair fell over her bare shoulders in what seemed to be the earliest one. She wore nothing above the waist, and her faded blue jeans were unbuttoned and unzipped just enough to reveal a tuft of light brown pubic hair. Her face was relaxed but serious as if lost in thought.

"Yes, who can take their eyes off her? And even now, in her sixties, she's gorgeous. Haven't you met Mary yet?"

Greg admitted that he had not, though he knew that Mary McCullough, wife of the dean for the sciences, was supposed to be amazingly beautiful.

"You'll recognize her at once at some reception or other. And here is the most recent I've done of her."

Ruth guided him down the wall toward a painting of the same woman. She had long silver hair, was fully unclothed, and was in a three-quarters profile. She was still slim and toned, though with softer curves.

"This was only last year. All the young men at Thornton

are in her thrall—not to mention some of the new women students!"

There were also male models, all of them young, some of whom looked like college athletes and some like working men.

"I'd like to paint you some time," said Ruth. "In any pose you'd like.

He demurred on the question of posing—he was flattered, of course, but intimidated and somewhat worried about what he would be letting himself in for. But he did say that he would like to *watch* her paint. Despite being an art historian, he was a mediocre painter at best, and he enjoyed seeing truly skilled people at work. It was like watching a dancer or a top-flight athlete. He did so wish to have reasons to return to the house on Okrent Lane.

11

The House on Welldon Street

THE WINTER QUARTER of his first year at Thornton was already nearing its end—time was flying. Greg had been so busy coping week to week that he could scarcely keep track of the shifts from quarter to quarter. Everyone, however, sensed the relief that was settling in among the male undergraduates now that the U.S. had finally extricated itself from the war in Vietnam. On that mid-February weekend, he would have Susan, Alex, and Susan's friend Dinah to dinner at his place. He had been across the street to their place countless times to eat and had finally gotten one of his chicken casserole dishes perfected enough to invite them. There was also something to celebrate; it was a somewhat sad occasion for Greg but happy for them. They had just closed on a house of their own and would be moving out of the little faculty cottage at the beginning of summer.

"You know, Greg," said Susan, "there is something that would be great for you, too. Jim and Nancy Hagarty (she's in Econ) are going to put their house on the market, but they'd prefer to sell direct. They offered it to us, but we wanted something bigger. It's a fabulous house, really near campus and Main Street, and if you act before they sign with a broker, you can get it for $40,000."

Dinah also knew the house on Welldon Street. She cat-sat for Jim and Nancy and described it in detail: the three bedrooms, small kitchen (no breakfast nook), screened back porch, living room, dining room, and detached garage. The little lot had a bonus: It backed onto the Otter Brook natural area, which had been bequeathed to the town by Angelo Accorsi, a now legendary grocer known in his day for the kegs he sold to the fraternities.

Greg objected that even at forty thousand, it was way over his head.

"Didn't they tell you about the Hinman loans? That's usually one of the things they push when they're telling you how great Thornton is. Their mortgages are always below market, and the way real estate is going, you'll come out ahead in time whether you stay there or sell."

Susan was the one with the financial smarts. A few years later, she got her MBA and launched a successful career in hospital administration. Fortunately, she enjoyed helping the clueless.

"I'll call my friend Dorothy in the treasurer's office. She can explain it all to you."

When he went to see the Hagarty place, Greg found that it was indeed in excellent condition. He decided at once to make the largest purchase of his life. The Hagartys and Greg signed all the papers for the sale at a small office in the Thornton

Savings Bank, which issued the mortgage. James and Nancy walked away with the check to deposit on the other side of the lobby in the Thornton National Bank. Greg walked away with his deed and arranged to move into the house in mid-July.

For the moment, Greg decided he would not need to repaint any of the walls, but there were a few essentials to purchase. A set of bookcases, a dining table (he had been using a folding card table in his rented place), and a real stereo system. On a Saturday trip to Burlington, he went to Pier One, found the table, and bought six matching walnut-veneer bookcases. When they were placed side-by-side in the downstairs bedroom that would serve as his study they would look almost as if they were built in. For the sound system, he headed to Tech HiFi ("Quality Components at the Right Price"). The two young men who ran the store turned out to be two hippie offspring of Thornton faculty members. One of them had even grown up on Welldon Street. They had shoulder-length hair and big handle-bar mustaches. Their ample nylon shirts and bell-bottom slacks gave the store a distinctly different vibe from the RadioShack a few streets away. They addressed him as "dude" and "brother" while explaining in eye-glazing detail the benefits and drawbacks of each turntable model, cassette tape deck, tuner-amplifier, and speaker, including the woofers and subwoofers. When Greg described his house, they suggested a Kenwood amplifier that could power two separate sets of speakers, so if he placed the amplifier with the turntable in the living room, he could run cables under the floor to the dining room and set up two smaller speakers there. Smaller was important so the sound would not overwhelm the tiny room.

And so it came about that in August 1973, only a year after moving from his room in the small white house on Park Street, that Gregory Byrne was well established in his new home on Welldon Street.

But he was not the sole resident for long.

As Greg began that second year at Thornton, there came a glorious autumn, the brief time of year in Vermont with all the splendor that compensated in advance for the rigors of the following winter. Since the house abutted Otter Creak, Greg could head out his back door, traverse the Shugart's back yard—thus avoiding the steep slope behind his house—and take the path into the nature area. In those first months of living on Welldon Street, he got into the habit of rising early and taking a brisk walk along the creek, returning ruddy-cheeked and hungry for breakfast. The last week in September or the first week in October was the apogee of Mayfield splendor. That was when the foliage was at its most vivid, and people prayed that it would not rain until mid-October. A rain would knock the leaves off and spoil everything.

So it was a risky and gutsy thing for John Wren in the Drama department to schedule a student performance in the Thornton Topos for that first October Saturday. Greg sat on one of the folding chairs set up in front of the sizeable glaciated granite boulder that appeared destined by nature to serve as a stage. It was smooth and level on top for a lateral width of about fifteen feet. One of his favorite students, Steve Santana, was playing the role of Schweizerkas in an abridged adaptation of Brecht's *Mother Courage and her Children*. The whole natural theatre was ablaze with the gold and red of a Vermont autumn—no need here for artfully constructed stage sets. The boulders formed a perfect stage and backdrop, and for this production a certain realism was imparted by having a goat and a couple of chickens next to the actors. The goat was tethered, but the chickens were wandering around, pecking at feed that had been scattered for them.

About twenty minutes into the play, a titter ran through the audience. At first, Greg had no idea what was funny, but then he noticed a small black and white cat peeking from behind a clump of tall grass at the same level as the stage. It was staring intently at the chickens. This captured the attention of the audience. People were wondering when the cat was going to pounce. The student players realized something was happening and attempted to shoo the interloper away. But they didn't want to interrupt their lines and eventually resigned themselves to the cat's being part of the scenery. The cat did not leap at a chicken but wandered away down the rocks, reappearing among the spectators. Greg saw it jump into the lap of a woman student at the end of his row. She must have been a cat lover because she made no move to remove the visitor when it settled in her lap.

Greg got absorbed once again in the stage action and forgot about the cat, until he felt something land on his own lap. It was the cat, which had seemingly decided to explore all its options for lounging. It looked up into his face for a bit, then turned in a circle several times before settling into a ball and falling asleep. Greg could not resist resting his hand on its furry little back, but at his touch, the cat yawned, stretched out its forepaws, and closed its eyes again.

When the play ended, he carried the cat out of the crowd, not wanting it to be trampled. He set it down near some bushes at the edge of the clearing. He wished he could do more for it. He thought for a moment about asking one of the performers if the cat had indeed been brought as a stage prop but then decided that their reactions had shown no recognition of the animal and even a particular annoyance. So he left it there next to the woods and took the path that led from the Topos toward Thornton Hall. There, he would pick up his satchel and head home. But no sooner had he gone thirty feet than the cat appeared *in front of him.* It must have found a shortcut through the trees and was now looking at him with its tail up. Greg squatted down to pet it, and it made a soft mewing sound before jumping onto his knee and, from there, in a flash, onto his shoulder.

They arrived half an hour later at his house. He carried the cat across the dangerous streets and then let it walk along with him. It showed no inclination to leave him but instead acted as if they had agreed to go to the same destination. Sometimes, it ran ahead, then sat down on the sidewalk and waited before getting up and walking forward again with Greg. When he opened the door, it walked inside without hesitation and started exploring. It clearly knew what a kitchen was, because he found it sitting in front of the fridge waiting for him to feed it.

In the following days he tried everything he could think of to identify an owner. He contacted the SPCA, read the classified ads in the *Mayfield American-Gazette,* and even phoned in a small "cat found" ad. Greg's neighbor Marilyn Shugart suggested that some student might have moved away and left the young cat to fend for itself. By the end of the week, Bogart had a litter box, a cat carrier, a name, and an appointment with Alcott Snow, the Mayfield veterinarian, for an examination and vaccinations.

The little cat did not seem to mind the name Bogart—he proved to be a movie lover. He would press himself against Greg's side when he watched films on television in the smallest of the three bedrooms, which served as library and media room. He looked particularly handsome with his shiny red collar. Among the many epithets he earned in those first months was that of "writing coach" because he liked to stretch out on Greg's oak writing table. He did not comment while Greg wrote and did not read what Greg scrawled in black ink on yellow legal pads, but he did walk across the written pages and liked to sleep on the pile of those that Greg had torn off the pad and laid nearby.

Mornings, after breakfast, Bogart made it clear that he wanted Greg to go to his study to write. Greg liked the company. Writing was, for him at least, a lonely activity, but it now became less lonely. He would sometimes ask, "Bogart, how am I going to fix this?" Bogart would look at Greg with apparent understanding, and although he didn't say anything, he would put his head down on his paw as if to take the time to think about it.

Greg could now understand why so many cultures believed in beneficent spirits that inhabited and, in a sense, animated dwellings—the Roman *Lares* or *penates* or Germanic *Kobold*. Bogart gave presence to the dwelling; he guaranteed that the place would never be empty. Once Bogart was there, coming home rose to the status of an event. And when Greg went out, there was someone to miss him and to look forward to his return. Greg felt meaningful because Bogart found the tiniest thing he did worth watching. If Greg put down a book, Bogart would come to check it out and rub his head on it. If Greg lay a shirt on the low counter next to the bathtub, Bogart would jump up and sniff it and then often warm it up for him by lying on it until Greg came out of the shower to put it on. Bogart observed Greg cooking. Surely he was hoping for something good that he could eat, but instead of showing up at the moment when Greg was about to serve, Bogart's eyes followed with deep appreciation all the preparatory gestures.

It was clear that they would make good housemates.

12

Drew's Lunch

REW'S LUNCH WAS the hub of Mayfield. It was a lunch place with stools at the low counter and booths along the wall opposite. Breakfast was served from 6 AM and throughout the day, but lunch items began to appear around 11. Business peaked towards 1, and Drew's closed at 3, except for ice cream in the summer, when cones and cups were available from a window on the sidewalk during the long, warm, and humid evenings. You could tell when Drew's was open for business when the blue awning extended over the sidewalk in front. There were no tables or seats outside.

Greg quickly got into the Mayfield habit of treating Drew's as an extension of his office. He often strolled over at lunchtime, sometimes with a colleague. There were other places to eat at noon, of course. Perkins Center had a small cafeteria in the midst of the art and theatre studios. Students generally had meal contracts with the Thornton Dining

Association, and so they ate in a large refectory near the grave-yard that sloped down towards Hubbard Brook, a tributary of the Lemon Fair river, but those who found themselves working on a stage set for a new student production or in a studio making jewelry or painting or sculpting could at the end of the morning use their TDA account in Perkins. For some reason, Greg always felt lonely eating at one of the little tables in Perkins. On the other hand, at Drew's, if he went alone, he would often find someone else sitting by himself—or more rarely herself—who welcomed company. The randomness of these encounters often led to new insights, such as when Jared Williams, a young classicist, changed Greg's idea of life in the Middle Ages, or at least during the decline of the Roman Empire.

As a typical product of the simplified political thought of the late sixties and early seventies, Greg viewed the feudal system as a barbaric system of oppression by a warrior class exploiting peasants. Jared explained to him that for the peasants, the presence of a professional fighter, accompanied by his armed subordinates, was an advantage, even a necessity, during invasions by Germanic peoples from the east at a time of widespread lawlessness as Roman institutions began collapsing. "You have it backwards, Greg," he told me. "The owner of a villa would try to persuade a strongman to take up residence in exchange for a large share of the harvest and of the produce of their herds. They would have security, a framework in which it was in the strongman's interest to keep the peace so that he would have food, textiles, and artisanal products. The local inhabitants would not fear slaughter by marauders passing through who just grabbed everything in sight and thought nothing of killing people and burning down their homes." Was Jared right? Greg did not know, but he felt that he had something important to think about as he ate a chicken salad sandwich.

Another time, Greg had a conversation that came closer to home. One rainy day during that warming known as the January thaw during Greg's second winter in Mayfield, he ducked into Drew's for lunch and found the counter fully occupied and no booth free. As he looked around, a corpulent balding man motioned to Greg from a booth, offering him a spot. The man introduced himself as Bob Wadsworth. Greg knew the name from advertisements on the local radio. Every morning, Greg woke to his clock radio, and among the lines drilled into his drowsy brain was, "Call Wadsworth, and don't worry about a thing!" He was an insurance agent who sold life, property and liability insurance, and annuities. Of course, he quickly told Greg that he could improve his financial situation with some of the products he carried. With astonishing rapidity, he pulled a business card out of his pocket and put it on the paper placemat in front of Greg. "I'm sure we have a product for you, my man!" This was the first time Greg had heard an insurance policy referred to as a "product." Given that Thornton College offered many such "products" in the form of group policies, however, Wadsworth fairly soon dropped the sales talk. Evidently, he resented the population of faculty members who were largely beyond his reach. Without using the word "parasite" he managed to convey his view that they were an unproductive lot of next to no use for society. Greg countered that, even from a strictly economic perspective, the college towns of New England stood out for their prosperity and for all the employment opportunities they offered. Then Wadsworth took direct aim at people like Greg.

"The thing about people like you is that you never grow

up. You're always just learning things. You look at everything from umpteen different angles, and you are trying to interest people in things that *enrich* their lives—that's what you say, right? You tell them that poetry is great."

Here, Wadsworth threw his hands into the air and waved them around. Was it meant to show that poetry was just a lot of wind?

"You say they should go to plays, ballets, concerts. That they should study macroeconomics and microeconomics and women's studies. *Women's* studies! What kind of a living can anyone earn with that? And you, what's your thing, anyway?"

His interlocutor paused with a forkful of mashed potatoes held suspensefully in midair as he waited for Greg to come up with something laughable.

Greg told him "art history" without going into further detail.

"So you spend your whole life just learning about art. Do you even *produce* art? Do you make stuff you can *sell* in a gallery?"

"No," he said, "but if people buy art, it's probably because they took a course with someone like me and developed a taste for certain kinds of beauty. They learned to understand and also developed some enthusiasm for art."

"*That's exactly right!*" Wadsworth said with an emphatic stab of his fork into the meatloaf. "You people are *enthusiasts*. You love to learn new things. You go from one new thing to another. You never really settle down and grow up. You know who's interested in new things? You know who finds every-thing interesting, even their big toe? It's kids. It's children. You people, you Ph.D.'s are just stuck in childhood. I see you all around Thornton with that rosy glow of childhood. I meet white-haired guys who tell me they have just discovered a *passion* for learning Greek! I mean, for Christ's sake, isn't that pathetic? What's he going to do with that?"

Greg couldn't help laughing.

"Bob, you just made the case *for* what I do. The college should put you on TV. Just think of what it would sound like: *Never get old! Learn Greek! Understand the calculus that you could never master when you were 19!* Why do you think that real estate in college towns costs so much? You sell homeowners insurance here in Mayfield. The old man with his Greek is probably one of your clients."

Wadsworth admitted that much. But he still had another line of attack.

"OK, OK. Sure, he started learning Greek at—what?—something like 72? But the guy I was talking about was *retired*. He did something productive with his life. After that, he can have a second childhood. I don't care about that."

"So what do you care about?" asked Greg.

"I care about—well, not really much of anything. Actually, I couldn't give a flying fuck. But it bothers me that you people spend your whole lives on this stuff. I mean you start out, as kids, just curious and playing and learning about things, and then you just keep on. You never stop and say to yourself: now I gotta work. You never settle down and just go into the office or wherever and do what you need to do as a mature person. Which is, as a real grown-up, that you don't do it because you are having fun doing it. You do it because it's what you don't *like* to do."

"So, Bob, according to you, if I didn't like teaching, it would be work. And that would make me an adult, right?"

"I suppose. But when I meet one of you, they are full of this *enthusiasm*. Am I enthusiastic about life insurance? Who could ever believe that? And in fact, I could never get anyone to buy a policy from me if they thought I was doing it because *I* liked it. They would not take me seriously. They need to see that I'm just doing my job."

This continued until it was time for them both to return and do their jobs.

He could see Bob's point, and he felt sad. They both needed to earn a living, and they both did things that their "customers" found beneficial. Yet Greg had the luxury of finding joy in everyday challenges. He did not dislike Bob, and maybe there was something about insurance that was intrinsically mortiferous. Greg thought of Kafka. He thought of Wallace Stevens. He thought of Charles Ives. They had worked for insurance companies and apparently needed to flee into something that brought them joy.

Could Greg ever help Bob Wadsworth to find joy?

13

"We don't need Byrne!"

I T WAS ONE of those sunny, dry February days during Greg's second winter at the college—one of those days when you need sunglasses to keep from being blinded by the sun reflecting off the crusty snow under the faded denim blue sky—and when life teaching at Thornton seemed a perfect heaven, Greg learned that someone had decidedly different plans for him. He felt a glow from the walk to his office as he took off his parka and his boots and put on the shoes that he wore inside Thornton Hall, although sometimes the puddles in the corridors from the tracked-in, melted snow made him think that shoes were not the best choice. He left the door ajar for anyone who decided to come during his office hours—but who would do that on such a day? The students would be outside skiing. The buses for the slopes were lined up outside Chandler Library.

Just then, there was a knock on his door.

"Mr. Byrne? Can I come in?"

It was Carla Ledyard, one of the best art history majors. She was taking her second course with Greg, and even though grading papers is notorious as the downside of teaching in the humanities, he always looked forward with curiosity to what Carla would come up with. In one of her papers, she proposed that many Baroque works intensified emotion by limiting what the viewer sees, thus making the viewer use her imagination.

"Sure, Carla. Already coming with your idea for the final project?"

"Well, uh, no. I'm not so far along yet."

She was quiet for a moment and looked troubled, and Greg worried that she was about to share some bad news. The week before, Alex Giannakopoulos had come to say that he would miss several classes to go home to Chicopee because his mom was ill. Greg hoped that all was well with Carla.

"It's something that came up in Mr. Kenman's course that I thought I should tell you about… If you haven't heard from someone else already."

The last thing in the world that Greg needed to hear was something about Kenman's antics. Had he set fire to the drapes in the classroom again?—the classroom they shared on Tuesdays and where the smell of smoke had lingered for weeks?

He told Carla that he wasn't up to date, and with some reluctance, she told him this: that Kenman had been carrying on about the *real way to learn about art*, which was to *feel it in your body!* "Kinetic learning" was the way to go, to take the flat, two-dimensional representations from the canvas or from the page and to go back to the "artist's inspiration" by assuming the poses and making the gestures and facial expressions that the painters tried—but in vain—to capture with the limited means at their disposal.

"But the thing that I really found shocking and wrong," said Carla, "was actually to attack people by name, people who teach at Thornton and who have different approaches. And a lot of us were kind of upset when he said, 'We don't need Byrne at Thornton! We don't need intellectuals like him. He's not the only one, but he's the latest! And soon we'll be overrun with them!'"

Greg felt as if he'd been punched in the gut. Obviously, not by Carla. He knew that if people were throwing punches, she would be on his side. Yet he was still living with the illusion of a veneer of gentility, of collegial politeness. His reaction, as he saw it in hindsight, was just another step in that gradual and painful passage from graduate student to young professional. Only now was he seeing behind the stage set, learning that the duels and ambushes were not only out there on the stage but in the wings.

Carla was looking at him with concern, and Greg realized that he had not said anything for a little while.

"Thanks, Carla. It's good to be kept up to date. I didn't think that I was upsetting people so much."

"You know, Mr. Byrne, I think he should have come to talk with you if he had a beef. That's the decent thing to do."

"Well, Carla, we all have individual styles. I guess I'd be less dramatic than Mr. Kenman. I thank you for coming to see me. And, by the way, I won't mention this to anyone."

No one else came to see him that afternoon, so he went back to staring out the window. The winter scene was still beautiful, but the mood had changed. Maybe he should enjoy the scenery while he could because there might not be many more seasons in Vermont.

But was he overreacting? Still, Kenman, intellectual lightweight that he was, remained an influential figure. To say that he was a popular teacher would be an understatement. By now, Greg realized that within the small world of Thornton College, Kenman was a star. There were newspaper articles about the "Kenman method" for teaching art history. The alumni loved him. The fund-raisers adored him. And even the tenured members of the department handled him with kid gloves. If he could persuade enough students to avoid Greg's courses, the department would see Greg as a liability. Being in his second year, Greg was only a year away from the detailed performance review to determine his renewal for another three years. Course enrollments, anonymous evaluations by students, and "service to the College and to the Department" would be taken into account, and some proof of scholarly achievement would be required. He would need to have a couple of articles and conference papers, at a minimum.

Yet the students would be the key. A dozen articles in prestigious journals would not weigh much if he did not have enthusiastic support from the students.

Fortunately, Ruth phoned him to ask if he would like to come to dinner. A few hours later, when the sun went down and it became frigid again, he walked over toward her place on Okrent Lane. Only then did he begin to wonder if Ruth, aware of everything at Thornton, had heard a version of Kenman's outburst.

They had a glass of wine on the winter porch, where Ruth managed to keep some brave cyclamens and anthuriums alive during the challenging Mayfield winter. Next to them stood the wooden garden nymph that Ruth had made from pieces of oak assembled into one large block and then lovingly carved and smoothed. She always brought it inside her studio in November to protect it and then took it back out in May.

"Oh Greg, you shouldn't let yourself be rattled by

Kenman. I agree with your student that it is shockingly unprofessional for him to say things about a colleague. But who will take him seriously? Carla—is that her name?—reacted well, and I'm sure that if he has any effect, it will be to make the best students interested in studying with you. You've told me so many things about your interactions with students that I know you are a gifted teacher."

He felt good hearing Ruth's reassurance. He was not worried about Kenman's influence on the students but rather on the trustees. More than anything, he was just plain angry. And as he sat there with Ruth—maybe the wine helped—he realized that the anger was a good thing, something that energized him. In his first two years at Thornton he had learned the rudiments of teaching, or even more than the rudiments: the *key* to teaching. It was not those few workshops on teaching back at Yale that taught him what he needed to know; it was the students. They asked questions. They made it clear when he was vague, when he had used some nice trendy term that came out in a lecture as mere filler. They made him understand the kinds of explanations that they needed. That definitions without examples were of little use. To his surprise, they also liked to hear him talk about theories, both those presented in the manifestos of schools of painters or sculptors and the theories developed by art critics. It helped them organize that massive inventory of artistic production into manageable pieces.

14

The Florence Assignment

BY THE MIDTERM of the spring quarter in 1974, Greg had yielded to the pleas of his Italian colleagues and several people in the dean's office. They desperately needed someone to lead the multi-disciplinary foreign study program in Florence. That person would need to handle the language sufficiently well to supervise the local teaching staff, deal with the host families with whom the students would be living, and take care of whatever came up in the notoriously complicated world of Italian banking and bureaucracy. Art History gave him mixed messages. His senior department colleagues went back and forth on the issue. On one hand, the Florence program drove future declarations of Art History majors. That was a plus. On the other hand, it meant that they would have to plug the staffing hole Greg left. And many of his more cautious friends, like Susan and Alex, used terms like "professional suicide" and "self-sabotage" as they pointed out the "waste of time" on the road to tenure.

"Look, Greg," said Wanda Andros, "it sounds great to spend a few months in Florence. Fine! I get that. But wait until you have tenure. Then you can do all kinds of fun stuff. It is important to remember that delayed gratification is a hallmark of maturity! Don't forget. You and I have books to write. We need to make our mark in the world of Art History. You will get *squat* done while you're in Florence. The students will take every single spare moment you have!" In his doubt, he telephoned his Yale friend Irene in Boston.

"It's completely and utterly and extravagantly crazy to direct such a program," she told him after he explained the deal. "That's why you should do it."

Greg first thought that Irene was being sarcastic. That was totally in her nature. Yet she defended her advice.

"Greg, has it ever occurred to you that you are one of the most boringly cautious people on the face of the earth? Well, probably not. But you are not someone who would go bungee jumping. That's why you need this chance at the academic equivalent of bungee jumping. You'll be scared to death. It will get your heart pumping. So I say: go for it."

As he tossed and turned the night before finally agreeing to go, he was not even sure how to explain it to himself. In many ways, it was childish. In other ways, it challenged him to be truly an adult, proving himself in a foreign country and taking massive responsibility for the students and the staff. In the end, it was probably the allure of Italy, where he had never been. A specialist of the Baroque who had never set foot in Italy! Who had spent his junior year in Paris and not even crossed the border? For an art historian to teach and write about the Baroque, it seemed absurd to pass up a chance to be within a short train ride from Turin and Rome, with their magnificent Baroque monuments. Florence, beautiful as it is, was not especially useful for the book he was writing, but writing about the Baroque would be a lot easier in Italy than in rural Vermont. And practice in Italian would be beneficial in the long run, especially if he could get a visiting teaching appointment at an Italian university someday.

Then, other times, he agreed with his friends. It was an insane risk for him to take. It was not just a matter of the language; there was everything that could go wrong when he dealt with three Italian faculty members he had never met, twenty American adolescents (most of whom had never been abroad), host families, excursions, the rental and management of the classroom space—all in the context of the notoriously, even laughably complex Italian bureaucracy and the likelihood of strikes, the ever-present risk of a *sciopero*. And he knew that being able to do any learning and writing for his career while directing the program would be next to miraculous.

Thornton was lavish in funding his preparation to lead the program. Beatrice, Larry Elliot, and the deans agreed that his current reading fluency in Italian would not be adequate for dealing with the local teaching staff and, especially, for him to teach an Italian culture course entirely in the Italian language. And they all knew that the student evaluations of his performance in that course would be crucial during the third-year review of his contract. They suggested the summer course of the Università degli Studi di Siena. In the dean's office, Peter Armbruster would ensure he got the financial support he needed. Thornton would pay for his tuition in Siena, food and lodging, and transportation. Arrangements for the classrooms and the continuing local staff in Florence were all taken care of. Margherita, who had directed the program several times, promised to find him a good place to stay in Florence.

And so, Greg took the leap that Irene had suggested.

In practical terms, he first had to rent his house to cat lovers to whom he could entrust Bogart. Greg could see that this was the biggest single hurdle for his travel arrangements. Who would be looking for a place to stay for only the summer and the fall? When he casually mentioned this problem to Jean Buxton one morning in the Art History office, she immediately pointed toward the solution. There would be hundreds of students who would be studying somewhere off campus during the winter and spring terms, according to the Thornton Plan calendar. They would be taking courses in Mayfield while he was in Italy, and then they would leave in December, just when he returned. So, all Greg needed to do was to ask the Study Abroad office to send out his rental/house-sitting offer.

Three sets of students contacted Greg and sent the information and reference lists he requested. He interviewed all three, and it was the last interview with four women students that was conclusive. The determining factor was the connection between them and Bogart. The cat's interview style was different from Greg's. First, about ten minutes of silent inspection from the safe distance of his columnar cat condo. Then a lazy saunter around the room as if looking for a lost toy. Then a sudden leap from behind the sofa onto the sofa back, where he washed his face with his right paw, then his left, before jumping into the lap of one of the students. Once there, he curled up and dozed off. Erin, Bogart's resting place of choice, caressed his ears and elicited purring that increased in volume until everyone but Bogart was laughing.

Since Greg had already checked the references, he was happy to give his decision right away. While the women filled out and signed the rental contract, Greg telephoned for a couple of pizzas from the sole pizzeria in Mayfield, Anything But Sardines. Sarah, who led the group, wrote out the check for the damage deposit and the first month's rent. Bogart got several sausage pieces from Erin's share, and a feline friendship bloomed.

After two intense weeks of packing, telephone calls, visits to the bank, and a farewell dinner at Ruth's, Greg left his car with his friend Wanda and took leave of Bogart, who was busy inspecting all the belongings of his new housemates as they moved in. At the Mayfield Inn, Greg got the Vermont Transit bus that ran from Burlington to Logan Airport via White River Junction.

From Malpensa airport, he took the shuttle bus to Stazione Milano Centrale. That July morning, when the train arrived in Siena, it seemed as if the long, wearisome journey was over.

Now, though, Greg ran into a spatial puzzle. The most exasperating part of the long trip was the two-kilometer walk from the Siena station to the student residence, where he had booked a room for the six weeks. Of course, he was tired and jet lagged, and it was hot, but there was a nightmare-like feeling and a reminiscence of an Escher engraving as he tried to transfer what he could see on his city map to what he could see with his own eyes. It was an object lesson in the misrepresentation of a three-dimensional world in two-dimensional media. What the map did not show (at least to the uninitiated) was the way the Sienese had adapted their dwellings and public spaces to the hilly Tuscan terrain. When he walked to the place where he was sure to find the via Fontebranda, he could see the street below him but could not see how to get down to it. He was at a considerable height on a street that passed above via Fontebranda. There was no staircase down, so he continued to an intersection where he hoped there would be a ramp or staircase down. No luck. He retraced his steps, hoping there would be some street parallel to the one he was on but at a lower level radiating from the station area. As he did this, a marching band of young men in vibrant Renaissance-style clothing blocked his path for a minute. Getting most of the way back to the station, he could see no useful-looking thoroughfare. He asked a man waiting at a bus stop, *"La via Fontebranda, per favore?"* The man shrugged and pointed in the direction marked "Piazza del Campo." After a series of further maddening twists and turns and vague directions from people he passed, he finally found the missing link. It was the via di Città, tracing a curve parallel to the Campo to the west. From there, he could easily descend via Fontebranda to the student residence.

The Residenza Sullustio Bandini had been created by opening the internal walls between two or three old brick and stone houses, certainly in part medieval. Inside, it was modern yet styled to harmonize with the original construction.

By the end of the first week in August, Greg felt sure enough of his progress in Italian to take a break to travel to Turin. This city had long fascinated him for its extensive Baroque porticos and churches, especially for the Piazza San Carlo with the twin churches. Knowing how crowded the trains were in Europe in August, he booked a seat on the northbound "Italicus" from Santa Maria Novella in Florence. He would take a morning train from Siena to Florence in plenty of time for the connection.

When he got to Santa Maria Novella shortly after noon that Saturday, the hot, humid air of the Florentine summer hit him hard. Siena was undoubtedly hot, but the air of the hill town was drier and not like the sauna that was Florence.

It was time to eat. He decided to walk towards via Bernardo Rucellai, where Thornton had rented classrooms for the program in the basement of Saint James, an American Episcopal church. There must be some small trattoria in the via della Scala less crowded than all the places near the station. Buco Enzo had some empty tables on the sidewalk. Inside, there was *climatizzazione*, but when he opened the door and walked in, Greg could feel that the crowd of hot bodies had already overwhelmed whatever cooling effect there might have been. So he sat outside and had a calzone and a glass of Chianti. Then he walked up Bernardo Rucellai as far as Saint James and then returned to the station. He was expecting the train to be the usual hour late. Still, when he heard that it would be more than two hours late and saw that a preceding train, also hours late, was pulling in, he decided to sacrifice his reserved seat and stand if necessary until Bologna, where he would have to get another train to Turin's Porta Nuova station.

All went well; the trains were not more than an hour late. He found a cheap hotel in the Crocetta quarter near Porta Nuova. He set his wind-up travel alarm so that he would wake up early on Sunday. He wanted to be up when the city was still mostly empty and planned to walk from Porta Nuova to Piazza San Carlo to see the twin churches and to walk under the porticos. It was not a long walk, and the streets were as empty as he had imagined. The map showed him that if he wanted to get the full effect of the churches, it would be best to enter the piazza from the north. So he walked up via Luigi Lagrange and turned left on via Maria Vittoria. Then he turned left again on via Roma into the portico-lined place. And there it was! As he looked across the length of the piazza, he recognized the Chiesa di San Carlo on the right and the Chiesa di Santa Cristina on the left.

He stood for a long while, taking it all in, then turned right and followed the porticos toward the churches. He came to the Caffè Torino, which was just opening. The waiters were setting up the tables in the broad space of the portico. Greg asked one if he could sit down, and he was instructed that he should first go inside to order. He ordered a croissant from one counter and a large *caffè americano* from another, following what apparently was an ancient traditional system, but then went to another person sitting on a high chair behind a cash register. Hearing his accent the cashier asked if he meant a *caffè americano americano* or a *caffè americano italiano*. When he asked what an *americano americano* was, she gestured toward a pot of brewed coffee of the kind he would see back in Mayfield at Drew's. Greg made it clear that it was the *americano italiano* that he desired, the one that would be produced in the large Marzocco machine behind the counter. When he paid and collected his *scontrino*, he was told that the waiter outside would bring him the coffee and the croissant once he presented the *scontrino*.

Outside, the waiter gestured toward one of the tables. Greg gave him the *scontrino* and sat with his notebook to write down his first impressions. It was a peaceful moment, and he felt lighter and more relaxed than he had in many months. He did not think about his urgent study of the Italian language or the challenges of encountering the strangers in Florence with whom he would work for the fall quarter. He simply enjoyed the light reflected from the porticos on the other side of the piazza.

Gradually, however, he became aware that two waiters standing at the door of the café were talking with unusual animation and were not laughing. He heard the word *strage* and tried to remember what it meant. He was sure that he had heard it in one of the courses he took at Yale. Suddenly, he remembered. It was one of the New Testament stories that had been the basis for famous paintings from the Quattrocento. Yes, that was it. He could now remember having identified and commented on Giotto's fresco, the "Strage degli Innocenti" in the Scrovegni Chapel in Florence. It meant "massacre." Clearly, the waiters were not talking about art history. He began to listen attentively now, and although he could not get all the words, he did make out *strage, treno, Bologna, morti, bruciati*—massacre, train, Bologna, dead, burned. He understood that people had died, burned to death because of a massacre on or near a train. Then he heard a word that made his blood run cold. *Italicus.* It was the name of the train that he was supposed to travel on. The one he had reservations for.

He closed his notebook and threw it into his backpack, and then he walked to the via Roma and found a newsstand. There were many newspapers on display, and all on the front page had in large, bold letters the words *Strage dell'Italicus!* He bought *La Stampa* and took it back with him to the hotel. When he entered the lobby, his eyes met the eyes of a middle-aged woman at the reception desk. She saw that he knew about the attack, and she just started weeping. And Greg felt the same impulse. He went up to his room and read what had happened. Twelve people were already dead, but many others were wounded. Several had been trapped inside a burning rail coach when a bomb inside the train exploded in a place called San Benedetto Val di Sambro, just outside Bologna.

He was too distracted to enjoy seeing Turin and checked out of the hotel. As he took trains back towards Bologna, Firenze, and finally Siena, he wondered whether he was on another train that would blow up. Shortly after his train left the Bologna station going south, he felt the train brake and then crawl forward. From the window on his right, he saw on a siding the twisted, burned remains of the *Italicus*. Which carriage would he have been in?

15

Autumn in Florence

B Y THE SECOND week of September, when he was to leave the Residenza Sallustio Bandini in Siena, Greg felt a trepidation akin to what he felt when he left New Haven for Mayfield precisely two years before. The move was like the delayed aftershock of an earthquake, as he once again moved from the summer's brief experience of being a student, strengthening his Italian, to a city where he would, as director of the program, bear the responsibility for students who would look to him for guidance not only in the classroom but also outside it.

Yet, as a last-minute surprise arrangement, his living situation in Florence would be almost unimaginably perfect. Thornton had rented classroom space for several years in the basement of Saint James Church. This was clear to him before he left Vermont. But then, in July, Margherita wrote that the church had also offered to rent a fully furnished and equipped apartment behind the church. The church policy was to rent this property for as long a term as possible, so Thornton faculty could not usually get to live there for the quarter. However, the next long-term tenant would not arrive until January 1975, and as a stop-gap, it would suit the parish to have someone take the place for the fall.

On his way to Turin, Greg had already checked out the short walk from Stazione Santa Maria Novella to Saint James in via Bernardo Rucellai. So, with a heavy backpack and two suitcases (one filled with books and papers), he entered the church premises and rang the bell of the *portinaia* and sacristan, Pruneta. She, a rail-thin woman of indeterminate age dressed all in black, took him next door to the apartment, which turned out to be much more than Greg had imagined. It was located behind the apse of the church and was almost as tall as the church itself. There was a spacious ground floor area that included a kitchen and laundry with a washing machine, a balcony with a sleeping area and a bathroom with shower, and a small study on a third level. One wall of the study had a large window that overlooked a private garden with lemon trees. Greg's "commute" to work, from his breakfast table to the classroom, would take less than a minute.

The next day, with his books and papers already organized in the top-floor study, Greg set out for the Steinhauslin bank in via Sassetti. He had a large check with him from Thornton with directions to open a checking account in the Steinhauslin bank, deposit the check, and use the funds to pay the host families with whom the students would live, the teaching staff, the "family placer" who located and negotiated with the host families, and to deal with other sundry operating expenses. His own per diem was included. It would have been convenient if Thornton had maintained its previous account in another bank. However, for reasons unknown to Greg, it had been decided to use Steinhauslin, a small, historic, private entity. He planned to get this done before noon, and then he could get acquainted with the classrooms back at the church.

As it turned out, opening the account took longer than he expected and gave him new insights into the Italian language and culture.

He was greeted politely in Italian, and the young woman to whom he explained that he wished to open a checking account, a *conto corrente*, said that would be no problem and that she would get *il dottore*, her supervisor, to help him do that.

The *dottore* was a round-faced man about a decade older than Greg, wearing a handsome suit and tie. He inspected the cashier's check from the special account in the Chase Manhattan Bank that Thornton used for its foreign programs. Showing no difficulty with the English, he read the letter instructing Greg to open the account in the name of Thornton College. All was going well until he asked Greg in Italian the kind of question that few people would be prepared for. Greg certainly was not.

"Certainly, *Signor Professore*. We can do that right away. But we need a proof of the existence of Thornton College."

Greg stood there pondering this. He understood that the account could be opened immediately, as soon as Steinhauslin had *proof of the existence of Thornton College*. What did this mean? There was the letter from Thornton. There was the fact that Thornton had an account at Chase. He referred to those two things as being self-evident proof. This did not work. Those things could have been spurious, the *dottore* said.

Still, this would surely be a minor delay. Pruneta, back at the church, had mentioned that the church had a big library of American books that Thornton students in prior years had used. So he walked quickly back to via Bernardo Rucellai, found the library, located in another part of the basement, and, as he hoped, there was a copy of the *Encyclopedia Britannica*. He made a photocopy of the article on Thornton College. It was a substantial article, ranging from the founding in 1750 (forty-nine years after Yale and nineteen years before Dartmouth) to the current degree programs in business, law, and medicine. He was able to return to the bank before the three-hour lunch pause.

This visit was even briefer than the first. The *dottore* told him, "That proves nothing, dear professor. It is from an old encyclopedia. It tells us nothing about the 'college' today!"

The U.S. consulate was only a twenty-minute walk from the via dei Sassetti. Still, Greg took a couple of wrong turns and arrived at the building on the Lungarno Amerigo Vespucci after the midday break had started. Greg was sure that once the offices reopened after three o'clock, someone could help him get out of this absurd situation.

Later in the day, the consulate reopened, and a friendly staff member gave him much more than he had hoped for. She had copies of the current Thornton College catalogs, not only for Arts and Sciences but also for the other schools. The consulate was well stocked because some of the wealthier and more enterprising Italians came to ask where in the States they could study. Greg took the Arts and Science and the business catalogs, declining the offer to let him carry away multiple copies. These were substantial, slickly produced volumes that would surely impress *il dottore*.

The bank was closed by the time he got back with this ultimate proof, but the next day, he started immediately, right after his *colazione* of coffee and toast. To his consternation, *il dottore* looked disdainfully at the catalogs, only admitting that they looked impressive: "Certainly, these are beautiful volumes. Expensive looking. But they have no official value."

So what *would* have "*valore ufficiale?*" asked Greg, who was becoming irritated.

" Well, clearly the charter, the constitutive document that founded the institution. Something official, *insomma!*"

The *dottore* was as exasperated as Greg. From his point of view, the American was just wasting time when the solution was plain as day. Something *official* like the college charter from 1750. Asking for the official document of the founding of Thornton was a tall order. Greg knew where it was and had seen it more than once with his own eyes in Chandler Library. It was kept behind tempered glass on display under reverently low light in the passageway to the rare books section of the library. It was issued by Benning Wentworth, colonial governor of New Hampshire, who had asserted the claims of the Colony of New Hampshire over territory to the west also claimed by the New York colony, a disputed territory that became Vermont. That parchment with its large red wax seal and blue ribbons obviously could not be brought to the bank in Florence, and Greg now understood *il dottore's* reasoning sufficiently to realize that a photo of the charter would not be official enough.

Really at his wits' end, Greg aimed for the basic concept of existence. After all, in terms of sheer existence, Thornton was more substantial and enduring than Greg himself. Thornton had been around for centuries longer than he and would be in the world also for much longer.

So, in his most elegant Italian, he defiantly asked *il dottore*, "Do you exist?"

His interlocutor replied, laughing, "Of course I exist!" (*Certo che esisto!*)

Then Greg asked, "And so *I*, too, exist!"

"Yes, most certainly—*certissimo*—You also exist!"

So, if both the *dottore* and Greg existed, how did the *dottore* know this?

Greg came out with the explosive, fundamental, metaphysical question. The question that Descartes had set forth as the starting point for philosophy.

"How do you know that I exist?"

This was it. Greg felt he had the banker against the wall. How did this man know, for sure, that Greg existed?

"It's as clear as day—*è chiarissimo!*—You have a passport!"

Aha! It was suddenly clear indeed. Greg had a passport! He didn't *exist* because he breathed, talked, and walked around. He didn't *exist* because people could see and hear him but because he had an *official* document.

So Greg pulled out his passport and walked out of the bank with the statement showing the deposit to the account of Sig. Prof. Gregory Byrne. He would be able to make withdrawals at any time and would have his own checkbook within ten days.

In the following week, Greg met with each of the local instructors: Franca Damiani, who would teach the Italian language course; Nicola Romagnoli, who would teach politics, history of Florence, and media; and the distinguished Luisa Becherucci, the director of the Uffizi, who would lecture during site visits. As often happened during those early years at Thornton, Greg had the sensation that what was happening could not be real. That he should be teaching alongside a historic figure like Becherucci! He knew some of her publications on mannerism. He knew about her heroic role in 1966, when she saved scores of priceless works during the *acqua alta* that flooded the Uffizi. And now he, like the students, would be able to hear her teach them about paintings, statues, churches, and palaces.

All of this was the dress rehearsal. The set was there; the cast had shown up, prepared. The programs had been printed (or rather photocopied in the church library). And now the doors would be flung open for the audience…

Despite the work and the worry, Greg found it good to be in Florence and to experience everyday life in a city with such a rich past and a lively present. He found a cinema near Mercato Nuovo that was showing a new Italian film, *We loved one another so much* (*Ci siamo tanto amati*), and it pleased him that he could understand the dialogue so well now. There were long lines near another cinema that was showing a French film, *Emmanuelle*.

16

Caterina

T THE LAST moment, Greg focused on what
was going to happen at the station on Saturday,
September 21. Up until a couple of days before,
the students had only been names on a list. Now, he began
to wish that someone more experienced than he could have
come up with a better solution for their first encounter.
Stazione Santa Maria Novella was a madhouse in even the
best of circumstances, but what would it be like when the
totally disoriented and presumably jet-lagged students min-
gled with the crowd and tried to meet up with him and with
the Italian host families? They had all been instructed to wear
some distinguishing Thornton garment—T-shirt, jacket, cap,
scarf—and the sticky paper badge with their name that was
sent to them with the rest of the orientation, insurance, rules,
and travel guidance. Yet, would they all follow through? And
would the host families all have their corresponding badges

with their family name in large red letters and their student's name in smaller blue ones?

This was the official rendezvous for all, regardless of whether they had come on one of the two flights recommended to them from Logan in Boston and from Kennedy in New York. If they took one of those flights, they would arrive at Milan Malpensa about the same time and there meet with the two student assistant teachers, Geoff Howe (known as Goffredo) and Sandy Murray (known as Sandro), who would do their best to get them on the bus to Stazione Milano Centrale and onto a train that would arrive approximately at 5 PM (17 *ore*), give or take an hour or so according to Italian custom. In any event, by whatever means they got to Florence, this Saturday meeting at 5 was the official and required start of the program. Though, in the case of inevitable emergencies, accidents and delays, they were to telephone Giovanna Fantucci, who was responsible for the placement with host families.

Greg could not help wondering how the U.S. press had covered the *Italicus* bombing. Nothing had come from Thornton about students dropping out of the program. Had anyone back in the States realized how dangerous a place Italy was?

As it happened, the arrival scene was no worse than a usual visit to an Italian rail station. With three exceptions, everyone expected was there. Students and families got sorted, and the stragglers arrived by the following noon. On Thursday, they all had time to settle in, check out the way they would get to class by foot or bus, and buy the required books. On Friday morning, the students were all present to recite out loud and in Italian their pledge to speak *only* in Italian except for true emergencies. Classes began. Greg sighed with relief.

Within a week, things were humming along. Franca

Damiani invited Greg to have dinner with her and her *fidanzato* Corrado—Greg soon realized that being *fidanzati* did not imply that marriage was to follow—and soon after had lunch with the Pistocchi, who were hosting "Maria" (Meredith—the Thornton students all came with Italian names that they had adopted as early as the Italian 1 course). For Greg, the complete immersion in Italian begun in Siena continued in an intensified form because he spoke only Italian with the program staff, and he was beginning to form real friendships. Meanwhile, one of his student tenants sent him a letter letting him know that all was well back in Mayfield. She enclosed photos of Bogart enjoying himself at home with his new friends. Goffredo and Sandro themselves had never been to Florence, but they were mature and dedicated. With them, Greg felt he had a kind of cabinet to discuss any matters affecting the students. The three of them recognized, however, that what they lacked was someone to speak from the perspective of the women students, and Sandro suggested Sheila Connor (Cecilia) for that role. She both looked and acted more mature than the other students, who looked up to her. Greg was happy to take this advice, and Cecilia's help soon proved to be crucially important, especially for what became known as "the Caterina rescue operation." This was a tense, serious intervention into student life, but it was mixed with moments of high comedy.

Caterina Camarata was an exchange student from Smith. Although Thornton continued to have exchange agreements with several New England colleges, those exchanges had diminished in number now that women could enter Thornton as freshmen. Before 1972, the exchanges served to test the waters of coeducation and to demonstrate to the more reluctant members of the faculty and the corporate board that women were not going to destroy the "great Thornton traditions" of manliness and life in the still north. In years to come, Caterina would be one of the few he remembered from those early years, though he knew little about her and had little interaction with her except for this one, dramatic episode. She was a pretty, round-faced brunette, fairly quiet, a decent student, but not someone who stood out in class discussion. She was so quiet, in fact, that if it hadn't been for her friend Daniella, maybe she would have covered up the whole matter. Who knows what would have happened?

The group was visiting the Museo di San Marco with Luisa Becherucci. Luisa was then seventy years old, and yet she would dash up staircases with an energy that left the teen-age athletes struggling to keep up. As usual, Greg was there to see the site and to learn from Luisa, but also to keep an eye on the students. Yes, they were young adults, and, yes, they were among the most serious of Thornton students (the advanced level of a foreign language required for the programs abroad winnowed out most of the party crowd), but the requirement to always speak Italian caused a perceptible regression in their maturity. At least, that is how he tended to explain it. Indeed, the fact of being away from campus induced a certain vacation mentality. Still, the limitations of what they could say in their still-new and limited Italian made them think in less complicated ways than in English.

Their last stop in the former monastery was the library, that beautiful space designed by Michelozzo on Cosimo de' Medici's orders. Cecilia came up behind him and whispered that they needed to talk. She was usually chipper and made light of almost everything, but she sounded serious. Greg and Cecilia left the group and walked out to the piazza. There was a problem with Caterina's family.

"C'è un problema con la famiglia di Caterina."

Rules are rules, yet hundreds of times, he was bursting to tell them just to tell him the problem in English. But instead, they needed to negotiate the hurdles of the Italian language. It took more patience to teach the language than to teach art history. His own vocabulary expanded in directions Greg never thought possible. Soon, he knew how to say "yeast infection," "hangover," "asthma inhaler," and "pulled muscle" in the language of Dante.

What Cecilia told him immediately made his blood run cold. It was one of the nightmares of faculty members tasked with accompanying students abroad: what to do when a student is sexually harassed. It was not just a bad thing for the student but potentially career-altering for a faculty member who needs to do *something*, but what? Back on campus, there was always someone to call, specialists who knew how to deal with the psychological and legal aspects of any allegation of harassment. But they were in Florence—far from help.

What Cecilia told him there on the sidewalk in front of San Marco was this: Caterina's best friend on the program, Daniella, had confided to Cecilia something that worried them both. Caterina herself, said Daniella, expressed a strange ambivalence. She had giggled as she told her friend that her "host father" had a crush on her. To all appearances, the family, the Martellis, was ideal. Giovanna Fantucci was proud of this "model family." The husband was a physicist with a position in a large corporation. His wife worked mornings in a law firm and was then at home when their two children, a boy, eight, and a girl, ten, got out of school at about one. They lived in one of the best streets in Florence and welcomed having a student, not because of the money, but because they valued international exchange. They were very fond of Caterina.

Too fond.

According to Daniella, the husband had declared to Caterina that he "loved her" and that "he had never felt this way about anyone else." She slept with a chair jammed up against her door. The wife gave no sign that she knew anything about this.

Greg and Cecilia decided that they needed to act right away. While he went to a taxi stand (knowing that one cannot just wave down a taxi in Florence), Cecilia went back into the museum to fetch Caterina. The class was breaking up, and the first of the students were already coming down the stairs. While Greg waited, he thought about what would happen when they got to the Martellis' place. It was now shortly after two. The father would be at work, but the mother might be home with the children. That would be an awful, awkward scene. On the other hand, it was a beautiful October day, and with luck, Signora Martelli would take advantage of the weather to spend some time outdoors. He could not remember the Martelli's street. He knew that they lived near Fiesole, and there was a wonderful park near there, the Parco Pettini Burresi. Since Caterina had no idea that she would be moving out, her things would not be packed. The sooner they got in and out, the better. Greg could handle the parents later, without the drama of a confrontation scene with Caterina and the children present.

Cecilia and Caterina arrived at the taxi stand. The driver was in a hurry to get started. Cecilia had filled Caterina in and told her that "they" (it was kind, he thought, that Cecilia was willing to share the burden with him) had decided that it would be necessary to extract her from the situation. They headed north up towards Ponte alla Badia, a far different neighborhood from the via Bernardo Rucellai. On this occasion, Greg decided that the emergency justified breaking the Italian-only pledge. His attempts to find out more about her situation provoked no expressions of alarm, just a matter-of-fact account.

"One morning, while Maria was busy getting the children ready for school, he told me that he had never met anyone like me before. There was nothing wrong with that, I thought. How many American girls had he met? I liked that he was paying attention to me and saying such nice things in beautiful Italian. Everything sounds better in Italian!"

"What nice things?" he asked.

"He loved my voice. He said that when I moved, it was as if I was always about to start dancing. He wanted to show me his favorite places in Florence. He said they would be especially magical to him if he was with me."

While Greg listened, he was trying to understand the route the taxi was taking. They headed up via Minzoni—that was obvious—and he knew that they would then have to take a right along the railroad tracks to get to the bridge over the tracks and then go back left, a maddening loss of time.

"Didn't you begin to worry that a married man was saying all this?"

"At first, it was just a little flirtatious. I'd always heard that Italian men were really… well, really into women and liked to just talk like that, you know, casually. Just showing off their masculinity and craving attention. So I actually really liked it."

"Did he do more than talk? How long did this go on?"

"He touches me now and then. Nothing sexual! Absolutely never in the wrong places. Just on my shoulders or arms, or sometimes running his fingers through my hair… It's just soft, very affectionate."

"And what about Maria in all this?"

"He doesn't do anything when Maria is around, or the kids. And I still think that I can handle it. The door locks, and I put a chair up next to it in case he has a key. It sounds dramatic, but I don't think he would do anything really aggressive. He says he loves me. OK, so he has a crush. Just the same, I think he will always want me to be the pure ideal on a pedestal. But Dana—I mean Daniella—just flipped out when I said a few things about him, about how I was having a real Italian adventure. She told me to watch out and to talk to you."

They were now heading east on Viale dei Mille, which does not lead towards Fiesole, before they got onto a street that turned out to be Passavanti, and they were at last finally heading clearly uphill toward their destination.

"You understand why I need to get you out of there, don't you? You *think* you can handle this, but you've never been in a situation like this before. It's explosive. What if he decides to get physical? And we don't know what the wife knows. Have they hosted women students before?"

They now turned off Passavanti and found themselves in a labyrinth of smaller streets. It was a posh neighborhood for sure, but Greg couldn't pay much attention to the surroundings.

"There was a Nancy. They don't talk much about her. Don't talk about her at all, except that the children tell me that they liked her and didn't know where she went. Just one day, they came home from school, and she wasn't there anymore."

That was all Greg needed to hear. A woman student who disappeared suddenly and whose name was not spoken. His pulse had started racing, unlike the taxi. They were barely inching along behind the *netturbini* emptying trash bins. There was no way to pass them, and looking at his watch, he saw that they had been driving around for forty-five minutes already. When he asked the driver if there was another way around to Filippo Brunetti, he made one of those gestures that means everything and nothing.

The three of them were now sitting silent. Greg almost took Cecilia's hand, needing some kind of comfort. Fortunately, he resisted. No need to create another problem! Caterina was calm and sort of dreamy-eyed.

Finally, the *netturbini* turned into a side street, and they accelerated. After a few baffling turns, they stopped in front of the little villa.

Greg told the driver to wait. He was not happy, but Greg told him that he would not pay him until they had loaded up and gone back down into the city. It was at that moment that he realized that he was so fixated on extracting Caterina from the Martelli's that he had not planned what to do with her later. Caterina was opening the door, with Cecilia right next to her. He heard Caterina call, "*C'è qualcuno?*"

It turned out that the house was empty. He let the girls go up to Cathy's room to pack while he paced the large living room with recognizable Roche Bobois furnishings. Physicists can apparently make good money. There was still the problem of a place for Caterina. Even though there was a sleeper sofa on the ground floor at Greg's place, he couldn't have anyone say that "she left her Italian family and moved in with the professor."

The Martellis had, of course, a telephone, and Greg could call Giovanna to ask if there were any host families in reserve. Yet besides the etiquette that one did not use someone's phone without asking permission—and in this case, necessity trumped etiquette—he was worried that someone as clever as Dottore Martelli could trace the call and find out where Caterina might have gone. He was going to have to wing it.

By the time the taxi had gotten down towards the center of town, just about at their starting place in the Piazza di San Marco, they were all hungry. Greg had the driver leave them in the via Cavour, near the *prezzo fisso* he knew. Although Thornton had given him a decent per diem, on evenings when he did not feel like cooking for himself, he went to a place with a cheap *prezzo fisso* menu. He soon learned that he should have upgraded the dining options in honor of Caterina's "escape."

They had ordered—easy to do with the limited menu— and had started devouring their pasta, when suddenly, oh horror!, the Martellis were standing next to their table, dragging a tearful Daniella behind, protesting that they had forced her to lead them to Caterina.

"They forced me to tell them! They made me find you for them," wailed Daniella to Caterina.

Those six words were enough for Cecilia and Greg to grasp the main lines of what had happened, and Daniella later filled in the backstory. The Martellis knew that Daniella was Caterina's best friend. They had even driven her home a few times. When they found Caterina's room empty and her key deposited on the kitchen table, they immediately went to find Daniella. Sandro and Goffredo had eaten with Greg a couple of times at this *prezzo fisso*, and apparently they had mentioned his frugal dining regimen to some of the students. No one needed to bring in Sherlock Holmes.

Signora Martelli took the lead, pleading with him and with Cecilia, whom she took to be his colleague, to return Caterina to them. Even after much reflection, Greg remained uncertain about the dynamics of that husband-wife duo. Did Maria Martelli know precisely what was going on all along? Was she indifferent to what Giancarlo was up to? Was she even his active accomplice? Or did a few minutes of tearful, angry, panicked explanation suffice to bring Maria up to speed and unite them in a common cause to save the family name?

Because this was Maria Martelli's opening gambit: the family would lose face. All the neighbors would wonder why the American girl had left so suddenly. They feared more than anything else losing face: "*Non vogliamo perdere la faccia!*"

They were not even addressing Caterina herself, and Caterina was the only one who looked calm, serene even, as she comforted Daniella.

At this point, Dottore Martelli asked Greg to come outside with him. He had left his car in the middle of the street. They left the wife arguing with Cecilia. As Greg walked with Martelli towards the door, they could hear the din of cars honking.

Greg was struck by the sight of the red Alfa Romeo parked in the middle of one of the narrow main thoroughfares of Florence during the evening rush hour. The noise of hundreds of cars honking was deafening. Standing before the immobile car was a traffic policeman in the classic dark blue uniform and white braids, a white helmet, and gloves with dramatic oversized white cuffs. He ordered Martelli to move his car, but Martelli was intent on persuading Greg that the beloved Caterina should return to the Martelli home. As the officer stood by, apparently transfixed by the vehement exchange between two professional-class men (*gente per bene*) speaking English, the physicist told Greg not only of his pure love for the American girl but also of an important step he had taken to set things right. He had gone to confession and been absolved. He then asked Greg if he was Catholic. When Greg said yes, Martelli seemed to think that henceforth the matter was settled since Greg would agree that the absolution meant that the repentant family man was now in a state of grace (*stato di grazia*) and could live without sin next to Caterina. Greg, however, recalling what he learned as a child about the sacrament of penance, replied that from now on, the absolved sinner had an obligation to avoid occasions of sin and especially—imperatively—the *proximate* occasions of sin. In the background, the noise from the cars increased in volume, and the policeman repeated his order to move the car. Greg pointed out that living under the same roof as Caterina was clearly a proximate occasion. Martelli turned to the policeman to ask for his opinion in this discussion of sin, forgiveness, grace, and obligation.

"*E Lei, Signore, cosa ne pensa?*" (And you, Signore, what do you think about it?)

The policeman, who had apparently been able to follow enough of the exchange in English, replied, in Italian, "I think that the professor is right. Now get the car out of the way!"

Faced with the united disapproval of the policeman and the professor, defeated in his theological argument, Martelli gave up. Now Martelli had to drive around the block to return to this point and get his wife. By the time Greg walked back to the table where Cecilia had held firm against the wife's pleading and where Caterina had managed to calm Daniella, it was clear that the Martellis' attempt to reclaim their American guest was unsuccessful.

Cecilia, Caterina, Daniella, and Greg remained at the table. Daniella had a bit of Caterina's salad, and it was decided that Caterina would spend the night with Daniella's family, who were, both of the students said, friendly to Caterina and accommodating. Greg would telephone Giovanna from his apartment, and then the next day would see that all of Caterina's belongings got to her new lodgings.

The scene in the middle of the via Cavour remained in Greg's memory as something out of an opera—the three male singers striving to be heard above the chorus of the drivers with their accompanying horns.

17

Bucharest

BY EARLY OCTOBER, Greg's life in Florence had become a pleasant routine. The courses were going well. Greg's colleagues and teaching assistants were all doing their part. He had many Italian friends, mostly from visits to the host families. He knew where things were—the *rosticceria* where he often got his lunch, the *prezzo fisso* that had basic no-frills fare, the little hole-in-the-wall produce shop where he could get the best tomatoes and fresh basil and other herbs, the best cinema—and he loved just waking up and walking through the city, smelling the coffee, the food being prepared, the freshly printed paperbacks in the bookstores. They were ten days from the fall break. The students were about to swarm all over Europe, and even though, to their surprise, Oktoberfest actually took place in September, Munich ranked high among their choice of destinations. For Greg's part, a few relaxing days in Rome without any responsibilities beckoned.

And then, one morning, he heard the phone ringing after walking the few steps from the classroom to his apartment. It was Peter Armbruster. All of Greg's conversations with Peter had concerned fastidious routine. This time, however, there was an unaccustomed urgency in the voice he now heard. Peter said that he was calling on behalf of Dave Bromley and, now that he had Greg on the line, he would transfer him to Dave.

This struck him as strange and a bit worrisome. Something must be wrong, but what? Had he unwittingly done something or failed to do something? Had they heard about Cathy's situation and his solution to it? As a still new assistant professor, he found anything out of the ordinary unsettling.

"Greg, it's Dave. What time is it over in Florence? Eleven? OK, good. Look, I'm sure that we startled you by getting in touch this way. It's nothing to worry about. It has nothing to do with the program you're directing, but we are contacting you because you're in Italy, so you're the faculty member who can best handle this matter for us."

He reminded Greg that one of the other college foreign study programs was a bit of an orphan—the one in Romania, with only eight students. At that scale, Thornton couldn't afford to have a full-time resident director. The rules required, though, that in such cases, the program had to be inspected on-site by a tenured or tenure-track faculty member. Greg thus qualified, and he was the closest.

Would he be kind enough to do it? Now, when a dean asks an untenured faculty member for a "kindness," the appropriate synonyms are "order" or "command."

"I know, Greg, that your program is going on a week-long break in ten days. Sorry for the short notice. But we'd like you to get over there for, say, three days. Talk to the students.

Talk to the relevant people in the Ministry of Education. And most of all, talk to Silviu Brucan. He's a big honcho, and we pay him a fee to serve as unofficial advisor to our students. We'll fax you all the details. Yes, I know you don't have a fax. We'll fax it to the US consulate in Florence. Naturally, we'll reimburse your travel, lodging, meals, etc. Then you can write a brief report and mail it to us. And… if there is confidential stuff you don't feel you can put in writing, call me. OK?"

Dave was sounding ingratiating and chummy.

"Well, Dave, anything for Thornton!"

Dave did not seem to detect the irony of Greg's hyperbolic affirmation.

Except that Romania was one of the Communist dictatorships slightly independent of Russia, Greg knew next to nothing about the country. In October 1974, all it meant to him was a significant inconvenience and waste of time, starting with a walk to the consulate to pick up the fax. That was the least of it. He was looking forward to going to Rome during the fall break. An easy train ride. Now, he needed to figure out how to get to Bucharest and back as quickly as possible. Did he need a visa? No, as it turned out.

Ten days later, he was at Santa Maria Novella waiting for the train to Milan, where he could catch a flight to Bucharest. Most of the students had left the evening before, also for points north. He saw Carolina and Susanna, who waved to him and then disappeared into another carriage. The professorial presence did not fit into their vision of a holiday.

With a reserved seat in a compartment without strong-smelling food, the trip began well. Since the train was only half an hour late leaving Florence, he figured that he would easily get to Milan in time for the evening flight to Bucharest. In fact, he did get to Milano Centrale with only eighty minutes delay. He had counted on at least that much. Ample time to take a taxi to Malpensa. He went down that massive staircase to the street and found taxis waiting. But when he asked a driver to take him to the airport, the driver just laughed.

"Would you rather sleep on a bench at the airport or in a bed?" he asked. And then the driver explained that the airport was fogged in at least until noon the next day. The hotels were mostly full, he said. Instead of the airport, he took Greg to a hotel near Porta Romana, far outside the small area near the Duomo that most foreign visitors knew. He got a crummy, cramped room with a window on a noisy avenue and was feeling testy that evening when he walked into a nearby pizzeria. The welcome was warm, the wine was good, and the Neapolitan-style pizza with fresh *mozzarella di bufala* was a consolation. The wine (on an empty stomach) had already put him in a good mood. He was hoping for a sound night's sleep before going to the airport the following morning.

The next day, the radio announced that the expected wind that would have swept the fog away had not come. The airport would be closed for at least another day. Travelers were advised to find flights from Rome or Genoa.

Around the corner from the hotel was a small travel agency. It was a shabby-looking place with sun-bleached posters of fjords, the Arc de Triomphe, and the Irish coast. The young man at the desk looked surprised and a bit alarmed to see an American walk in. The agent diligently looked through large volumes with flight schedules of airlines flying to Bucharest—there was not much choice. Finally, he told Greg that there might be a chance through Vienna—another whole day of travel away. He made a couple of phone calls and booked Greg on a flight on Austrian Airlines. He said that Greg needed to catch the next train from the central station. *Subitissimo!*

Greg paid with a check from the Steinhauslin bank, rushed next door to the hotel to grab his bag, and got a taxi from the stand at Porta Romana. The train was predictably late. That suited him fine because otherwise, he would have missed it and would have needed to wait another six hours. As it was, he grabbed a *panino* and found his reserved place in an eight-person compartment.

The following ten hours were a drowsy litany of names. Brescia, Vicenza, Venezia, Udine, Villach, Klagenfurt, Graz, Wiener Neustadt, and finally Wien.

Flying from Wien-Schwechat airport, he got to Bucharest Otopeni. Everything would now go smoothly.

He thought that.

He thought that until he got to the U.S. Embassy on Tudor Arghezi Strada. It was in a vast old fairy-tale castle of a house in a small park. The ceiling paintings, ubiquitous ornate fireplaces, and marble staircase balustrades from the 1920s or 1930s might have held Greg's attention at any other time. Still, right then, Greg needed the help of the consular staff to direct him to the hotel room they were to have reserved for him.

The receptionist knew who he was. She stood up, shook his hand, and addressed him in excellent, American-sounding, and only slightly accented English.

"Welcome to Bucharest, Dr. Byrne. We have been expecting you, and the Thornton students are eager to see you."

He apologized for being later than expected, explained the delay, and said that he hoped his late arrival had not complicated things for the hotel.

"Ah," she said, "the problem with the hotel is not resulting from your arrival. We have done our best, but the leadership of Romania is having an international congress and all hotels have been reserved for the… congressists."

She saw the look on his face and added, "We are working on it right now. What is best is that you leave your bag here with me while you talk to Mr. Randolph, the interim consul."

Randolph seemed to know all about the resident Thornton students.

"This is their home away from home, in effect, because except for the university, they don't have any gathering places. We're not involved in the academic side, of course. Brucan takes care of that. We're happy to see them show up so that we can verify that they've not gotten in trouble with the Securitate. By the way, the secretary you have just spoken with is excellent, really smart and helpful. You should be aware, though, that the Securitate debriefs her at least weekly. They know just about everything that happens in our embassy, outside the secure room."

Greg asked him about Brucan.

"He's probably the most complicated man in Romania, and I can't explain to you what I don't understand myself. He's a professor at the university, even though he himself has no university degrees—he wasn't allowed to study before the war because he was Jewish. He was the deputy editor-in-chief of *Scînteia,* the official Communist newspaper. His wife is a judge, feared throughout the country because of some death sentences she pronounced. I'm frankly amazed that Thornton is lucky enough to have him advising the students. They know that they are not supposed to mention Brucan to anyone. And you should follow the same rule. *Never mention Brucan.* You're going to meet people in the Ministry of Education. They know all about Thornton working with

Brucan, but when you are talking with them, don't say his name. Understood?"

Greg nodded, while thinking how many different meanings "understand" can have.

Leaving Randolph's office, he found six of the eight students waiting for him. There were Jared, John, Olivia, Richard, Mark, and Alison. Only Amelia and Wesley were missing because they were in class. They knew about the hotel snafu, and a couple of the boys joked that he should stay with Amelia because she had the largest bed. When he pointed out that he was not supposed to share a bed with a student, they suggested that he could have one of their beds and the lucky guy could stay with Amelia.

They gave Greg various pieces of practical advice. One that stuck with him was: never throw your newspaper away because you'll need it for the toilet.

He was feeling pretty exhausted at this point. So he really appreciated the next person he met. It was Noah Fields, the assistant cultural attaché, who offered to let Greg sleep on his sofa. His place was near the embassy, and they could walk over there any time he was ready.

First, though, Greg needed to contact Brucan. He returned to the friendly receptionist and asked her to call the professor. She would obviously have his number since Brucan was involved with the embassy and the students who hung out there.

"I will be happy to dial his number for you if you give it me," she said.

As he looked in his satchel for the sheet with instructions, Greg found her request odd. He started to show the paper to her so that she could dial it.

"Please do not show me the paper. Just read the number to me."

She dialed as he dictated. The phone rang, and she handed the handset to him. After a while, a woman greeted Greg with something like the French *allô*. He tried asking in French for Professor Brucan, but the woman, noticing Greg's accent, replied in English that the professor and his wife were out but would return soon. Could he please call back?

He found Noah in his office, and they strolled over to his place. It was modern and spacious for a single person. Noah said he enjoyed living there because there was space to do his artwork. The sofa Greg was to sleep on was in his studio room, and the walls were covered with Noah's colorful watercolor renderings of the older houses and churches of the Old Town and the Uranus-Izvor neighborhood. They reminded Greg of the work of Chaïm Soutine, and Noah felt sure that he would quickly find buyers for those paintings. Already, people were talking in hushed tones about Ceausescu's megalomaniacal project of leveling the whole area to build the Palace of the Parliament. If that happened, Noah's might be some of the last paintings of a forgotten world.

Noah offered Greg a bottle of Ursus beer, and as they sat near a window overlooking a quiet side street, Greg had a strange and unfamiliar feeling. Thinking about it, as they talked, he realized it was a sense of relaxation. Here, in Bucharest, he was not responsible for anything. No problems to solve. He was simply to look around and report back. And Noah Fields was the perfect host.

"It's quiet and safe here in Bucharest," said Noah. "Everything is watched. Everything is controlled. The Securitate and Ceausescu are aware of everything. Of course, you could be mugged or pick-pocketed, but it would only be on orders from above. It's a pretty city, the pace is slow, the language is not so hard, and my responsibilities are reasonable.

If you get tired of grading papers, see if you can become a cultural attaché—or even better, an *assistant*."

After a while, they returned to Tudor Arghezi Strada. Noah pointed out the drab, four-story building across from the embassy.

"You can see the strange configuration of the windows on the top floor. It's all set up with cameras, listening devices, and motion sensors directed at the embassy. They can follow everything we do."

Greg found the helpful receptionist at her desk and asked her to please redial Professor Brucan.

"Yes, with pleasure, Dr. Byrne. Can you tell me the number?"

He could see from her eyes that she knew the number perfectly well. Nonetheless, he complied with the ritual, took out the paper, and read the number to her.

This time, he was in luck. Brucan himself was on the phone. There were no niceties, no ceremony.

"Can you meet now?" he asked.

"Yes."

"Where are you staying?"

"I'm at the embassy."

"No," he said impatiently, "where are you *staying*?"

He gave him Noah's address.

"Good. I'll meet you near there with my car at 3:15. Be at the corner."

What followed on that sunny, mild autumn afternoon long remained for him one of the most baffling experiences of his life. It shaped Greg's view of Baroque performance and display. And when, a couple of years later, he was teaching a Humanities course in which they read Poe's "The Purloined Letter," he thought of Brucan, using openness as a tool for concealment.

Greg made sure to be on his way to the meeting spot early since Brucan's instructions had an air of command about them. Just a few minutes after 3 p.m., he was nearing the corner when a small brown-and-white car resembling a Morris Mini stopped abruptly beside him. The driver pushed the door open and motioned impatiently for Greg to get in. It was clearly Brucan, and his expression made Greg feel that he was late even though he was more than ten minutes early.

Brucan asked a few perfunctory questions about Greg's trip. He showed no interest in why the college had sent as emissary a junior art historian with no connection to Romania. Still, he said that the students were doing well, assuring Greg that he was taking care of them.

Having no clue about the city's layout, Greg just drank in the sights of this picturesque but shabby city, expecting to arrive at the house of an influential professor at any moment. When the car stopped, they were not near a home but in a parking lot next to a fairly large lake.

They got out of the car and started walking on a path that curved around the lake through a landscape of pine and poplar. It must have been the peak time for well-to-do residents of the city to have their stroll, their *passeggiata*, or whatever they said in Romanian for a social time for strolling. All greeted Brucan with great deference.

"*Bună ziua, Doctor!*" they would say and make a slight bow. No one said anything beyond that, and although Brucan apparently recognized these people, he simply nodded in return. As they walked, he filled Greg in on the ongoing negotiation with the Ministry of Education. For years, the Romanians had wanted Thornton to officialize its presence in Romania. So far, the Thornton students had simply been "tourists." Beyond that, there were issues far beyond Greg's pay grade. As a private institution, Thornton could not exist in a country in which the state was supreme and where "private" enterprise, schools, churches, etc. were non-existent. So, for Thornton students to be recognized, the U.S. government would have to get involved, and some entity, presumably the State Department, would have to start talking with the Romanians. This, he understood, the State Department did not wish to do. So his obligatory visit to the Ministry would be a vain exercise in politeness.

"And," added Brucan, "do not use my name or in any way refer to me."

By now, they had walked to the other side of the park. They exited onto a residential street of two-story villas. Quite comfortable looking, though not showy. Eventually, they reached Brucan's.

He led Greg into a living room with two ample sofas, a coffee table, and a well-worn leather easy chair with a good reading lamp nearby.

"We have, as you see, made a substantial collection of icons," he said, drawing Greg's attention to an especially large one with an image of the Virgin. He picked it off the wall and brought it closer to Greg. That struck Greg as a strange gesture since he could easily have approached the wall to look closer. He looked at the icon Brucan was holding. Not being especially informed about Orthodox icons, he could only recognize that they were old and fine in detail. He turned it over and saw that it was incised, painted, and gilded on the back. Perhaps that is why he took it off the wall.

"Go, you can choose any you would like to look at more closely. Feel free to take from the walls," he said with much emphasis.

To satisfy his host, Greg examined several up close and

removed a small one from the wall. After turning it over, he replaced it on its hook. Later, he wondered whether the walls, rather than the icon, were the point. Did he want Greg to feel that he could inspect everything for listening devices? It would have been a fool's errand anyway. There were so many ways a bug could be planted in such a large and complex house.

Brucan called for a housekeeper to bring them coffee and some sweet cakes.

"It is a pity that my wife, Alexandra Sidorovici, cannot be here. She always enjoys meeting visitors from abroad, but her work at the tribunal is taxing. We have the unusual privilege of being able to travel to the States, to Britain, and so forth, as a couple. And, as you can see, we get the *Times* and the *Economist*. So we stay in touch."

He gestured toward the coffee table, where there were recent issues.

Over coffee, they talked about the courses the students were taking, Brucan's assessment of their ability to understand lectures in Romanian (very good, he thought), his custom of writing a one-page report about each of them that he would send shortly after their return home at the end of the quarter. Greg immediately wondered whether Brucan would have someone from the Securitate ghostwrite the eight reports.

They walked back to the car by a shorter route that did not lead them through the park and then drove back to a street corner two blocks from the embassy.

Brucan's last instructions to Greg were quite detailed.

"Please tell Dave Bromley that everything is going as we agreed in April."

Greg assured Brucan that he would let Dave know that everything was going well.

"No, please. That is not what you should say. Tell him that everything is going as we agreed in April. Do you understand?"

"I should say that 'everything is going as we agreed in April,' is that right?"

"Yes. Exactly those words. And only to Dave directly. Not in a letter or on the telephone, please."

18

Halftime

GREG WAS BACK from Florence in time to get a fir tree from the Thornton Co-op, one small enough so that he could walk back with it the two blocks to Welldon Street. Bogart observed a tree magically appearing inside his house. The Christmas gifts that Greg had bought in Florence had not suffered from the trip. Now Greg needed to get festive wrapping paper, as well as some decorations for the tree. As he walked along Main Street at about 4 PM, the sun was already setting, and the windows of Drew's Lunch, the bookstore, Cranston's Clothing, and the newly opened Peter Pagan's café shone brightly in the gathering dark.

Shoppers were coming out of the stores with bags and boxes, but it was somehow strangely quiet. Greg paused to look around. He felt an inexplicable malaise, as if something essential were missing. Pausing in front of Drew's, he looked around. Everything was the same as before his months in Italy, yet he had a queasy, uncanny feeling. It was something about his body that did not feel right. It was not the cold, but something else. Suddenly, he realized what was wrong: nobody was pressing against him. The nearest person must have been ten feet away. He was having a sensorial withdrawal from the crowded life of the Italian city.

The remaining two weeks of December passed quickly. The Christmas Revels in Perkins Center were like a homecoming party, where he saw almost everyone he knew in Mayfield. Even Bob Wadsworth, the grumpy insurance agent he met at Drew's, was part of the Revels. It pleased Greg to see that Bob had found at least one thing to be enthusiastic about, a role for which his silhouette destined him: plump Saint Nicholas. There was Clara Marsh from the library; there was his neighbor Marilyn Shugart with her daughter Megan; John Wren from the Drama Department; even President Chauncey was there on the stage as one of the wise men. At the end of the performance, the whole town was dancing in a winding line, holding hands, whirling around the auditorium to the Shaker hymn "Lord of the Dance," which kept going until everyone was out of their seat and dancing out onto the Green. Greg now felt thoroughly back at home.

And yet, as the bells on the college chapel greeted 1975, Greg was acutely aware of the mounting suspense. There were months of sleepless nights ahead, for in spring of that year, according to his contract as assistant professor, would come the dreaded "third-year review." It was then that his department and the Dean's Promotion and Tenure committee would determine whether he had the makings of a career member of the college. He was to be judged on three criteria. First, at least in all policy documents, came the quality of his teaching. Second came the essential demonstration of scholarly ability, the ability to create new knowledge in his field, as judged by more senior art historians. The third was the vaguest and, therefore, most potentially lethal criterion: departmental and college "presence." This was parsed in a kaleidoscope of ways. "Do you pull your weight?" "Are you reliable as a colleague?" "Are you fun at department parties?" "Do you get your name in the newspaper (for good reasons)?" One remarkably frank older professor told him, "It just means: do I like you?"

If he were distributing eggs and placing them in three baskets, he had clearly bungled the job. There were lots of eggs in the first basket. Whether the eggs would pass inspection or not, there were a lot of them there. His students really liked him. Now, there were terms of anonymous written evaluations in his file. In the main, there was consistent praise. And the smaller number of consistent criticisms could also be helpful. "He is really demanding." "He expects too much." "When we were in Florence, we had almost no time to party." "My friends at UVM don't need to do half the work I do in art history." It made him feel good when he saw that many said things like "When I go to his office hours, he always seems happy to see me, unlike a lot of professors," "The comments on the papers really help me," "When I was having trouble thinking of a topic for my final paper, he actually remembered a question I asked in class and said it would be a good thing to write about. And it was!"

The third basket—"presence"—held a nice mound of eggs, though due to the nebulous definition, maybe some of the eggs would do him more harm than good. The department must recommend continuation towards tenure. And yet Greg had let himself be swept away by the enthusiasm (yes, his acquaintance the insurance agent was right) for a liberal arts, interdisciplinary education. Colleagues in Italian and Humanities and members of several college committees would vouch energetically for him. And some of this group, such as Larry Elliot and Charlie Woodruff, were senior and influential. Support from the department, on the other hand, could go in either direction. On one side, they would say, "He's increased the visibility of the department throughout the college. And he's attracted many students." And on the other side—a minority, he thought—they would argue, "He's acting as if he already has tenure. He teaches fewer art history courses than any of the rest of us."

Greg did not like to glance in the direction of the second basket, innovative scholarship. By the time he arrived at the threshold of the tenure decision three years later, he would need a book, if not published and in bookstores, at least accepted with a contract from a reputable press. So far, there were three accepted articles and one more pending. To make matters worse, he had a split psyche. Coming from grad school, he was proud of himself. One-half of his brain tingled with confidence—that was an effect that Yale instilled. On the other side lay the constant terror of making a misstep. When you make a mistake in print, the evidence of your stupidity or carelessness is there in black and white forever, available to anyone with access to a good university library. He needed to publish, to have articles that could be counted. The problem was that he dreaded having anyone—anyone at all—actually read those articles.

His better-balanced Yale friends lived by the mantra, "Get yourself noticed!" They wanted to make a name for themselves, to publish in the most visible places, and even to get their work criticized if it enabled them to be part of a talked-about polemic. This was Irene's forte. Whenever he went to Boston, he always got together with her, and besides talking about old times in New Haven, they traded news about what they were doing. The two of them had a completely divergent approach. Irene wrote caustic reviews of books by big-name scholars. Her articles staked out speculative positions that even she admitted to Greg were "really pushing the envelope" and "would get lots of push-back." But *everyone* in twentieth-century art scholarship knew Irene Bishop's name. She got invited to give papers at conferences because the organizers knew that the room would be packed to see Irene Bishop, even if they loathed what she wrote. She was *someone*.

How could he survive, she asked, living in the shadows? Greg did not dare admit to her his own logic, what he called (to himself) the "polar approach." He decided to publish in what he perceived as respectable backwaters. These were journals that did indeed have stringent criteria and a good track record of decisive contributions to the field, but they were not household names, at least from his point of view. It happened that several of them were published near the North and South Poles, such as the *Konsthistorisk tidskrift/Journal of Art History* in Stockholm and the *New Art History,* in Australia, and the *Finnish Review of Art Studies*—hence the "polar."

Even if that handful of articles were taken into account, by crunch time in 1978, he would not have the talisman, the book. It was true that if an article or two were miraculously must-reads, cited throughout the profession, he might be able to squeak by on the basis of the rest of what he did for the college. Greg's morale plunged when he heard that Cynthia Collins, a brilliant, serious, and hard-working person, failed to get tenure in Spanish. Although he did not know her well, he knew she had several articles and the complete manuscript of a book. The press, however, had not yet come to a decision about publication. His own timing now appeared worse than he earlier feared. The program in Florence and the time it took to prepare for it had been a foolish detour.

There was something even worse about what happened to Cynthia, as Greg learned one evening when he was at the Farringtons' for dinner. Bill, like Greg, had done his Ph.D. at Yale and had taken Greg under his wing. Greg was grateful, but Bill's "tough love" guidance consisted of pushing him relentlessly to get himself noticed in the rough and tumble, competitive world of scholarship. Art historians were not always "nice" to one another. As Bill used to say, "The smaller the stakes, the more vicious the game."

"Talk about vicious!" said Lizzy, Bill's wife. "You heard about Cynthia?"

"Yes," Greg said. "That scares the hell out of me. If her book wasn't good enough, what chance do I have?"

"Oh. There's more to it than that. It's not just that she didn't get tenure. It's how she learned about the decision. You weren't close to Cynthia, I guess. She was discreet about her cancer. She has, they say, only a few days to live. And Marta, as chair of Romance Languages, could have delayed announcing the department's decision. Instead, she showed up at the hospital in Burlington. She came smiling to Cynthia's room as if she were making a warm and compassionate gesture, knowing that she might never see her junior colleague again. Cynthia's husband Marty was next to the bed but left for a few minutes so Marta could be alone with his wife. About twenty minutes later, he came back to the room, and Cynthia was alone, shaking and sobbing. Can you guess what that bitch had said to Cynthia?"

It took only a couple of seconds before the shock appeared on Greg's face. "No way! She didn't tell her! What a sadist!"

"Marty went ballistic. He screamed he would 'off the bitch!' The hospital called the police. They picked Marty up and questioned him but then let him go with a warning.

Now the Mayfield police have someone standing outside Marta's home."

Lizzy, Greg, and Bill were quiet for a moment, just fathoming the lack of humanity. Then Bill said, "Too bad you had to hear how cruel it gets, Greg. But the fact is, in the plainest of terms, you've got to get your fucking ass in gear and publish some of your goddam shit!"

Greg liked to write, but it was lonely work without the immediate payoff, the kick, that he got from teaching. Teaching was absolutely addictive—despite, or because of, the emotional rollercoaster that it entailed. The day before a class, whether lecture or discussion, he suffered through waves of anxiety. He would get his main points down on paper, just a short list. As he told himself, if he could impress upon the students four essential ideas, four things that would be new to them and that they probably had not yet perceived, it would be a good class. Next, he would find good illustrations for those points. By this time, panic usually set in, and he could not bear to think about the class. He would go to extremes to find other "urgent" things to do that would plunge him into a kind of anesthetic cloud of distraction. Often, these "urgent" things were book orders for a course that he was going to give the following quarter, or a letter that he owed a friend, or even changing the litter in Bogart's box. Then, about an hour before class, this blackout period would end, and he would have a finite number of minutes to combine the four points with the examples and to find the "leads," the questions that he would raise so that the students themselves would perceive what he was getting at. By being involved in the discovery, he knew, they would retain the ideas and the examples much better. And they would soon themselves locate other examples and—for the best of the students—objections and refinements to the conclusions from class.

He would leave a successful class session so pumped up, so joyful, that it made up for the previous anxiety. Endorphins, that was what must make him feel that way. On the other hand, when a class failed, he would sit on the steps of his house, staring into the gravel driveway until the pain began to fade.

Teaching was not the only thing that gave him a distraction from the solitude of writing. And not the only thing that gave him moments of satisfaction.

He was considered in his department, as Emily Latouraine told him, a "glutton for punishment."

"You haven't learned to say no yet. People keep dumping things on you, and you jump at them like a squirrel running after a crust of stale bread."

It was true that Greg felt himself drawn to things that other people found tedious and a waste of time. It astounded him, for example, that already in the middle of his third year at Thornton, he was his department's representative to the Executive Committee of the Faculty, a body chaired by the president of the College that met at least once each month during the fall, winter, and spring quarters. There he was, sitting at a rectangle of tables with colleagues from all the departments and with the Dean of Faculty, the Registrar, and the Provost. Many important policy decisions were voted on after lengthy discussion. Some departments sent junior faculty as representatives, while others sent senior tenured faculty members. Clearly, Art History thought that this was just drudgery that an underling could dispatch.

The Executive Committee met in the large front meeting room of Perkins Center, overlooking the Green. On the west wall, the Thornton motto, *Vox gaudentis in silentio*, was painted in large Thornton-blue letters. When the whole faculty of the College got together, the room was respectably full, but this smaller group would have looked forlorn in such a space, so dividers were put up behind the president, dean, and other bigwigs. Though seating was not assigned, Greg almost always sat with his back to the Green and thus usually found himself next to a young member of the Romance Languages department, David Feighery, who taught French and Italian. They amused themselves by commenting *sotto voce* in Italian on the more comical moments of the proceedings.

Even though it meant losing a good chunk of many a Monday afternoon, Greg found much of interest. He thought, though, that he would have gotten even more out of it if he had majored in anthropology. The rituals of a formal meeting, with the approval of minutes, the careful following of the agenda, the motions and votes, and especially the discussions, were like something out of a Dickens novel. The president, Chauncey, being a philosopher of mathematics—and this in itself was instructive for Greg that there was a *philosophy* of mathematics—was fond of metaphors from that field. The "Markov chain" was often mentioned, leaving Greg entirely in the dark, even after he asked one of his own student advisees, a whiz in science, to explain it to him. "Well," she said, "when you are analyzing a stochastic process, you recognize a Markov chain when it has the Markov property, that is, when a process is memoryless and depends only on the present state." Fortunately for Greg, the dean, Lawrence Dwight, who sat next to the president, translated most of the sibylline utterances into English.

One topic had a particular impact on Greg. It was a discussion about "grade inflation." The registrar, Douglas

Borden, had gotten the topic inscribed in a meeting agenda for the second week of spring quarter. Borden was alarmed because the grade averages, particularly in the humanities, had shot upward in the previous year. The Thornton grading scale, as Greg now knew well, had not only the usual A+/A/A-levels but also the peculiarity of three levels of F (skipping over E). So there were F, F-, and "F with flagrant neglect." On the other end of the scale, the As and Bs could be filed "with citation." The citation did not affect the calculation of grade point average but remained as a statement (of no more than fifty words) in the student's personal file. Another quirk, that came up in the course of that discussion, was the rule allowing students with either of the two "higher Fs" to retake the course for a passing grade. Some faculty members preferred to give a D rather than an F because even though the D was technically a passing grade, it was a permanent stain on the transcript.

Borden believed that some faculty members were simply giving As to all of their students. Without identifying the person or department by name, Borden gave the example of a habitual offender who had consistently large enrollments and no grades below A. From the registrar's perspective, the person in question simply wrote A automatically next to each name. Wallace Donetz, a member of the philosophy department who looked like an older image of Max von Sydow, objected to this description by asking, "How can you be sure that this person is simply writing an A next to every name? Maybe he just has good students." Borden asked the members of the committee to call to mind the computer-generated sheets that were sent to all teachers shortly before the examination period, the sheets that had perforations down both sides so that the printers could spew them out. The student names were on the left, and there was a column on the right for the faculty member to write in the letter grade. Borden then said, "I know exactly how this person fills out the sheets. As usual, it was a large class, and therefore, the instructor had four sheets of names. The names on the last page came only one-third of the way down the sheet. As I see it, he spreads the four sheets out so that only the last column of the final three pages is visible, the one on the right where the grades go. When he dropped off the grades in the large envelope, my office saw that he had continued to fill As into the last column all the way down the fourth page. In other words, there were more As than there were students."

This description of the "scene of the crime" provoked great hilarity. Donetz had no come-back. Other members of the committee probed a little further, asking Borden just when did this rise in grades begin?

"I first became aware of it in spring 1973," he said. "That's when I noticed it, but looking back, I could see that already the grades from fall 1972 were significantly higher than for the previous fall. At first, I thought it was a fluke and that grades would regress to the mean, but they did not and have not. It's only gotten worse. The faculty are derelict. They are not grading with the rigor we once had."

Alan Lord, a senior faculty member in English, said, "Isn't it obvious? What happened, dear friends, in the fall of 1972? I warned you years before, that the arrival of women would do this. It would drive up the grades. We've lost the treasured ambiance of the Thornton we knew. Remember when the lads would rush out of our classrooms when they heard the alarm from the firehouse—so many of them members of the volunteer squad? Remember how sparse the classes would become in mid-November, when so many of them went hunting? All that happy good feeling is now history! All the camaraderie, the challenge of the great outdoors, all those things that formed *character!* Christ! Now, what we've got is people buried in their books! And…"

At this point, president Chauncey, seeing that Alan had gotten himself launched into one of his rants, said, "Thank you, Alan. Let's hear some other voices." He recognized Marlene Guthrie from the history department.

"How much of this macho bullshit do we have to listen to?" she asked in a loud baritone that was the hallmark of her interventions in faculty meetings. "We're not a hunt club. This is a college. Reading and writing are good things. Ranting and writhing, Alan's specialties, belong in the dustbin of history."

David Feighery turned to Greg and said, "Well, they're off and running!" And they relaxed and watched the show.

The Executive Committee got Greg interested in parliamentary procedure, and he began to study *Robert's Rules* in the recent seventh edition. And this discussion about "grade inflation" gave him something new to be curious about. He thought about its relevance to the situation in his own department. Since arriving at Thornton, students in his courses had achieved a massive number of A's and A+'s, often with citations. The overwhelming majority of the students in his foreign study quarter in Florence had received A's, with the egregious exception of David Lumpkin, who had gotten an F with flagrant neglect. Lumpkin's F could have signified "freak" because, at every opportunity, he demonstrated his contempt for Italy, Italians, and language learning. The "no English" rule applied to books and newspapers in class, as well as to talking. Yet Lumpkin would show up, again and again, defiantly carrying the *International Herald Tribune,* folded so that the front page title and headlines were showing. It was as if he carried it with him like a shield to prevent anyone from mistaking him for someone who spoke Italian or read Italian newspapers. Anyway, Greg wondered, except for Lumpkin, if the grades for his Florence program had been too high. Or had the students just learned an amazing amount of Italian?

The following week, he asked Jean if she could share with him the grades for Art History courses from 1969 until the present. That would be three years before women matriculated as regular students—though some women had studied at Thornton as visiting students before fall 1972—and then two and a half years since the beginning of coeducation.

She spent a week compiling all the material, explaining that she only arrived in 1971 and that much of what Greg wanted had to be found at the registrar's office.

"By the way, Greg. When I told them who wanted to see the grades, they said Registrar Borden would be happy. He's been saying for years that Art History is among the worst offenders—even before women arrived."

This startled him. Greg had gone on the assumption, shared by many on the Executive Committee, that the arrival of women students, numerous in his department, would occasion a spike in grades. Thornton had a longstanding and implicit assumption that men came to this northern outpost of American academia to enjoy sports and the rugged outdoor life, bond with their fellows, and look forward to jobs in their fathers' or uncles' corporations. What did they care about grades? The life of the great Northwoods drew them, the days working on maintaining the trails for the Thornton Outing Club, the boisterous evenings as they sat in front of a blazing fire in the TOC cabin on Rams Head Mountain. This was the bucolic, rugged, masculine life, the treasure that Alan Lord and his partisans wanted to preserve.

Jean and Greg talked about how to handle the mass of data. "I wish there were a machine for this sort of thing," she said. Instead, they designed a model page with columns and boxes that they could photocopy. It would have the course numbers in one column, the instructor in another column, the time of day, the quarter, etc. That would spare a lot of redundant writing. Then Jean, in her neat hand, would insert the numbers.

Once all of the figures were in front of them, they could see a significant rise in grades beginning with the fall quarter of 1972. It was lower than the percentage increases mentioned in the executive committee. If something had increased dramatically in Art History, it was the overall enrollments. First, there was an increase of 10% in the fall of 1972 at the introduction level (AR1). The following winter quarter saw an increase of 15% in AR1, while the students who had taken the introduction in the fall continued with one of the intermediate-level courses. The figures that Greg and Jean had were not broken down by gender. To get to that level, they would have to study the class lists and hope that the given names followed the traditional naming of boys and girls. Jean pointed out that with her first name, it would be a problem if they came across a "Jean Thibodeau" or a "Mackenzie Carter"—the latter being the name of one of her college roommates.

Even though they could not separate out female and male enrollments and thus prove that women had directly driven up the GPA, one of Greg's assumptions was unfounded. There was a widespread perception that women took more of the morning classes. They were more diligent than men in many ways. And Greg supposed the really gung-ho fraternity brothers would shun a 9 AM art seminar. In short, he hypothesized that the early morning courses, dominated by women, would have the highest grades. Yet, in fact, the *highest* art history grades came from two mid-afternoon courses, both taught (in alternate quarters) by Justin Kenman. The average grade in both his courses was A, or actually slightly above when letter grades were calculated numerically, factoring in the A+. So, this is why Douglas Borden complained about grade inflation in Art History. Kenman again!

Greg knew that this work that he gratuitously took upon himself was wasting his precious time. But he could not help himself. He lived alone with Bogart, and projects like this kept him distracted. They were the most insidious form of procrastination. And besides, it was fun to work with Jean.

Towards the end of the winter term, Greg had a glimpse of another side of Thornton when he was invited to a reception at Keller House, the building for the upper echelons of the college administration, to honor a donor to the Italian program. Apparently, his term directing the Florence program earned him the privilege of hobnobbing with important people. The building was impressive in its sober, solid New England aesthetic. When he gave his name at the front door, one attendant took his coat, and another ushered him into a large room with a stone fireplace. Everyone was wearing suits or dresses, and Greg felt shabby in his blazer and gray slacks. The only person he recognized was Margherita, from the Italian section, but she assured him that a few others he knew would be there.

"There's someone who very much wishes to meet you," she said. Taking his arm, she navigated through the crowd towards a man he immediately recognized as Edward Constable Adams, the keeper of the Thornton flame. Greg was flabbergasted. Why would Adams want to meet him? Why would Adams even know that Greg existed?

"Ah, Mr. Byrne," said Adams, taking Greg's hand with what could pass for a smile. "I am so pleased to meet you at last! We are so grateful for your help in the fall when you took time from your demanding schedule in Florence to go to Bucharest. I've heard that you were very good with Brucan. And very discreet! You should come to see me sometime in Chandler. We need young men like you. Very pleased!"

At that point, Adams turned to talk to a distinguished-looking gray-haired man who approached him with an air of deference. Bewildered by the whole incident, Greg followed Margherita to the bar to get a glass of wine—costly wine, as befitted the company.

"What was that all about?" he asked her.

"I don't really know myself. I simply got a call from the president's office to make sure you came and that Adams got a chance to see you. You haven't been here very long and probably don't know that Adams isn't just the College librarian. He has just about nothing to do with books. If this were Italy, I'd say he's like the pope. The college president has to treat him with great respect because Adams has connections worldwide through the Thornton network. He pulls in a lot of money and can solve many problems. Or cause a lot of problems. I'd say to keep on his good side, but don't get too close."

19

A Summer in Boston

AFTER THE AUTUMN in Florence and the winter in Mayfield, Greg was thirsty for a big city, for a city with rich museums, large libraries, and streets full of people, with cafés and cinemas. Of course, Mayfield was a small, attractive town, but after the long winter, he knew he had to be somewhere else. And wherever he was, he would have to devote himself to writing. The third-year review was behind him, but he made it by the skin of his teeth. There were votes in his own department against the evaluation committee's favorable recommendation. Douglas Sykes had told him that some people thought that Greg had neglected his obligations to Art History, that he was too quickly "distracted" by his contribution to the Italian program. His handful of articles (and even "handful" was said to be an exaggeration) did not allay the doubts about his competence in the discipline for which he had been hired.

Larry took him to lunch at a new pub in Bolton Valley,

where they would be away from Thornton for a few hours, and tried to boost his morale.

"You made it, Greg. That's the important thing. There are almost always detractors who find something to grumble about. But now you'll finish your book, and your real-life immersion in Italy will enrich it. Just keep your eye on that terrific project on baroque visual narrative. Worrying is just a waste of time."

Larry's voice was mellow and reassuring. When they were together, Greg and Larry usually avoided the college's micropolitics and plunged into whatever they had recently discovered, whether in books, art, films, or theatre. So, this was an unusual topic for them.

"Yes, I suppose…" said Greg. "That's the Stoic way to look at it. Just clear away distracting *phantasma* and focus on what is right there, right in front of you."

"Isn't that also the essence of your discipline, Greg? Seeing what is *in* the painting, not what is *supposed* to be in the painting? Not what people have *said* is in the painting?"

Larry's encouraging words—live *in* the moment, *seize* the vision of the painting, do not fill your head with myriad fantasies of what could go wrong—were in his mind when he dialed Irene. Chances are she would be heading elsewhere for the summer, leaving her lovely little apartment near Copley Square. When they spoke, Irene reminded him sarcastically, "You're the one who wanted that job at Thornton, remember? I warned you it was a shithole." She told him she had a no-cats policy.

"You are probably planning to bring Bongo with you, right?"

"It's Bogart," said Greg, sure that Irene had deliberately mangled his cat's name.

"Well, I'll find you something and call you back."

What Irene found for him was far better than her place. It was an apartment on Hemenway Street, surrounded by the Northeastern University campus. The graduate student who wanted to sublet it for the summer had nothing against cats. The location could not have been more perfect. The Isabella Stewart Gardner Museum was only twelve minutes away, and the Museum of Fine Arts was even closer.

On the first weekend in June, Greg parked his VW on Hemenway Street, lifted Bogart's cat carrier out of the back seat, and rang the bell of the stone-and-brick apartment building. The man he was renting from was eager to get on his way. He showed Greg the appliances, handed him some typed pages with instructions, gave him the three keys (one for the apartment and two for the street entrance), warned him about parking problems and possible solutions, took Greg's check, and headed out the door.

Looking shocked at the change of scene, Bogart began an eager and thorough exploration, with particular attention to nooks and crannies, the space under the sofa, and the closets. Greg was in and out, bringing boxes of clothes and books and his typewriter. By Greg's fourth return, Bogart had discovered that he had a view of the street from a perch on the back of the sofa. It was not Welldon Street, but there were still birds and squirrels.

Greg wasted no time getting himself organized for a summer of work. He would make the Public Library, which was only fifteen minutes away, his central workplace. He would not be there every day because he would also spend time in the museums, but he would try to have forty hours for writing. Beyond that, he would burn out. So, in the evening, he would go to the cinema, read for pleasure, and see friends.

The day after his arrival, Greg finished his coffee, made sure that Bogart had fresh water and a bowlful of dry cat food, and walked up Huntington Avenue to the library on Boylston Street. He had never been inside, and as he walked up the marble interior staircase, he saw the frescoes for the first time. He paused and looked upwards and around. The paintings were visible on three sides—three panels each on his right and left and one large panel stretching across the wall he was facing. He needed to grip the brass handrail because he realized that he was starting to lose his balance. It was unmistakably the work of Puvis de Chavannes, whose murals in the Panthéon Greg remembered from his undergraduate days.

Then, he remembered that his priority was setting up his summer work situation. He continued up the staircase and into the vast main reading room, Bates Hall. The rows of long tables, illuminated by lamps with green glass shades and seats for eight readers at each table, were precisely the setup he had imagined. It would be impossible to be distracted here. Whenever he glanced up from what he was writing or reading, he would see hundreds of other people working quietly around him, and he would feel the energy and example of their effort. This had been the effect of the reading room in Sterling Library back at Yale. It got him through his dissertation. Now, this place would get him a big way through the book. He walked around the entire room, to familiarize himself with the reference works available. That way, whenever he needed to confirm the location of a specific painting, the artist's dates, or an iconographic detail, he could find the information rapidly and get back into his seat.

But where would he sit? This was not a trivial question. Greg knew that, at least for him, the habit of writing required comfort with the place, and in such a big room, he needed to take possession of some spot. He could not "own" a seat, but he wanted to find at least a table that could become his regular location, his *Stammtisch*. One of the corners would be good. He tried the northeast corner, then the southeast, and when he got to the southwest, he sat down and felt at home. "Why?" he asked himself. It was probably the morning light that greeted him there, slanting across the huge, airy space from the windows on the east side. The sun would shift throughout the day, but a warm greeting first thing would get him off to a good start.

He took a folder from his satchel and looked over his planned table of contents. The introduction would be the last thing to write, and the first chapter, the one on the theory of iconic narration, would remain a collection of bits and pieces for now. He knew that he worked best by building on case studies, or thick description (as he recently learned to call it). He had already published three articles of that sort, and by the end of the summer, he was sure to have several more. He sank into a reverie about the book, imagining what it would look like and picturing himself as someone picking it up in the "new arrivals" section of the Rockefeller Library at Brown. What would the book offer a reader interested in European art history? It would add *life* and *depth* to each scene. It would remind the reader that, just as for a stage play, what was immediately visible was only the entrance into a three-dimensional world in which the visible characters lived. That invisible world which motivated everything they did could become perceptible to the viewer of a painting only through the work of an informed imagination. That was now Greg's task: to create in words a palpable world that was once real, meaningful, and pregnant with promise or threat for any human figure portrayed.

By 12:30 Greg decided that it was time to walk back to the apartment for lunch and to check on Bogart. For the first few days, at least, he would need to have lunch at the apartment so that his little friend would not feel abandoned in the unfamiliar space. When he opened the door, he had a huge fright. In one of the two screened windows of the small living-dining area, the screen had been pushed out of its frame, and there was a gap on the lower right side. A gap big enough for a cat! Greg knew that there had been no gap when he left. He looked down towards the sidewalk but realized that he could not see the ground next to the wall without leaning out, and the screen was in his way. As he tried to figure out how to unfasten the screen entirely to check, he heard a loud meow from behind him. He turned around and saw Bogart peering out from under the sofa. Apparently, the cat had pushed at the screen and then became frightened. Greg closed the window and picked up Bogart for a big hug.

They had a celebratory lunch together. They had survived their first morning of that working summer.

By the second week, the screens were all secured with new screws, Bogart had made himself thoroughly at home, and Greg had established his daily routine. Early breakfast, a brisk walk to the library, arriving at nine on the dot, working until 1, bus 39 back to the apartment, lunch with Bogart, the bus back to the library, and then, after three hours of work, a stroll home (unless the weather was bad). He knew it would be more efficient to bring a sandwich on lovely days and eat outside in the park across Dartmouth Street, but it was lonely for Bogart in his still unfamiliar dwelling. In the morning, as he came up the stairs towards the reading room, it was a great encouragement to be greeted by the largest of the Puvis de Chavannes frescoes, "The Muses of Inspiration." That was what he needed.

One Saturday, when he felt secure in his working rhythm, Greg met Carla Ledyard for lunch in an Italian restaurant she knew on Newbury Street. He almost did not recognize the confident, cheerful, well-dressed woman who rose and smiled from a table near the back of the long room. She hugged him and then asked, "Should I still call you Mr. Byrne?" They both laughed and sat down to babble about what had happened in their lives since the day of her graduation on the Mayfield Green.

"Greg, when we met, you had just arrived at Thornton. For me, you were a 'professor,' and you seemed *so much older* than I was! Now I realize that we're not that different in age and that I'm now about in the same position you were back then."

"Well, I was doing my best to pretend I wasn't a graduate student anymore, but everything was an improvisation. All my classes, whatever I said during office hours, being in committees…I hope I fooled you into thinking I was an authority on Renaissance and Baroque art."

"You absolutely did! But about the improvision. That was the best thing about your courses. I hope you haven't given it up. Every time we started on a topic, you made us feel that we were discovering things together. You didn't seem to be just telling us 'Here's what you need to know.' It was more like, 'How can we describe this? How did the painter make this work? What must it have meant for the people who first saw it?' You made us work for the answers."

"So, do you feel as if you're improvising now? After all, to go from Art History major to assistant curator is a leap."

"Not really so much for me. It's different, I think, for the people in contemporary art. They interact with the artists and gallerists, knowing their acquisition decisions can change a career. I do tend to be more conscious than ever before of art objects as part of a marketplace, even though I'm not remotely involved in acquisitions. Most of what I do is like preparing papers for an art history course, but with much more time to do it and with more resources. But what about you? Back at Thornton, we talked about the 'tenure clock.' It must be a lot of stress."

Greg explained his writing routine at the library, and when he mentioned "The Muses of Inspiration," Carla laughed.

"You're joking, right? That's Puvis de Chavannes? He's just a footnote in art history, someone who couldn't figure out where art was going! He was a contemporary of Manet and Courbet, and they showed us what the world looked like. And after them come Monet, Turner, Sargent…The people who really made modern art."

"Well, Puvis is an acquired taste, I'll admit. And I've never taught, written, or even thought very much about his work. But you can make a case for him precisely because he does *not* show us how the world looks. Modernity has as much to do with turning away from everyday life, from sense impressions, as it does with representational art—to use a rather misleading term. Think of Gauguin, think of the Douanier Rousseau, and then later Magritte or De Chirico."

Carla looked unimpressed.

"Yes, we can turn towards symbolism and surrealism and cubism as important paths of modernity. But if it comes down to taste, then Puvis's bland, languid, flat paintings look dead. Did he even know anything about perspective?"

"I understand what you're saying, but we all have a dream life, an otherworldly life, where it's warm and peaceful and unhurried. And for me, as I'm about to sit down to write and turn away from the world where I have to do the laundry, take out the trash, and worry about my cat falling out of the window—I'd like to imagine myself into that peaceful world for a few hours. So for that, Puvis is a great gateway artist."

Carla laughed and said, "Well, once I'm a senior curator and you have tenure, we can do a Puvis de Chavannes retrospective together. He's so ignored that we could make big news by putting on a show. We might be able to get a cosponsorship with the Public Library—as a curator, you need to think about things like that. But let's talk about what these 'Muses of Inspiration' are doing for you. What are you writing?"

Greg began with an example, as he almost always did, in class, as in his articles. "Do you remember that landscape by Poussin…"

"I *knew* you were going to bring up Poussin," said Carla, as if she were winning a bet she had made with herself, "but excuse me for interrupting."

"The one called 'Landscape with a man killed by a serpent'?"

"No, that's not one I remember."

"It's often spoken of as if it were just a landscape, and if you look at it quickly and casually, you might just admire the crepuscular light, the foliage, the distant hills. You might think of it as a serene, idyllic moment unless you read the title or pay attention to the small human figures. Yet, if you look again closely or read the title, you realize it is a moment of terror. Something awful has happened, and perhaps the danger is not past. A woman is kneeling next to a light-colored object, a bundle of some kind. She seems to be calling to a man running towards her (though we do not immediately know why she is calling out), and this man has turned his gaze towards something in the shadows to his left, something difficult to make out. Looking closer, it seems that a truly huge snake has wrapped itself around *another* person. Then the whole scene becomes a horror story, but *what is* the story?"

"Well," asked Carla, "just what *is the story*? You certainly got my attention!"

"Unfortunately, I don't know. But that's precisely my project—I hope my book—is about. It's about how much of Baroque painting contains implicit or secret but perhaps indecipherable narratives. While only a single instant appears, the painting sends the viewer searching for clues about what has happened or is about to happen. Of course, this is only one part of the book because there are other paintings, such as much of the religious art, in which the narrative is clearly already known to the average viewer."

"It sounds like just the opposite of Puvis," Carla pointed out. "Almost everything of his that I've seen is serene, bright, without depth or mystery, rather pompously conveying an official message."

"That's a good point. And perhaps that's why I find a dose of Puvis reassuring as I prepare to sit for hours scratching my head about what to say about the mysteries of the Baroque."

As they walked back towards Mass Avenue, where Carla would get the T, Greg was glowing from his lunch.

"You're the reason I want to get tenure at Thornton," he told her. "Even if I only have one student a year—or even every couple of years—like you, it makes everything worthwhile."

Before her train came, Carla shared some more personal news. "I've met a really nice guy. So, I'm not always talking about art and art history! He works in city hall. Our chemistry is terrific together, even though he's not interested in art. But urban planning is important, too. Boston could use some fixing-up."

Several weeks later, under a blazing August sun, it was time to return home. Greg got Bogart back into his cat carrier. Bogart was so unusually calm about being shut up in the little box that Greg could only surmise that his smart little companion knew they were going home. As they drove north on the interstates through Concord and White River Junction, the car radio played again and again songs from a new album by someone named Bruce Springsteen. He sang of dark and depressing circumstances of a town full of losers, and yet throughout it all, there was a thrilling pulse of hope, of energy and optimism. Greg felt sure that he, too, was driving on Thunder Road and that he, too, was going to win.

20

Ralph Sawyer

ONCE BACK FROM Boston, Greg saw his modest home with new eyes. He was lucky to have a place well situated and suited for him. He wanted it to look its very best, and clearly the front yard could use some work. The only feature of that tiny space that made it in any way picturesque was an old tree, taller than the roof of the house itself. Several large boughs were dead; clearly, the tree was overgrown and neglected. Something must be done. Greg looked in the Midvalley Yellow Pages and found the Ralph Sawyer Tree Service, "celebrating twenty years of solving all your tree problems." Two days after his phone call, an aged Mercedes Benz pulled up in front of the house, and a large, round-faced man in olive-green work clothes, matching shirt and pants, got out.

"You Gregory Byrne?" he asked, and then, turning away from Greg's answer, he looked at the tree.

"This tree has problems. It needs some thinning. We'll

prune, then we'll inject some nutrients into the soil. You—well, maybe not you, but someone—neglected it for many years. We should get it done soon. Two hundred fifty dollars for the whole thing, and we'll take away the cuttings. You OK with that?"

Greg thought that the tree was some kind of maple. Sawyer told him that it was a boxelder, basically a "trash tree."

"But given that it's all you've got, I figure you want to keep it."

They shook hands on that, and Greg didn't think any more about it until two weeks later when he saw two orange trucks with SAWYER on the side park in front of the house. He was sitting at his bedroom desk organizing slides and writing notes for his course on Baroque and decided that no welcoming gesture was required. About ten minutes later, the phone rang. It was Sawyer himself.

"The guys there yet?" he asked.

Greg assured him that they were fueling up their chainsaws. One was fixing cleats on his boots and was almost ready to climb the tree.

"Good. That's all I needed to know."

Greg went back to organizing the notes. Bogart stretched out lazily on a corner of the desk. The fall quarter had just begun, and the previous week, they had talked about Wölfflin, the general concept of the Baroque. Was it accurate to call it "the Jesuit style"? Indeed, in the north of Europe, outside of immediate Catholic influence, there were many celebrated Baroque religious buildings and even some civic buildings that today are considered Baroque. How should we account for this?

The first angry grunts came from a chainsaw. Bogart jumped off the desk and disappeared, probably to the basement.

Soon, the chainsaw roar was overwhelming. Without looking, Greg could make out three going at once, with different pitches and rhythms as they went from outright screams to grunts and soft, resting putters. Pruning was a lot of work.

He walked over to the front window. They had worked really fast, and the top mass of the tree was already significantly thinner. The climber had dropped the boughs on ropes to the ground, where the two others were cutting the wood. Nearby was an orange machine with a chute angled toward the back of a dump truck. It looked like this was for grinding up the fallen boughs, but it was not yet used.

Back at his desk, Greg searched his memory for good examples of northern baroque buildings. He thought of Nancy, for a French example, and of the Winter Palace in Saint Petersburg and the Zwinger in Dresden. When he looked in the binder that listed the slides in the Malvern Art Library collection, there were no slides for those listed. He made a mental note to request slide purchases before he taught this course again. On the other hand, several of the listed slides in Malvern made him realize that he was concentrating too much on buildings. Decorative landscaping was a significant concern of princes, bishops, aristocrats, and enriched merchants and bankers. The gardens in the Scandinavian, Lutheran, countries were spectacular. He chose several of the Jakobsdal in Carlsberg and Frederiksborg Slot castle in Denmark and started a new page with questions for the students. What would Wölfflin say about them? Did they correspond to his requirements of "painterliness" with the related concept of movement? And what about massiveness? It was a lecture course, but Greg wanted to keep the students on their toes, fighting against the tendency to think that for art history, all you needed to do was relax, sit back, look at some pretty pictures, and then recognize the images later and reproduce snippets of their lecture notes with names and dates.

The chainsaws were roaring and whining in a hellish symphony. How could that be?

Greg went to the window again. It was difficult for him to believe what he saw. The top half of the tree was entirely missing. Or rather, it was not missing. It was on the ground, mostly cut into firewood-length pieces. One of Sawyer's workers saw him at the window, smiled, and gave a thumbs-up sign.

With hands trembling with shock and indignation, he dialed Sawyer's number.

Ralph Sawyer answered right away.

"Sawyer," Greg said, "what do your guys think they're doing?"

"They're pruning your tree, just like we agreed."

"So why is half of the tree on the ground? There are no branches left, just a trunk. And they're still at it."

At the other end of the line, silence. After about thirty long, soundless seconds, "Shit!" Then more silence.

"What are you going to do about it? The whole idea was to keep that tree."

"I'm down in Windsor. I can get there at three. Will you be there?"

Greg told Sawyer he would be waiting. He couldn't bring himself to watch the rest of what they did to the tree. But he also couldn't collect himself enough to work on the course.

He went down to the kitchen and got himself a tea. They must have felled the trunk in one piece because a thud reverberated through the house and shook the glasses on the shelf over the counter. There was some loud shouting outside. Greg heard a resounding "Fuck! You trying to kill me?" It turned out that one of the workers had managed to jump out of the way a nanosecond before the mass of boxelder hit where he was standing. Greg only learned that later from talking to Sawyer.

As Greg sipped his tea, he realized he needed to have some strategy for dealing with Sawyer. He would try to weasel out of damages, and besides, how was he going to replace a whole tree? Greg did not want a sapling that would have no visual impact until…well, probably until he was long gone from Mayfield. Could Sawyer bring him a tree? Was it even technically possible? If it was possible, it was going to cost lots of money. Sawyer would not want to shell out for that.

And there was no written contract! They had shaken hands. Sawyer could deny that Greg requested pruning and that it had been clear that the agreed-upon job was to remove the "trash tree."

At this point Greg had an inspiration. He could almost feel one of Bernini's angels hovering over him, like the one in Sant' Andrea delle Fratte, the one holding the inscription. As if he were reading the marble scroll with the inscription, Greg saw the name "Deborah."

Just across the street from him lived a couple about his age, Deborah and Bruce. Both already had law degrees. Bruce had decided that he also needed an MBA, and was studying at the Walter Luck Business School (known familiarly as the "Good Luck" school), a part of Thornton College. Greg saw little of Bruce, but he talked often with Deborah, who had been an art major in college and whose dream job was to work for a prominent art museum. Greg found it interesting to hear about art from her different perspective. To stay busy while Bruce got his degree, Deborah had taken a job with a local law firm, Thibodeau and Weiss, doing whatever came along.

Greg called Deborah and asked if, by some miracle, she could be free at three. Surprised, she asked what was up. After a quick summary of the situation, Greg told her he didn't think she would need to do any lawyering. He hoped not.

"But if I introduce you as my attorney, it will put Sawyer on his best behavior. You may not even have to say more than 'Hello'."

"Sure," she answered. "I was planning to work at home this afternoon anyway. Why don't I just come over when he arrives? What will he be driving?"

"An ancient Mercedes."

And so it was. Sawyer arrived punctually, and Deborah came across the street. She took her role seriously. Greg's idea of working-at-home clothing was jeans and a sweater. Deborah, however, was wearing a dark blue pantsuit and low heels. She was a good-looking woman, and Greg realized with satisfaction that her appearance might distract and confuse Sawyer. On the other hand, Greg began to doubt his plan to ask Deborah for help. Would Sawyer take a young woman, especially a pretty one, seriously?

Deborah was at Greg's side only a minute after Sawyer got out of his Mercedes.

"Mr. Sawyer," Greg said, using a formal tone that had not characterized their previous dealings, "this is attorney Deborah Hoover. I've asked her to help me in this matter."

It was immediately apparent that this approach was promising. Sawyer's body language became strikingly deferential as he said, "Good afternoon, counselor."

Already confident that Deborah would not have to say much, Greg was astounded that he did not have to restate his indignation at what had happened.

"Counselor and Mr. Byrne, I want to make this right. I

promise to replace the tree that was stupidly taken down. I guarantee it will be one with the equivalent visual impact. We'll locate the tree, plant it, and ensure its health for five years. Will that be acceptable?"

Deborah glanced at Greg, and her eyes told him to agree. Greg managed to keep his face from expressing excessive satisfaction, and he did not have to pretend—after all, the incident was distressing and a waste of time. He was still worried that Sawyer would try to foist a sapling on him.

"That was a big tree. How are you going to replace it?"

"You're right that it won't be easy. But there are tree farms here in Vermont and New Hampshire. We may even have to go to Massachusetts. We can get something you'll like. It won't arrive at the same size as the tree you lost, but it will be a large tree and of a superior species. It will be a much better tree than a boxelder. You'll like it, and it will be beautiful in foliage season. And you will see it and approve it before I buy it and move it here."

So that was that—another handshake, witnessed by an attorney.

After Sawyer drove away, Greg offered Deborah a drink, but—a big piece of news from her side—she was two months pregnant and not drinking alcohol. She did, however, accept a tea. Over tea, as they laughed about the brief afternoon's work, she declined Greg's offer to pay her for her legal services. He began to look forward to buying a handsome baby gift.

In the following weeks, Ralph Sawyer came to know Greg's class and office hour schedule well. They were to drive around Vermont, New Hampshire, and Massachusetts. The time spent actually looking at the trees was minuscule compared to the hours they spent riding in the aged Mercedes. It was a good time to choose a tree, because the foliage was shifting from green to the rainbow of autumn. They needed, said Sawyer, to make the choice before the leaves all fell. Of utmost importance was that the tree be dug, transported, and planted in Mayfield before the snow came and before the ground froze. Although he was resigned to this waste of his time, Greg did not relish the prospect of hours of Sawyer's company. He alternately imagined hours of sullen silence and hours of tortured efforts at finding something they could talk about.

During the first of their expeditions, as they pulled onto I-89 going south towards White River Junction, a heavy rig passed them at high speed. At that moment, the sight of the truck caused Greg to think of the recent death of a popular high school assistant principal, Dwayne Mead, whose Toyota had been crushed by a tractor-trailer ten days before. A front-page article in the Mag occasioned many letters to the editor. The letters praised Mr. Mead's kindness and skill as an educator, decried the dangers of large trucks, and some called for lower speed limits. The description of the crash was based on the initial Vermont State Police accident report, which concluded that the driver of the Toyota had been inattentive and had somehow not been aware of the large truck behind him barreling along in the left lane. Skid marks showed that the truck driver had braked as much as he could without going out of control, but the small car was crushed and thrown far into the median strip. Mead must have been killed instantly.

Greg told Sawyer, "That was a terrible accident that happened last week right about here."

That simple sentence led to an hour's worth of discussion.

"You call that an accident?" said Sawyer. "When someone does something deliberately, I don't use the word 'accident.' Maybe that Toyota driver thought it would look like an accident, but it was clearly a suicide. He planned it. I don't mean that he was necessarily targeting that particular truck—you never know—but he knew there would be trucks, and he seized the occasion."

"But how do you know he didn't just get distracted? How do you know he wasn't lost in his thoughts and didn't pay attention to what was around him?"

"The guy, as I understand it, was a school principal of some kind. He was a smart guy. Used to dealing with lots of things. He just wouldn't go and do something stupid. Look, I may not have a Ph.D., but I can tell shit from Shinola!"

This exchange went back and forth for a while, and Greg was amazed at Sawyer's stubborn insistence that humans invariably make conscious choices. Sometimes stupid choices, he admitted, but "it's what they think is the best at the time."

The tree farm they were to visit that day was in Orford, New Hampshire. At White River Junction, Sawyer took the ramp onto I-91. It was only a few miles before they exited the interstate at Norwich, crossed the bridge, and passed through Hanover to turn left onto NH 10 towards Orford.

"There's your competition, Byrne. Dartmouth College, the 'Big Green.'"

Although Greg knew of several art historians at Dartmouth, he was too busy to come visit. Seeing the Green and Dartmouth Hall standing over it, he thought it looked like a clone of Thornton.

Among the Norway maples that they found in Orford, Greg saw two that appealed to him. They were the size he hoped for. Not as big, certainly, as the boxelder had been, but he knew they would grow quickly. Sawyer's reaction surprised him and gave Greg a new appreciation for the man. Sawyer said that the trees Greg liked had structural defects. Greg would see it split in a few years if they took one. There was no remedy, and the seller knew, said Sawyer. That was the reason for the low price. Surely, thought Greg, Sawyer would prefer not to spend another day driving around. It would have been in Sawyer's interest to get a cheap tree quickly and wash his hands of the matter.

Leaving Orford, Sawyer drove south down Route 10 until they could cross the river to East Thetford and then down Vermont Route 5 towards White River. They stopped at a diner, and Sawyer bought them lunch. Greg found that the chore was turning into something much more interesting and even entertaining: a guided tour of the Connecticut River Valley with an emphasis on trees.

Ten days later, they again drove down I-89, but this time, turned off at Bethel, Vermont, and took Vermont 7 towards Bennington. Once again, for Greg, it was like a tour of New England college towns that he had not seen. The tree farm was a few miles south of Bennington, near the Massachusetts border. Much of their conversation concerned borders—not the one with Massachusetts but the Vermont border with Canada. Ralph Sawyer, Greg discovered, had another important occupation. He was head of intelligence for the Vermont National Guard.

"When you think of Vermont, Byrne, you probably think you're far away from danger. But we're living here on the front line. We've got an almost completely porous border. Think about it. It's not ICBMs that we, in intelligence, worry about; it's the man with the suitcase. That's right. Just one man, with one suitcase. And that suitcase could contain enough radioactive material to destroy a city, a big city. Come through Vermont, go down to Boston or New York. It's not a pretty picture."

The trees at Pownal, Vermont, looked good to both of them. There were some standard Norway maples and some Crimson King, which would grow a little more slowly but would be a brilliant red and, at maturity, a large and gorgeous tree. Greg decided on the Crimson King. They drove back to Mayfield and shook hands.

The tree arrived only two weeks later. It came with a parade of vehicles. There was a flatbed truck carrying a backhoe. Another truck had bags of soil and mulch. And the third truck carried the tree itself. The root ball of the tree was held by a tree spade, a large pointed steel bowl that could open to deposit the tree. Sawyer had contracted with a company that specialized in precisely this work. Within a few hours, all the vehicles had departed, leaving a medium-sized maple neatly surrounded by dark hardwood mulch.

21

Les Bergers de l'Arcadie

THE FOLIAGE WAS gorgeous in the fall of 1975. Everyone said that it was only slightly less splendid than the year before while he was in Florence. All the more reason for Larry Elliot and Greg to carry their trays from the cafeteria in Perkins Center out the door to the terrace facing the Anthropology building so that they could enjoy the scene.

It was always a treat to spend time with Larry. He was one of those restless souls who flew from one topic to another, from the Renaissance to the twentieth century in French literature and then back to the Renaissance, but this time in Italian. Such intellectual wanderlust would have led to superficial dilettantism in most people. Yet Larry dove into things with such focus and energy that he had already written several respected books on lyric and novel, as well as two widely-praised articles on French tragedy. When Larry suggested that they pick up lunch at the Perkins cafeteria Greg expected to be surprised, and he was not disappointed.

It was an overcast October day but warm, and the bright orange, red, and yellow foliage was in the last days of its splendor.

"If only Verrazzano could have seen the New England coast at this time of year!" exclaimed Larry with the delight that he always manifested when he was heading down some new scholarly path.

"Verrazzano, the one the bridge is named for?" asked Greg, startled by Larry's sudden interest in American geography.

"What a pity that people working on the French and Italian Renaissance don't look at the treasures sitting right under their noses! I've begun reading for my senior seminar in Italian…"

"But that's not until the spring," Greg pointed out.

"Sure, but I'm doing a new topic, and there's lots to read," said Larry.

"Travel literature," guessed Greg.

"Close. The literature of exploration, a subset, if you will, of travel literature. So besides the books that got published, there are reports and letters of various kinds that exist only in manuscript."

"How can the students get access?" asked Greg.

"Well, we can get microfilms and make print-outs."

"That's asking a lot of undergraduates."

"They're *seniors*. They are about to enter the demanding world of graduate school, law school, the corporate world."

"So Verrazzano wrote a letter," interrupted Greg.

"Exactly! And do you know who he was writing to?"

"Someone back in…Florence?"

"No! It's much more intercultural. He was working for

the French. Verrazzano wrote in Italian, but François the first, who was fascinated by Italian culture—and envious as hell, competitive with the Italian princes and cardinal—spoke and read Italian perfectly. This letter, *"Del Viaggio del Verrazzano Nobile Fiorentino al Servizio di Francesco I,"* is in the Morgan Library in New York. I'm considering proposing as one option for a final project that they make a critical edition. Several could work as a team, transcribing, making explanatory footnotes, and mapping the ship's route down the coast. There's one letter that would be perfect for that treatment…"

"Ambitious!" said Greg, thinking not only about the students' challenges but also about Larry's need to provide them with a lot of guidance.

"They'll learn so much! And I'm learning so much myself. It's a pity that the navigator's name has shrunk down so much that people think he only saw what is now New York, but the Florentine described the coast from Nova Scotia to North Carolina. He found it so beautiful that he called it 'Arcadia.' The reason this pops into my mind right now is that he told François that he gave it that name 'because of the trees' (*per ragione degli alberi*). And Verrazzano missed the gorgeous autumn display because he passed along the coast between winter and summer, completely missing the autumn."

That evening, as Greg sat eating supper at his kitchen table, with Bogart nearby waiting, as usual, for a few pieces of lamb from the lamb-olive ragù, he returned in thought to Verrazzano's idea of calling the American wilderness "Arcadia"—because of the trees. Did the explorer spend much time on shore? Did he learn how the inhabitants obtained food? How did they manage their habitat? He would have to ask Larry. For years, Arcadia had been an important name for Greg, the name of an ancient place that had grown into a significant and productive Renaissance myth and one that he found helpful as a way of immersing students in the master-pieces of early modern European painting.

Some paintings, statues, and drawings seemed to teach themselves, works for which the students' enthusiasm was quickly kindled and had many comments and questions. At the top of his list was Poussin's *Bergers de l'Arcadie,* "The Shepherds of Arcadia." It was not surprising that this painting worked for teaching because it is a painting about discovery. About a painful discovery that the young will someday make.

There, in the center of the scene—or, to be more pre-cise—slightly to the left and below the center, are the pointing fingers of two shepherds as they seem to attempt to decipher an old inscription on a large stone monument, presumably a sarcophagus—a third shepherd standing on the left watches. One of the three draws the most attention for several reasons. Between his pointing finger and his face lies the horizontal center of the painting. He is also the only one turned fully forward towards the viewer. His left arm (used for pointing) is one of the lightest value points. His bright red garment is one of the two most intensely colored areas of the painting (lightest and most brilliant hue). He is also the only one of the three shepherds interacting with the fourth, most promi-nent, and clearly most powerful personage in the scene. This magnificently dressed woman stands closer to the front plane of the painting than any of the others. She designates the red-clad shepherd to our attention by laying her right arm on his shoulder, and he, in a complementary way, draws atten-tion to her by looking towards her. It seems evident that he is seeking the help of this imposing woman (or goddess) to understand what he is pointing to. She, however, is looking neither at the shepherds nor the monument but downward as if lost in thought.

Do the other shepherds even see the female figure? Is she visible only to the viewers of the painting and to the shepherd whom she favors with her touch? The scene is crepuscular. It is dark in the back at ground level, though light falls on the figures from the left. The sky is lighter on the left than on the right, but is it sunrise or sundown? At any rate, there is nothing in the scene that suggests rejoicing.

Only with the greatest attention can the viewer discern the words that deeply concern the shepherds: "Et in Arcadia ego." Sometimes, this phrase serves as an alternate title of the painting itself. Scholars suggest (or assert) that the words should be completed by adding the verb "to be," but the tense and even the number can be disputed. Should it be *sum* (I am) or *fui* (I was) or *eram* (I was, imperfect tense)? And who is the "I" the *ego*, presumed to be the subject of the utterance? Is it the deceased whose body lies within the sarcophagus? In that case, one of the past tense forms would be appropriate. Or is it Death itself that speaks in the present tense to remind the shepherds, and through them us, of their and our mortality? And are the shepherds literate? Could they be reading the words and asking for the meaning, or could they be asking simply, 'What are these strange scratches on the stone'? For a literal-minded historian the answer would surely be that they cannot read. What percentage of the ancient population of Arcadia could read? Almost assuredly, no one. It was a notoriously wild area, regarded as backward by other Greeks. On the other hand, such a literalist reading would be absurd since "Arcadia" was a literary fantasy place, the setting for Theocritus's idylls. And although the poet evokes a hard, rustic life, the language of the idylls is exceptionally refined.

Hence, when his "shepherds" sing, they use a language that belies their rustic state.

And yet, even after we have come to some conclusions concerning the inscription, what further questions will the shepherds have? What do they hope from the woman or goddess? What should they make of the discovery of mortality if that is what they have discovered? What, then, is to be done?

Greg found that this painting engaged the students more immediately than any other and without the slightest effort on his part. Greg did not have to ask the students questions to provoke discussion; the painting shows people of the students' age asking questions. This always worked, and many of the students' compositions, for which they could choose the topics, included *Les Bergers de l'Arcadie* in one way or another. Some of the most perceptive pointed out that life at Thornton was a kind of Arcadia, an artificially "natural" place where they escaped from the life of the city, from the duties of careers and families, and, in the papers of one or two of the male students, the War in Vietnam. Even in the bucolic setting of Thornton, they could not forever escape the prospect of death. Three years before, students had been shot and killed by the National Guard at Kent State University. There seemed little chance that the Vermont National Guard would come to Mayfield except for recruiting purposes.

22

Why did you call
her a woman?

I T WAS MARCH, and the time had come to announce the choice of the Rathberg Lecturer for the following fall semester. This was a huge event for the Art History department, and the Rathberg attracted an audience not only within the college but also from all over New England and even New York.

The arts at Thornton had surprisingly good resources for a college so distant from a large city. Wealthy alumni took enormous, ostentatious pride in donating paintings, or at least placing them on long-term loan, after returning from vacations in Europe. Several donors collected sculptures from Asia and Africa. These filled several rooms in Hunter House, as the art museum was called. The museum's principal benefactor and namesake, Keith Hunter, had lived for many years in Paris during the Belle Époque and had purchased an almost unimaginable number of Impressionist paintings, with a predilection for Monet. Yet Hunter House was not the only beneficiary of this largesse. The Art History department had received endowments for a range of purposes. There was one that paid each year to allow an art history major to study abroad. There was another that subsidized faculty research expenses. And there were several that underwrote lectures by distinguished art historians and critics. The Rathberg was by far the most prestigious. In alternate years, it brought an artist and either a critic or historian of art.

The three-person committee tasked with selecting and inviting the lecturer for the following fall was ready to reveal the name of an art critic or historian at a meeting in March. The committee had maintained complete secrecy during the selection and negotiation process, and from their smiles, it was clear that they had made an impressive catch. Just how amazing could be gauged by the sight of the champagne buckets on a side table to fête the event. Douglas Sykes dispatched the routine business as quickly as he could, keeping them strictly on the agenda and allowing no news, announcements, or digressive questions as the group ticked through the first five items. The fifth, approval of the course schedule for the fall, took 48 seconds by Greg's watch.

Then Jay Curran, speaking for the committee, began teasing his audience, building suspense by describing the achievements of the invitee. He started by saying, "No one could have predicted that from such humble beginnings in a working-class family, she would become one of the most sought-after curators in Europe and North America…" There was already a lot of information right there, but from the expressions on his colleagues' faces, Greg could see that no one had an inkling yet. He certainly did not. "Her approach to the formal qualities of visual art has provoked criticism from those who view the creation of artworks primarily through an economic lens." Greg saw some people smile with satisfaction—satisfaction with themselves, of course, for their perspicacity, not necessarily from agreement with that approach. "We have all, and I mean *all,* made use of the catalogs she has produced for exhibits characterized by their bold juxtapositions." Lorna leaned closer to him and whispered, "Maybe Majewski?" And Jay managed to keep going this way until he finally said, "Erika Berg."

There was a round of applause at that, and from around the table came the plaudits: "First-rate choice!"

"I can't believe you persuaded her to come all this way!"

"How did you do it?"

"I'm amazed."

"A truly brilliant woman!"

Suddenly, they heard Emily Latouraine ask ferociously, "Why did you call her a *woman*?"

It was Frank Kellenberger who had spoken of a "brilliant woman." At Emily's comment, he looked around, stunned, pulling his head back defensively like a turtle. And apparently, they were all stunned because it was now totally quiet.

"Well, she is a woman, and she is brilliant. I'm not sure what else I could say…"

Emily was fuming. Her face folded itself into a scowl. "That is *so* sexist! *So* blatantly sexist! You could have just said, "She's brilliant."

Frank contemplated that for a moment and then shrugged and said, "Yes, I could have said that. But if I were talking about someone else…maybe, like, Gombrich, I would probably have said, 'He's a brilliant man.' So is it all right to say 'a man' but not 'a woman'?"

"You're implying that there is something unusual about a woman being brilliant. That's exactly what you're doing. You can say someone is a brilliant man, and no one will think twice. But when you say someone is a brilliant woman, people will obviously think you're making some token gesture. You're being patronizing and condescending. You should just shut up about women!"

To that, Frank just said, "I'll try to remember."

With this exchange, the festive atmosphere leaked out of the third-floor seminar room. Meanwhile, Jean and her helper Paige had come in with the bottles of champagne. Greg had a glass and congratulated Lorna on her guess: "You came close. Majewski and Berg have lots in common." They chatted a bit until Dirk approached them and suggested they move on.

Lorna, Dirk Ellsworth, Greg, and Wanda had formed the habit of getting together after department meetings to let off steam and, as Lorna said, "to debrief." They had gone to the Latrine many times but a new place had caught their fancy, Caffè La Fragola, partly because it was more private. It opened for lunch and dinner five days a week and stayed open for tea and coffee afternoons. It was just slightly off the beaten track, and many people did not even know it was open in mid-afternoon.

Wanda being away, there were just the three of them. Greg got a tea and scone.

"That was the most rollercoaster-ride meeting I can remember," said Dirk. "Emily comes out with some pretty far-out stuff, but that must be her masterpiece. She actually implies that the term 'brilliant woman' is an oxymoron. Who among us would think that?"

"Well," said Greg. "I'll be careful not to call Emily a woman. But I'm also not likely to call her brilliant."

"I think she had a point," said Lorna, "although I think that she made the point as an afterthought to cover the real source of her anger. Frank is among the most hidebound of the old-timers, and if I or either one of you had said that Erika Berg is a brilliant woman, she wouldn't have exploded. Instead, it was Frank. Whenever I hear Frank start up, I can feel my body tensing for some unfortunate attempt to deflect from his legendary opposition to the admission of women. Remember when he said that we should put some 'disability art and women's art' in AH1?"

"I wasn't around to hear that one," said Greg. "That is an unfortunate juxtaposition. It's fascinating how he can take a progressive idea and make it sound bad. But Frank and Emily both freeze up the discussion. I can't figure out whether Frank is completely tone-deaf or is being sarcastic and fighting a rearguard battle against the changes we're all part of. Emily makes me feel that I have to be so constantly on guard that I can't try to talk an issue through thoughtfully. Arriving here at Thornton, I feel as if I'm walking across a battleground, caught in the crossfire."

"What issues do you want to talk through?" asked Dirk. "What would you be willing to say here, with us, that you would not say in a meeting?"

"Well, for instance, I know that in English, they are fighting over whether it is better to take the traditional course on Renaissance poetry and include more women writers or keep that course as it is and have a separate trans-historic course on poetry by women. Personally, I think they should both modify their readings in the existing course and also create a new one, but it's not my department, and it's not up to me. But we really need to review the syllabi here in our own department, and I'd like to brainstorm without getting shouted at."

"Welcome to the crossfire, Greg," said Lorna. "Ever since I set foot in Mayfield, I have had to watch what I say. Being without tenure. Knowing that the Kellenbergers and the Kenmans of the department are going to decide my professional future, and knowing that they see me as an aberration. It's not that they consciously dislike women; it's just that when they look around at the recent Thornton, they say to themselves, 'What doesn't belong in this picture.' And it's obvious that Emily, I, and all the other women hires are in that category. It just looks weird to them."

"But I get it from the other side," said Greg. "Here's an example. Remember last fall, there was a talk about women in varsity sports?"

The reference meant nothing to Dirk or Lorna.

"It was a speaker from Michigan who had just published a book on the sociology of sport. As you have probably both guessed, I have zero interest in sports. At Brown, I went to a grand total of two football games; just because I had a visitor from Boston, I wanted to impress. And the only thing I recall, besides her, is the great view of the fall foliage nearby. So I had no intention whatever of going to that talk. But Marlene Guthrie approached me after an executive committee meeting to urge me to go. When I asked why, she said, 'You've got to show up to show your support for women at Thornton!' I answered that I don't choose the lectures I attend based on the speaker's gender. That would be a textbook case of sexism. That's what we're fighting. And Marlene said, 'Yes, you're right. But it's *good* sexism. We can't just all live in a state of repressive tolerance. How naïve can you be? Haven't you read Marcuse?' But I stood my ground and didn't go, and now I'm on Marlene's shit list as an enemy of women."

"Well, Greg," said Lorna, "I guess I'm on the same list. I didn't go. But one thing I think we can all agree on is the song."

"What song?" asked Greg.

"Man enough," said Lorna.

"You mean the one they play at sporting events and that there's such a ruckus about in *The Voice*?

"Almost all the alumni and more than half of the male students want to keep it."

Dirk, who had been at the college much longer than Greg and Lorna, began to sing softly,

> *Boy, are you man enough for Thornton,*
> *Upon the Mayfield hills? Where now we*
> *Strive to keep the flame and live as*
> *Brothers all…*

"Cut it out, Dirk," said Lorna. "That's disgusting!"

"It's so bad it's almost good, good for a laugh, at least," said Greg.

"You know there is speculation that it was written as a parody?"

"No way!"

"Yes. Larry Elliott told me that the student who wrote it in 1912, a guy named Fred Greene, was also the editor of the humor magazine they had then, the *Thornton Madman*. Of course, you can say that he liked writing and could write both serious stuff and comic material. From what Larry found out, it was submitted to the contest for a school anthem and got chosen. Larry's idea is that Greene sent it in as a prank, but then, when it got selected, didn't dare admit it."

"It's not impossible," said Lorna. "There are stories of

people who do things hoping they'll fail. Have you seen *Putney Swope?*"

Greg had seen *Putney Swope* at Yale, and he remembered the clever plot set-up—the members of a corporate board needed to choose a new chairman. The bylaws prevented them from voting for themselves, so each of them secretly voted for the person they thought had no chance of being elected, a black man named Putney Swope, who had been appointed to the board purely as a token. The upshot is that Putney Swope was elected.

Then Dirk said, "You know, our conversation just proves how inward-turning Thornton makes us. Here, we have just had fabulous news that one of the luminaries in our field is coming to this remote place to give us a chance to drink the elixir of the world of ideas, and here we are talking about faculty squabbles and student doggerel."

By now, they could see that one of the servers had started setting up tables for the dinner service, and the three of them realized that it was time to move on.

23

Peter Armbruster

G REG DID NOT hesitate when the Italian program asked him to return to Florence in the fall of 1976. He was fired up for all things Italian and attended the meetings of the Italian club, the *Circolo Italiano*, twice a month in Perkins Center. This time, he would not have to sacrifice months of writing time to bring his language skills up to speed. And he had stayed in touch with many of the people he met on that previous trip. After the graduation ceremonies in June, Greg was invited by Peter Armbruster to spend an hour or so preparing the program budget. Peter was the assistant in the dean's office who made all the financial arrangements for the multiple off-campus programs. He was a jovial, round-faced balding man with heavy-rimmed glasses who had never left Mayfield after he graduated from the college a quarter-century before. Without any direct experience of the wide world, Peter dealt on a daily basis with banks in Paris, London, Copenhagen, Nairobi, and many other cities. Greg had heard that men in Peter's family had had distinguished and even heroic careers in the military. Yet Peter himself had never served.

They would review all the expenses for faculty and host families, the arrangements with the Banca Steinhauslin, and policies concerning faculty duties. Then, the talk went in a different direction.

"I certainly hope I won't have to pick up and head to Bucharest again," said Greg.

"Oh, I don't think we'll need to call on you for that. There will be Wendell Winks in Vienna for the new program there. So, short of some real misfortune, you should be undisturbed in Italy."

"I still can't fathom why we have this tiny group of students in Romania," Greg said. "It's not as if Romanian language and culture were a big trend. I've heard that you people in the administration have to offer various inducements to get four or five students to volunteer. I've heard about the special scholarships…"

"Well, Greg," said Peter with an ingratiating smile, "this is not a for-profit institution. Sometimes, we have to step up and do our part for the greater good."

"But what is the greater good, Peter? I haven't seen the Bucharest budget, but beyond the scholarships there must be payments to Brucan. And since he is such a big deal in the Party, not to mention the power his wife wields…He doesn't come cheap; I'm sure of that."

Peter smiled and said nothing for a moment. "Well, there's no reason for you to worry about those things. Just between you and me, it goes all the way to Adams. I doubt that Chauncey even knows much about the international side of Thornton. With Adams's network of Thornton clubs…

Well, let's say that some parts of our operation may seem to lose money. On the other hand, there's what we're getting for the money. That's the value. And it's beyond our pay grade. Please don't lose your charming innocence. I really love naïveté in a handsome young man. Although, if you'd like to lose some of yours, you could come by my place this evening at about 7."

Greg did not take up Peter's offer, which reminded him why Peter had not followed in his father's, grandfather's, and great-grandfather's footsteps. The Thornton tradition managed to combine a genteel and undercover gay culture with a hardcore cult of physical strength and the acceptance of the hardships of life in the northern woodlands. Peter had deviated from that tradition on two counts, bending neither to the requirements of the "undercover" nor to the hardships. And Peter had teasingly lifted a veil, but for too short a moment to allow Greg to grasp what lay behind. There was that expression, "What we're getting for the money." But what *did* Thornton get for its money? Or perhaps the question should be, "Who are *we*?" Yet soon Greg got caught up in his evening routine, feeding Bogart, cooking his own meal of chicken breast cooked following Marcella Hazan's recipe for rabbit in the pan, then eating it in his small dining room and, necessarily, letting Bogart (alias "the food critic") have a small portion, then undressing for bed and watching a film on Vermont Public Television.

The other essential part of planning for a fall term in Florence was locating people to care for Bogart and the house. He was going to advertise to students who might find a single-term accommodation useful. Then, as both of them were working in their yards, he struck up a conversation with Bob Shugart. Bob said that he and Marilyn had a real problem.

They had lined up a contractor to do extensive painting and other renovation work in their house.

"It's beginning to show its age. But we can't live in a construction site!"

"How long is it going to take," asked Greg.

"The whole fall quarter."

The rest was easy. The Shugarts would stay in Greg's place and pay for the utilities. Greg declined rent. The house would be in good hands, and he would not have to find and interview prospective tenants. Bogart would love the idea since Megan Shugart was one of his favorite people and his occasional cat sitter.

24

Kunsthistorisches Institut

T HIS TIME, GREG felt almost at home in Florence. It had been a crazy, risky thing to do that first time, two years before, taking responsibility for twenty-three college students, intellectually mature for the most part but living outside of the institutional and family structures that they had lived within for their entire lives. The first time around, he felt much the same himself. Like them, he lacked the constraining presence of superiors and peers. He lacked the time-tested curricular structure, the conventional classroom spaces. What focused his attention was fear. If they were distracted by Italian life, by meeting young Italians their own age, by the temptation to spend the weekends traveling instead of studying, by too much *vino*—what could happen to them? A grade of C+? But for him, the stakes were much higher. He faced non-renewal—the euphemism for being sacked—and thus would find himself back on the job market with a complicated story.

This time, however, Greg knew he could do it. He possessed confidence, information, a spatial orientation to the city, experience of the bureaucracy, vastly better language skills, and, most of all, friends. The teaching staff were, with one or two exceptions, the same. He would use the same basic structure for the Renaissance culture course that he taught, which would be coordinated with Luisa's lectures and site visits. Now, he better understood what worked and what did not.

Their classroom space was now in via Gino Capponi, more centrally located. He and Margherita had chosen it, for it really was an excellent location for Americans arriving in Florence. It was only eight minutes from the Academia and from the Museo di San Marco, twenty minutes to the Uffizi, and a little less to the Bargello. All those could be useful for his course, but for him personally there was a bonus: the Kunsthistorisches Institut was practically next door in via Giuseppe Giusti. Since his first semesters in graduate school Greg had been hearing about this renowned German institution, the oldest research center for art history in the whole world. It was founded in the late 19th century and had survived two world wars. It was in a lovely setting in the university quarter and right next to the Giardino della Gherardesca. Although he was sorry that he could not once again have the lovely three-level apartment behind the church in via Bernardo Rucellai, he found a place in a cheap but good pensione in via della Mattonaia, the Ginevra, more or less opposite the prison.

One Thursday, three exhausting weeks after classes started, he walked from the pensione out into a beautiful October morning, determined for one single day to leave all cares about the program behind. A few mothers and nannies watched young children playing in the Piazza d'Azeglio. He settled his back into the curve of a wooden bench under a plane tree. The faint traffic noises in the distance, the laughter and screeching of the children, and the bird song underscored the general quiet. There was no place like this back in Mayfield. No place to be anonymous and idle, and for twenty minutes or so he reveled in the sense of blending into the scene, of being a disembodied consciousness without identity. He watched workers on scaffolding applying new render to the façade of a building on the north side of the piazza. A delivery van from a produce vendor went down the via Giuseppe Giusti. For him, it was all pure spectacle. And yet, the sense of time began to leak back into his thoughts. There was a new hit song that he couldn't get out of his head, the slow and melancholy "Margherita." The lyrics that ran through his head were *"Io non posso stare fermo con le mani nelle mani, tante cose devo fare prima che venga domani"* (I can't stand waiting here, there are so many things I need to do before tomorrow comes). Administrators at Thornton bandy about the term "tenure clock." To them, it is simply part of the impersonal jargon of the academy, like "exam schedule," "fiscal year," and "classroom management." For him, however, it was a real clock. It ticked, and when in his mind he heard that ticking, his own heart began to beat faster. He remembered that he needed to *produce*. It was good that his students liked him. It was good that many people at Thornton were grateful to him for agreeing to lead this study program. Yet the clock did not stop when he landed in Milan. Each month without progress on publications brought him closer to the end of his six years as assistant professor.

His thoughts followed the delivery van, going down Giuseppe Giusti past the Kunsthistorisches Institut. That is where he needed to be. He needed to get off the bench. During his freshman year, he heard Bates Lowry talk about this institute. Then, in the fall of his last year at Brown, he heard about the devastating flood of November 1966, which damaged irreplaceable artworks and millions of books in the Central National Library. In the institute, at least ten thousand books had been covered with muddy water mixed with heating oil. Many Americans came to join the volunteers frantically working to salvage what they could as the waters receded. They were called the *Angeli del Fango*, the angels of the mud. This was Greg's chance to see the place for himself.

He retraced his steps to the pensione to get the folder with letters from the dean and from the chair of the Thornton Art History department. There was also a copy of his application for the NEH fellowship. The institute would require at least that much documentation to give him access to its collections and reading rooms. Would that be enough? Back in Vermont, he had not worried much about credentials, but now, seeing how thin the folder appeared, he wished he had written to his dissertation director for a letter. It would have been good to have something from someone in Germany, like Markus Zweig, whom he had met at that conference in Bonn. He also decided to put on a tie but then thought that that would be a mistake. It would make him look too eager to please, too lacking in confidence. He took off the tie.

As he walked back across the piazza his worries became even more acute, and more trivial. Should he think of a polite greeting in German? How should he present himself, with what title? Then, all of a sudden, common sense began to reassert itself. This was Italy. Even though the institute was a German organization, its employees would likely be Italian and abide by the age-old Italian norms. So he would find himself filling out a form, showing some documents, and then he would be told to return in a week to learn if his application had been approved. The person he would be speaking to would be a secretary with no interest in art or in him. This was a discouraging thought but oddly calming.

With a sharp buzzing sound followed by a click, the door from the street into the lobby area opened. In the lobby, a middle-aged Italian woman smiled at him and asked in Italian how she could help him. This was a good start. In France the question might be the same, but without the smile. At his response, she immediately understood that he was an English speaker and offered to use that language, but he continued in Italian. As he expected, there was a form to fill out, and she invited him to sit at a smaller table on one side of the lobby while he completed his request. The printed instructions were in Italian and German. While he worked on the form, he saw several people enter from the street and pass through the lobby, each carrying a book bag or briefcase. They seemed to be known to the receptionist, who nodded to them on their way inside. He noticed one in particular, a tall, slender, pretty young woman with short, light brown hair, carrying a large, much-worn leather bag. She glanced at him quickly as she walked past. She had an earnest, focused look, clearly intent on her research in the center. Hers was the kind of face he would not forget.

He returned the application and his CV, a copy of his Yale transcript, which indicated his completed Ph.D., three letters of recommendation, and a two-page typed summary of his project. At that time, the title was "Narrative Programs in Baroque Painting and Sculpture." The receptionist looked over the form, put it on her desk, and then read through the documents, seeming to have no difficulty with the English.

From time to time, she wrote something in one of the portions of the form that was reserved for administrative use. She then asked him for his passport, and after looking at it, she made another note on the form.

She told him in Italian that the only thing lacking was the two passport size identification photos. He was annoyed with himself that he had not brought some, since his student experience in France had taught him that the photo IDs were a bureaucratic obsession.

"I'll bring them tomorrow," he answered. Surely, at the Italian pace, tomorrow would be soon enough. There were photo machines at the Santa Maria Novella station, and getting a strip of photos there would be easy.

The woman answered that it would be much better for him if he brought one before three in the afternoon. She explained that the assistant to the director, who must approve each application, would be leaving Florence for a trip to London and would be gone for a week. Surely, he would like to work in the library as soon as possible.

With relief and gratitude, he thanked her and promised to be back shortly. The passive aggressiveness of the average French bureaucrat had apparently not spread to Italy, or at least not to Tuscany. He saw that if he could get the photo in time, he would have his card by the end of the day.

It was only a few feet from the Institute to the via Gino Capponi, where he turned left, then turned right onto the via Guelfa. His mood was much lighter now. It was good to feel the useful urgency of his walk. There were many people from the university there, going to classes or laboratories or sitting outside at tables in front of tiny cafés. Although many came from other parts of Italy, he heard much of the distinctive Tuscan accent, the *gorgia toscana*, that so amuses Americans when they hear of someone drinking "*Hoha Hola*" or physicians or biologists talking about "*anti-horpi.*"

When he reached the via Nazionale, the proximity of the station was evident, as he saw people with suitcases and backpacks coming towards him. He knew there were photo booths in Santa Maria Novella. They would be on the side with the taxis. As he passed the newsstand near the photo booths, he saw headlines about the student who had died when the bar Angelo Azzurro in Turin had been attacked with Molotov cocktails. Even though this had happened relatively far from Florence, Greg could not help but wonder and worry. What if one of his own students had been the victim and had been killed or maimed? The news recently had been full of violent attacks of that sort, and he learned a new Italian word, *gambizzazione*, knee-capping. He later thought it was unfortunate that he had seen the newspapers before taking the photos. His picture showed him looking grim and worried. He was back with the required photos in little more than an hour. The receptionist cut the two required pictures from the strip and assured him that he could return by five o'clock to pick up his reader's card.

It was not until the following Tuesday morning, however, that he could use this privilege. The Palazzo Capponi-Incontri was an early nineteenth-century palace with room after room of books in elegant wooden bookcases. Behind it were gardens with a history from the sixteenth century. It smelled of old books, old leather, and polished furniture. The building itself was impressive, almost intimidating, in a different universe from his life in New Haven and at Thornton. And Greg could also feel the energy from the people around him there. Everyone working in the library was an art historian, at least at the graduate level, and most were either finishing a dissertation or beyond that. He knew some had the luxury of a year or more of uninterrupted time to spend there. For him, the number of hours he could afford to take away from his other duties over the next few months was tiny in comparison. He looked over the bibliography that he prepared for the NEH fellowship application. Only a tiny fraction of those books and articles would be available back in Vermont, so he would have to work quickly, reading with ruthless speed through what he found, with no time to admire the elegance of the writing. He felt paralyzed by the need for haste, like one of those dreams where you try to run, but your feet will not move.

First, he needed to examine the cataloging system that a young librarian named Bruno had shown him. Then, he would need to get a feel for the storage space of the books themselves. He felt like screaming as he pondered the start-up time that would be required for these two steps before he could actually start reading and taking notes.

He went back to the catalog room. He did not consider himself a demonstrative person, but something of his distress must have been visible. A soft female voice from nearby behind him said, in lightly accented English, "You look as if you could use some help."

He turned around and recognized the tall young woman with short brown hair whom he had seen entering the palazzo the week before.

"Show me what's on your list, and maybe I can point to the best place to start."

She was clearly not an employee but a fellow researcher. His immediate impulse was to decline. He felt ashamed to be so clueless, and the fact that he found her so pretty made him wish even more not to look dumb and ignorant. In the second or two he took to figure out what to say, she reached out and took the list from his hand.

"Oh, you work on stuff that's much different than me!" she said.

She paged through the bibliography, which was several pages long.

"It is OK that I write on this? You have other copies, surely?"

He agreed, and she began to mark in pencil the different catalogs he should use for books of specific periods. Some were in large binders on shelves, the binders color-coded depending on the year of acquisition. Others were in card catalogs. She put the markings on the first two pages of his list and told him that he would see the pattern and could continue on his own for what followed. Then she took him over to the wall, where there was a chart showing how the number in the catalog, the *Signatur*, related to the location in the different rooms of the Institute. At first, he was going to ask what *Signatur* was, but then he realized how dumb that would sound. It clearly meant simply the call number. In five minutes she made everything much clearer than Bruno had. Some books and bound periodicals needed to be requested the day before or even two days before he needed them.

"Will you be coming every day here?" she asked, adding, "For how long are you in Florence?"

He explained to her that he could only come two days a week, though he would try for a little more.

"I'm also teaching," he said.

"At the University?"

She sounded impressed. He laughed.

"No, I'm with a group of American students. They need a lot of my attention. And I will have to leave before Christmas."

"With your bibliography, it's unreasonable to try to do all that. You need more time."

He shrugged and just said that he was hoping to get a grant for an entire year off, maybe next year. They both stood there in silence for a moment, and then she said, "It's time for the *pranzo*. Why don't we go out to eat and maybe we can see what's best for you to do. By the way, I'm Anja."

She led him to the Buco Pietro, in Borgo Pinti, and on the way they talked about how each of them in different ways had come to be in Florence. She was completing her Ph.D. at the University of Stockholm. She had a scholarship for a whole year to do the research for her dissertation on Cimabue and his relation to Byzantine art. As she said, this was different from what he did. He explained that only a couple of years before, he had completed his own dissertation on seventeenth-century painting at Yale.

"Yale? That's an important university! Lucky you that you have your doctorate already."

He was pleased at her reaction but pointed out that moving from the state of graduate student to that of assistant professor was in some ways a decline.

"Before," he said, "it was all about helping *me prepare* for the profession. But now that I'm supposedly prepared, it's not about me. It's my turn to work for *them*. This is why my time at the Institut will always come second. It's the time left over from my real job. Or rather, it is *part* of my real job, but it takes place in the background."

Buco Pietro was a good place. It was lively, traditional, picturesque, and even though they were sitting at a table with two other people they didn't know, it was a fine place for a conversation. It helped that the others were talking in Italian and he and Anya in English, so the two communication channels sorted themselves out.

Anya asked, "What is it like teaching American students? And why do they come here? Are they all interested in art history?"

"It's difficult for me to tell you about American students because I don't have a basis to compare with students in other countries, like Sweden. But your question about their interests could reveal some differences. All my students are 'undergraduates,' and most of their courses give them a general cultural education. They also devote between a quarter and a third of their time to some specialization, which could be art history, mathematics, economics, sociology, etc. So I'd say that most of the students with me now are a little bit 'interested' in art history but have not yet chosen it as a specialization."

"Doesn't it bother you that they are not more advanced?" she asked. "What they study must be far from your own researches. Does it not bore you to have to explain all manner of basic concepts?"

"I'm almost never bored," Greg said, and laughed. "It's not in my nature. The wonderful thing about teaching students who know so little (even though they are very smart) is that I learn from them."

"That's either a joke or just nonsense! What are you learning?"

"I get a chance to revisit the concepts we specialists take for granted. We are often content to assume that Wölfflin, and Saxl, and Panofsky have perfectly created the framework within which we must think, and write, and teach. But with my students, I have to start from scratch, and that gives me ideas for new things to write about."

"So you are reinventing the wheel all the time," she objected.

Greg just laughed. "Maybe I'm making a better wheel. Besides, maybe we should all check our wheels more often."

He also asked about her work on Cimabue and whether all the "wheels" for Cimabue studies hadn't been invented. Was there anything new? He asked her about the time she spent "out in the field" looking at the artist's paintings and about getting access to study the objects themselves when there were no crowds of tourists and school groups.

By the time they walked back to the Palazzo Capponi, Anja had volunteered to gather up some of the preliminary information he needed, and to get the books brought to a table in the reading room for him, so that on his free days he could plunge right into reading and taking notes. When he pointed out that this would take time away from the work she herself needed to do, she replied, "I procrastinate a lot—is that good English? Like *temporeggiare*? I just can't do hours after hours of reading about Cimabue. And it would be better for me to look up your articles for you than to read the newspaper or go out for a smoke."

At the Institute they both got back to work. While Anja went back to reading about Cimabue, following her indications he broke up the list into the necessary catalogues and got through locating about twenty items on the shelves before it was time for the library to close. He would see her again on his next free day, Tuesday. Walking back to the via della Mattonaia he hardly noticed his surroundings. He was absorbed by the puzzle that was Anja. Why did she so quickly volunteer her help? Surely it was not that she was immediately attracted to him. His looks, he knew, were average, nothing special. Could he have looked so distressingly disoriented that pity drove her to help him, just as she might spontaneously have rushed to the aid of someone who had fallen in the street? Certainly she did not act out of loneliness, not a lively, smart, good-looking woman living in a country where such a woman would be swatting away the men who swarmed like fruit flies. This image, however, led to a possible explanation. Perhaps, he conjectured, she found in him a defense against incessant male attention. Perhaps, she had detected in him a reserve, a reticence, that would make him tolerable, and with him by her side the fruit flies would swarm elsewhere.

The one thing that was certain, he knew, was that in one day his whole experience of Florence had shifted onto a new trajectory.

25

Discovering Anja

O N THE DAYS when he was not teaching, Greg had one cup of *café americano* at the pensione, and then headed towards the little hole-in-the-wall café where he would meet Anja. There was no place to sit, and as the Florentines packed in to have their dose before going to their offices or their classrooms, just getting over to the counter to order the coffee and the greasy, sugar-coated *ciambelline* was a kind of sport. Wedged in as they were, no one could ever have fallen over, and in a way this was a pleasant opportunity for Greg and Anja to be literally face to face as they drank and munched. They arrived among the very first at the Institut and put their bags at the place they had chosen near the window overlooking the garden of the Gherardesca with its fountains. Working next to Anja, Greg felt a special motivation to stay on task. He wanted her to take him seriously. It even passed through his mind that this was something he cared about even more than actually making progress on the book. Fortunately for him, these two things coincided and reinforced one another. Around noon, if it was a nice day, one of them would head out to a nearby *rosticceria* and buy sandwiches, and they would sit in the garden. It was a sweet but short break in the routine of reading and making notes.

On Tuesdays and Thursdays, when he taught, he would usually be finished by two, and they would explore Florence together. They discovered Masaccio's frescoes of Saint Peter's life in the Brancacci chapel. Greg had studied them in books, but seeing them *in situ* and thinking about what it must have been like to live with them every day made it seem as if he was walking into Saint Peter's story.

"You actually never came here before," he asked Anja with surprise. "You've been here several months already."

"I was saving it for you!" she said. "A vision told me that I would meet a handsome man from across the ocean, and that I would show him the wonders of the *oltrarno*."

It became their joke that she was mysteriously appointed to be his guide, and they returned several times to the quiet, neglected *oltrarno* area and came to know the Santo Spirito church and the streets around it quite well. Anyone seeing them walking hand in hand, close together, would have assumed that they were *fidanzati*, but in fact their life was frustratingly chaste. Anja lived quite literally in a cloister, in a convent near San Lorenzo. The nuns rented rooms to visiting women scholars. Male visitors were, of course, not permitted—Greg could not picture himself climbing over convent walls or disguising himself as a gardener to penetrate into the secluded space as did Boccaccio's characters. Greg could not invite Anja to visit him in his boarding house. Because of the proximity of the Mattonaia prison, there were women waiting (for professional reasons) in the street to greet men released from custody and eager for sexual release as well. This made the owners of the "Pensione Ginevra" extremely punctilious about women visitors, lest their establishment should lose its perfect respectability.

In the evening they often had dinner and went to a film. Anja got them tickets to a play one Friday at the Teatro della Pergola, the complicated, moralizing play *La Ragione degli altri* (*The Reason of Others*) by Pirandello. Afterwards, having a drink nearby, they saw that they reacted differently to the story, which concerns a husband's extramarital affair, the child that is born, and what the man's wife does about it. Though they agreed that the outcome was awful (the mother gives up her child to her ex-lover's wife), Anja detected in Greg the kind of craving for respectability, the quest for social approval, that was a major theme in the play.

"Come on, Greg, you know you are *super* respectable. You are basically such a Puritan. Isn't where you teach the place where they burned 'witches' and people can get arrested for what anyone in Sweden would consider just normal fun? I read that when you work in an American university you have to sign a contract saying you won't engage in 'moral turpitude.'"

Greg felt unfairly accused. He said it was ridiculous to associate him with a religious group that had disappeared two hundred years before his family even arrived in the States. The European use of the term "puritan" was a ridiculous generalization anyway. He could not understand why she connected the play in any way with him.

It was the first time they had had anything like a quarrel, and even though Anja gave him a quick peck on the lips, he went back to his place feeling out of sorts. They did not see one another for several days after that. On the weekend he accompanied the students on an excursion to Assisi. He had rented a bus and had invited Anja to come along, but she told him she would be in Rome for a few days, visiting friends. On Monday, when he went to the usual café, Anja was not there. He assumed that she was still in Rome, and so he was not surprised that she did not appear at the library of the Institut. When she was not there on the next day he had free for research, the Wednesday, he was disappointed. She had not told him how long she would be gone, and so he thought it would be only for the weekend or a little more. The convent discouraged phone calls for residents, but he dialed the number nonetheless, and the *suora portinaia*, who was the one assigned to deal with the outside world, told him curtly that Signora Persson was not available.

Although he knew that it was unlikely that anything they had said to one another on the night of the theatre had made Anja prolong her stay in Rome, he could not stop associating the two things. When Anja reappeared at the morning café on the following Wednesday, she greeted him as if she had just seen him the day before. When he said, "You must have enjoyed your stay in Rome," she looked at him blankly at first, and then smiled. "Sure. It was great. Super, in fact." He realized that she was more important to him than he was to her.

As they worked at their regular table, she sat deeply and placidly absorbed in her reading, unlike Greg, who was antsy and disappointed. At lunch he expected to hear more about Rome, but she just talked about what she had been reading. She was very focused and said that she had never perceived the paintings she was studying as vividly as she now did.

"And Rome?" he asked. "How was it? Any new discoveries?"

"I just hung out with friends. Didn't get out much to see stuff."

In the following days they followed the old routine, and

Anja gradually began once again to show signs of affection, walking very close to him, sometimes holding hands, taking the initiative to propose new places to explore, films to go to, and one time a club where they danced close together. He did not want to pester her with questions about Rome, that odd caesura in their habits of being together. It had seemed, for a while, that they lived in a little bubble of their own. Anja had endless amounts of time for him, she never showed up with other friends, nor did she talk much with other people at the Institut.

Then one afternoon, on one of his teaching days, when he did not go to the library, he saw her from a distance with a very well-dressed man who did not look at all Italian. He might have been in his early forties. Anja and he were walking arm in arm—the way she walked with Greg—and laughing. It was a shock. And a reminder that he knew really nothing about her outside of what she shared about her studies and about living with her parents and her sister in Malmö.

He walked back to the via della Mattonaia hating himself for being so stupid.

The next day at lunch, it all came tumbling out. Anja was wearing an expensive-looking sweater, a style that he had seen in the Max Mara window in the via de' Tornabuoni, and Greg asked, "A gift from your friend from Rome?"

Anja looked at him with real hostility. He had never seen such an expression on her, and he felt as if he had been hit with a fist.

"Is that the sort of nonsense that you dream up in your little adolescent brain? *What* friend from Rome? Do you mean my friend Axel, from Malmö? Were you spying on us? And what does that have to do with Rome?"

"Well, what were you doing in Rome all that time when you were just 'hanging out with friends'?"

"Here I try to be kind to a lost-looking American guy, completely *goffo*, irritatingly clingy, with no initiative, just full of his 'important' job at some American university no one ever heard of—and I try to show him how to use the library and show him a little bit of Florence, and now he thinks he owns me! Just like the Americans think they owned Vietnam! That is just *skitsnack*!"

Greg just stood there letting it all wash over him, washed with shit, with *skitsnack*—he did not need to know Swedish to get that much. Instead of trying to defend himself, he dug himself in further. His curiosity was too strong.

"But what about Rome?"

Anja laughed so hard that she looked as if she were going to fall over. She grabbed his shoulder to steady herself.

"That had nothing to do with Axel! In fact it's the opposite of Axel, who is mature beyond his years and doesn't go for exploring new stuff. In Rome I dropped acid with some friends from Sweden and Norway. It was my first time, and it was really wild—terrifying for a few moments, but beautiful a lot of the time. It took me a few days before I felt like coming back to work here. And it made me feel peaceful, focused, and happy."

"But that's incredibly dangerous!"

"You are just so timid, little Gregorio. And I'm not stupid. I was with experienced people who guided me through and took care of me. You are just scared of everything!"

It was not really an argument. Greg was embarrassed at his own infantile jealousy. He knew she was right. He should have concentrated on being grateful for the time he spent with her. He was, he recognized, full of himself. And out of his depth. For a moment he almost cried, so much did he wish to go and hide himself in his little house near Otter

Creek. Yet he pulled himself together and suggested that they go for a walk in the Gherardesca to cool off.

Both of them apologized, and both of them agreed that they had spent no time really talking about themselves.

"It's actually good that you asked about Axel," said Anja. "Because you shy away from anything personal, as if you have something to hide."

"Maybe it's because I don't have anything much to hide. My life is pretty dull, when you come down to it."

"Well, mine isn't."

They talked for a long time, and by the end of the afternoon, Greg understood that Anja was a generous, warm person who offered to make his life about something other than his work and worries. He realized that affection could take many forms, including compassion and the desire to help the afflicted. He thought about Bogart. Had he rescued Bogart? Or had Bogart rescued him?

When he wrapped up the program in December, Anja accompanied him in the train to Milan. They laughed about the name of the place they stayed that last night, the Jolly Hotel.

26

Back Home

GREG PRESSED HIS back into a pillar in the chaotic boarding area for the Alitalia flight to Boston. Malpensa airport was not generous with seating, and it did not help that so many travelers—especially the large family groups heading to the U.S. to celebrate Christmas with relatives—had used every stratagem imaginable to circumvent the limitations on carry-on baggage. One woman appeared to be wearing an entire wardrobe in layers that bulked her up to look like the Michelin tire man or a raggedy Italian impression of a snowman. It was clear that she was using her suitcases to hold gifts. Greg had paid to check an extra bag that had small gifts for the Elliots, for Ruth, and for the Shugarts. Once in his seat, he buckled his seatbelt and fell asleep, not even waking up during takeoff. When he woke, they had already been flying for some time. He saw the flight attendants picking up the platters from the meal they had served. Mercifully no one had bothered him. All the fatigue of the months in Florence had hit him suddenly. He was a limp rag, the tension of being always on duty for the students, the excitement of meeting Anja, the spectacle of the city and its smells, had drained away. For the first time in months he was alone—the planeful of passengers didn't count. He did not know them, they had no story together.

He lay in a daze looking out at the clouds. And the clouds led him to think about randomness, about wispiness, about why clouds form and come together. Why these clumps of white and grey instead of a world full of endless, uninterrupted swirling mist? How do things come together? For everything that happens there is an infinity of things that do not happen. He ended up spending the fall in Florence, and not in Vermont. And he worked at Thornton, and not at Chapel Hill or Ann Arbor. And suppose he had not met Anja that day in Palazzo Capponi? How totally different his experience of Florence would have been. The past three months seemed so solid, so vivid, so unquestionable and yet they all stood on… nothing but cloud, or nothing but a sheet of ice or of glass.

Sometime later he woke up again. The image of glass had persisted into his dreams, but instead of being something he walked on, it was what he himself was. In the dream he was a man made out of glass, like the character in that story by Cervantes, "The Glass Graduate," who had to be transported in a cart padded with hay. He was so afraid of breaking. There was much more to the dream, Greg thought, and he felt that if he could remember it, it would unlock some key source for the book he needed to write. Even just the fragment that reminded him of Cervantes was intriguing. In that novella, even after the graduate is cured of his illusion, he is plagued by people from all over Spain who come to see the "man of glass." What do they expect? Do they really think that there can be a man made out of glass? Or do they want to see an ordinary man who *thinks* that he is glass even though they can see that he's not? And how would that be represented in a painting? It seems like an impossible thing that would be also impossible to represent. He remembered that Descartes mentions Cervantes's works more than once in his *Discourse on Reason*—not by name, but the references are unmistakable. Greg was too drowsy to be able to formulate anything coherent from this, but he remembered later that his thoughts were about all the things that did not happen but were lurking behind everything that happened—about visualizing the network of possibilities that could have become real. And then he thought about Anja again, and how *unreal* it was that he had met her. That was his overwhelming thought, the scary thought: meeting her and finding her so kind and welcoming was much *less* likely to be the thing that became real.

That evening, back on Welldon Street, Greg saw the surprise in Bogart's eyes and felt the small, warm body rubbing against his legs. The cat sniffed Greg's shoes, slacks, and hands and could smell that Greg had been somewhere quite different. He purred when Greg gave him some of the good cat treats. Both Greg and Bogart knew that life was back to normal.

The next morning, as Greg woke with surprise in his own bed, reality hit him in a new, unpleasant way. Although it was the festive season, and he got back to Mayfield in time for the Revels, and he would go to Ruth's and to the Elliots' for dinner, and they would drink sherry and laugh—emerging from the focused, frenzied experience of Florence Greg now felt in his very bones the passage of time. As he lay there in bed, with Bogart next to him, Greg remembered those verses from his high school English class: "But at my back I always hear / Time's winged chariot hurrying near." He heard the inward tenure clock ticking much louder in Vermont than in Florence.

He made himself a quick breakfast. The Shugarts left his kitchen stocked with fresh milk, fruit, bread and coffee. There was the shopping to do, but also a trip to Thornton Hall to see what mail had come. Greg had agreed with Jean Buxton that she would forward nothing except personal letters since he could do nothing about his professional business from Florence. The response about the two articles he sent off just before leaving would surely be waiting. If they had been rejected, it was just as well that the news did not spoil his time with Anja.

27

Valentine's Day

IME'S WINGED CHARIOT had sped Greg into 1977, and it was already the middle of the winter term. For Valentine's Day he mailed a card to Stockholm, although he didn't know if the Swedes had that holiday, or, if they did, what they did for it. Then, on the day itself, Anja called at noon. It was great to hear her voice. It was the first time since Christmas. "'*Glad alla hjärtans dag!*'— that's what we say here," she said. They talked, but not too long. Greg reminded her how expensive these calls were. It was six o'clock in Stockholm, and she and her friends were cooking a special meal and Anja herself had made the cake. "Maybe next year, Greg, you'll be here to see *alla hjärtans dag* for yourself and lots of other holidays."

What would next year be like? He was in his fifth year already, but he was acutely aware that he should have been at this point in his work at least a year before. He was paying the price for agreeing to do that second round in Florence.

An article had recently been accepted, the one on the narrative moment in religious art that was to appear in Australia. The other one, which attempted to show how still life could be construed in narrative terms, had been sent back by the bulletin of the Société d'histoire de l'art français with vaguely encouraging suggestions for a rewrite. He needed time! He thought bitterly about that Irish saying his mother had been so fond of: "When God made time, he made enough of it." If there was so much time, why wasn't there more in his own life?

A little over two weeks later, a letter from Larry Dwight arrived in his Thornton mailbox. Larry wrote that in answer to his petition, Greg would be allowed an additional year to finish his book, though without funding. This was the compromise that the deans had worked out, trying not to set a dangerous precedent. When Greg reached that point in the letter, it occurred to him that the adjective most often associated with "precedent" must be "dangerous." Stopping the tenure clock, Dwight wrote, was something usually reserved for medical emergencies or childbirth, and there had been a lot of debate in discussions with the provost and even with the assistant to the president. The administration did understand that Greg had been unselfish and assumed a significant risk to his career by directing the Florence program, especially when he did it the second time, knowing, as he did, that his time as an assistant professor was getting short. It was understood that he would be on leave from teaching during 1977-78. The tenure clock would start again on September 1, 1978, and the Promotions and Tenure committee would expect his completed dossier no later than June 1, 1979.

This was tremendous news! Instead of grading, Greg gave himself an evening off, sipping a beer and relaxing on the sofa in front of the fireplace with Bogart. He listened to the new song "Hotel California" and thought that if he could travel for the following year, he would not be staying in a frightening place like that.

The next day came the letter from the NEH. Greg realized even before opening it that the news was good. It was a standard nine-and-a-half-inch by four-inch business envelope, but what he immediately noticed—not just on sight but by holding it in his hand and feeling it—was that it was thick. It contained several sheets of paper. If it were the type of letter that began, "I regret to inform you that…", one sheet would have sufficed. The letter started, "On behalf of the Endowment, I am pleased to inform you that you are the recipient of a Fellowship for College Teachers…" The other papers included a set of rules and requirements and a form to fill out with his social security number, the date at which he planned to begin his year of research leave, and so forth. He must also send them a letter from his institution granting him a release from duties for the corresponding period.

No sooner had he perused the packet than the phone rang. Greg thought at once that it must be Wanda Andros. If it had not been for Wanda, Greg would not have applied for the NEH. He considered it a real long shot. But she told him that she had received two application packets and insisted on putting one in his mailbox. "Let's do it together. Come on! It will be a blast. I'll read over your proposal, and you can read over mine. Let's go for synergy!" Proud of her Greek heritage, she reminded him that *sun* and *ergon* meant working together.

He lifted the receiver from the phone on the kitchen wall, hoping more intensely than ever that Wanda had good news. If she didn't, he knew he would feel sad and ashamed to share his own news.

"Professor Byrne," said Wanda's voice, "I suspect that you have received good news. Am I correct?"

From her usual joking tone, he knew at once that they had both gotten the same letter.

"Did you get one of the fat ones too?" he asked.

"Absolutely! So now we both face the urgent, important question."

"What's that, Wanda?"

"Should we go to La Fragola or Trillium this evening to toast our synergic success?"

They decided that Wanda would phone Trillium, and she volunteered that she and Ian would invite Clara Marsh. Wanda often teased Greg about having a crush on Clara and about finding many pretexts to request interlibrary loans. Greg would neither confirm nor deny this, but Clara was always fun to talk with, not only because of what she had to say but because there was something warm and alluring in her alto voice.

They had plenty of privacy at Trillium since it was the break before the spring quarter would begin at the end of March. As they sipped their *apéritifs* in a booth near the soapstone stove that was the glory of the restaurant, they talked about how the fellowships opened a world of possibilities. "Are you going to stay here?" asked Clara. "Or will you head back to Italy or to Paris? I know that if I had a year to do research, you would not find a trace of me in Mayfield. No way!"

Ian, ever the contrarian, played the devil's advocate.

"When I'm writing or feverishly taking notes for a book, any distraction is poison. What is there to distract me here in Mayfield? Nothing to do except Thursday night movies at The Jewel, ice hockey and football games, the Winter Carnival…

So, utter boredom. *But…*Boredom is good! It's a prophylactic. It forces me back into my work. But think of being in Paris, London, New York, L.A.! A refugee from Thornton would go wild in places like that. How could I sit still?"

"So what will it be, Greg?" asked Wanda.

Greg admitted that he hadn't thought about it. He just knew that he would not be living off his meager savings and a loan from Thornton (more debt!) and could travel. He had not said much to anyone about Anja. She was back in Stockholm now, and if the choice was his, he really wanted to be near her.

The following day, after his morning class, he dashed off a quick note to share the news with her. If she were free, they could choose any place to live together—Italy, France, Spain or even the U.S., where Anja had been for only a single summer of study at the Getty. They had been writing regularly since his return to Vermont. It took five days for an airmail letter to reach Florence, and now, more recently, Stockholm, and then five days for her reply to get to him.

27.3.77

Trädgårdsplats 30

Dear Greg,

I'm writing to you from my new abode—Trädgårdsplats—FRONT ROOM as opposed to maid's quarters. My school friend "Ping" has occupied the remaining rest—quite an extraordinary person—totally different from Jude and I—lots of variety—lots of fun in the flat. In fact she had both of us running round, organizing and reorganizing and cleaning like two little chars—you've got no idea what degree of variety that was!

Now that we have a dining room table we take great pride in having formal meals which means that everyone has to be out of their pyjamas by 6 p.m. We also thought of making this two hour interlude reasonably useful. Jude has been wanting to learn Italian so that if the great day should arrive she would be able to receive you in the proper manner—that's assuming that Americans don't speak English!

So you see I don't have the problem of talking about you—I say anything I want to, and they all believe me implicitly.

The slides from my Sicily trip have just been developed. Colour wize, camera wize quite good but I've still got a lot to learn about the layout of a slide. I saw them for the first time in a café and to everyone's great amazement uttered a shriek when I came across the two slides taken in the Rome airport—their existence had totally slipped my mind and so, once again, Gregory Byrne had caught me unaware.

Greg, should you decide to come to Stockholm…! Well, there's just too much to say about that, and I must get this letter off before the post office closes. The sooner I send it, the sooner (I hope) I'll get a letter back. So till then…

Much love,

Anja

A situation that he had not dared fantasize about now shifted into the range of possibility. Greg felt a barrier in his thinking suddenly give way. Until then, he refrained from imagining a year in Stockholm because he did not know that he would have the freedom to leave Mayfield and did not know how he could possibly pay his way. And Anja had also, despite the intense rhythm of their letters, only given vague hints that she would make it possible for him to live with her. The radio was playing a song that fit his mood, "Good Times." The lyrics could not have been more straightforward: "Good times, these are the good times, leave your cares behind, these are the good times."

Greg now began to focus on the details. Anja had just moved into a new place. She had two roommates with whom she was close. One of them was already talking about—probably jokingly—speaking Italian with him. They would not be moving out, he was sure, and so where would he fit in? Would he and Anja be in the "front room" together? Probably. And where would he sit and write? Could he get access to a good library, one where he could sit? Yes, sit, and write on his usual yellow legal pads, the way he always did, with the bizarre numbering system that only he could fathom, but he could surely not bring his Olivetti to a reading room in order to type up a readable clean copy. The clacking and ringing of a portable typewriter would get him thrown out of the library at once—*sehr schnell* or whatever they say in Swedish—and that would leave him where? The dining room table? And what about Bogart? His faithful cat had tolerated Greg's previous absences, but the two trips to Florence had lasted only three months each, not a full academic year. And crowded into the apartment, could he and Anja remain on good terms? And what about the possible resentment from Ping and Jude? The more he thought, the more it seemed that he and Anja should find somewhere else to live, perhaps staying in Stockholm to avoid disrupting her life too much. But then, could he bring Bogart…

28

Stockholm

WAS IT SPRING fever? It was that time of year in Mayfield when the snow had melted except in the deepest pockets of shade under the pines and spruce trees but when the hardwoods were still bare. It was mud season. On many days, Greg found it difficult to concentrate on his classes and marking, particularly the meticulous commentaries that he insisted on writing for each of the student papers in AH 55. His mind just drifted to Stockholm and Anja. He now had an image of her apartment in his mind, even down to the color of the walls.

In one of her letters, Anja wrote about her decorating project.

15/4/77

Dearest Greg,

I guess I'm not exactly unfolding a passionate love letter by asking for information regarding the state of your walls. I don't mean whether they're wall papered or plastered (they're probably both, or alternate, or something) but as always—just skimming the surface—I just wonder if you have any pictures around.

I've just completed the process of re-re-redecorating my room and also undergone a similar process concerning my attitude to decoration and ornament. Simply I started from an empty room—cluttered it up and now want to go back to square one. Why? Probably because I'm untidy—excuse the profundity. You see how easy it is—just answer the above mentioned question—you'll be sized and appraised (and I'll get my room ready).

Still part of the process of keeping up (with you) I've taken a book about Poussin out of the library. But even though I've never spent so much time reading as I seem to now—a sure sign of spring fever—the book on Poussin remains untouched.

I'm still continuing with the university reform projects, going to assemblies, etc. After being so free in Italy, I'm very sensitive to a lot of the restraints on me here, such as my thesis director leaning on me to take his approach instead of leaving the discovery process up to the individual. I know that Gregory Byrne would never deal with his students that way!

Enclosed are two photographs, having just been obtained after a hectic afternoon in town. Even in Stockholm I'm an incompetent road crosser. (You'll see from the photo).

You'll probably laugh at this, but I write a good many more letters to you than I actually send. You're like my "soul mate" to whom I write in the dead of night, purely in order to clear up my own mind. The frustration of letter writing is that it's much more difficult to turn a blind eye rather than a deaf ear to my monologues.

Greg, I can't wait to know for sure whether you are coming to Stockholm! Or must I resign myself to a correspondence until we're eighty?

Please write soon!!!

Anja

Greg reassured her that whatever she chose to decorate her walls—no, *their!*—the room would be fine. He wrote back immediately, as he always did, although often he wished he had waited and written an even better letter. He did not really write, as Anja said she did, more letters than he sent. But there was always a kind of draft letter in his head, a silent mental stenography of the experiences, discoveries, and feelings he wished to share.

Oddly, a couple of weeks passed before he got a reply, and this time it was astoundingly brief.

30/4/77

Dear Greg,

Sorry I haven't written in a while. There's lots going on. Nothing important, just the usual stuff...

It continued in this vein but lacked the usual humor and loose, flowing conversational grammar. It was stilted, he felt. On the other hand, he did realize that she also had a demanding life with her studies and involvement in student organizations.

But then there were no letters for two weeks. Only something really drastic could explain that—an illness, an accident. One evening, in sudden, urgent alarm, he started to make a long-distance call to Stockholm. He started dialing before realizing that it would be a really late hour at night there, so he resigned himself to calling first thing in the morning. Instead of his morning run, he would stay in and phone before breakfast.

There were the usual multiple different tones as the signals made their way from the middle of Vermont through whatever switching points and then cables over to Sweden. Finally, he heard a recognizable European ringtone. After about a dozen rings, someone picked up. A woman's voice he did not recognize. He asked for Anja and said that he was Greg Byrne.

"Oh, Greg, yes. This is Jude. Anja's not around just now. Can I take a message?"

"Well, I'm just calling to see if she's all right. I haven't heard from her in a while."

"She is fine. It's just that she's been busy for several weeks now. I'm sure she'll write soon, Greg."

"Could you have her call me? I'd like to hear her voice."

"I'll leave the message."

The call had not been reassuring after all—just the opposite. Even Anja's roommate sounded abrupt and less friendly than he thought she would be, given all that Anja had written about "Jude, our chatterbox in residence." But as the day went on, he tried to persuade himself that Jude, too, had been busy. His call reached Stockholm in the early afternoon when they would be busy.

No call came, at least not when he was around to get it. And not the next day, either. At least he knew now that she was not sick.

Then, six days after his call, he found a familiar blue

light-weight envelope in the box inside his door. He resisted the temptation to rip it open because he wanted to sit down and enjoy this news after such a long time. So he fed Bogart and gave him fresh water, and then he went to the living room and settled on the sofa. The envelope had the reassuring thickness of a long letter of multiple sheets.

22/5/77

Greg,

This is such a hard letter to write. Actually I've started it at least five times and thrown the crumpled pieces away. Now I'll just write straight thru, even though it will be sloppy and there will be many words crossed out. There is just no good way to say what I have to say.

Greg felt a bad, indescribable discomfort flood his body and broke out in a sweat. He stood and walked to his bed, where he lay down. He must have fallen asleep or passed out because the light was different now. He lay there for a few minutes with his eyes open, and then he resolved to go back and read the letter all the way through, no matter how painful.

I've met someone. It didn't seem as if that could happen. I mean, it didn't seem as if I would react to someone else so strongly and so quickly. The fact is that he's not nice at all, really. I can't talk with him the way I can with you—even writing letters to you is a way of talking, not so much like writing. He doesn't even listen to me and besides, he knows nothing about art and just laughs when I bring up my work. But he just sweeps me away. I've even, in my mind, tried to share with you, my soul mate, this feeling, because we share everything (it seems to me), but I realize that this is one thing I can't share with you. It's not just that it would hurt you, but it's that I can't explain it to myself, so I can't put it in words for you.

Jude and Ping think that I'm crazy. They are cross with me, and they don't like…him. I won't name him. I think that's best. It doesn't matter to you and I don't want you to have a name in your mind that you will find ugly and painful.

I know this is horrible timing. You are making your plans for next year, and now I've gone and made a complete bollocks of it all. Even now it's hard for me to get out of my mind all of the things I was planning to show you here, and the food I wanted to share, and the places to go for walks. I do hope you will not hold it against Stockholm. It's a beautiful city, and you should come sometime. But I imagine that you'll not want to come now, during your leave time. You'll go back to Italy, maybe to Florence. I hope that the memory of me won't blight the city for you. Someday you'll go back there, I know, because the city will still be there and be beautiful and the hurtful memory of me will fade.

I'll ALWAYS remember you, Greg, and keep your letters and that photo of us that your student took.

How can I end this? Just please forgive me.

Love,

Anja

Greg finally realized that Bogart had been rubbing against him, trying to get his attention. Greg went out for a long, pointless walk. Wasn't everything now pointless?

29

Sir Anthony Blunt

REG HEARD AGAIN and again that being on leave should be great. He heard that from his friends and colleagues, except for Ruth, Wanda, and the Elliots. They were the only ones he told about the fiasco with Anja. Now, there was a year of research leave stretching ahead of him in all its emptiness and lack of structure. He would have been less lonely, he knew, if he had classes to teach. Ruth suggested he get away from home for the summer, but she advised him not to return to Florence. Not yet. There would be too many bittersweet memories.

Paris was a good idea. He had not been there for more than a few days since graduate school, and the change helped him get out of the funk of the breakup with Anja. Though disappointment still burst into his consciousness sometimes. When he walked on those summer days in the old familiar places—the Luxembourg, the Palais Royal, the rue Mouffetard, the Place Dauphine, the Montagne Sainte

Geneviève—he caught himself thinking what it would be like to show them to Anja. It amazed him to think that she lived so close in Sweden, from his point of view, and yet had only been to Paris once. Those moments were the hard ones, but often, he could think back further, back to his student days in Paris. When he did that, it brought a milder, sweeter form of melancholy. Towards the end of June, however, tensions in Paris rose when a bomb exploded in the palace at Versailles, destroying paintings and statues and blowing a hole in the roof of one wing.

Greg returned to Mayfield in late August, like those of the colleagues who were preparing to teach. But he planned to seclude himself as much as possible. Now, it was time to get going. Really going. For the 1977-78 college year, Greg had agreed to let a series of visitors use his office, knowing that the office was the last place for doing sustained work—it was a place to avoid at all costs. Instead, he got one of the coveted studies in Chandler Library on the fifth floor of the stacks, where most of the art history books were stored. Few people got a stacks study. There was a long waiting list. Fortunately Larry Elliot had had the kindness to suggest to him, as early as 1974, that he get his name on the list. The timing turned out to be perfect.

To be in the stacks study was like committing one-self voluntarily to solitary confinement. Greg would enter Chandler from the Green, cross the lobby, enter the stacks at level two, and then go up the stairs to level five. He then went through a maze of shelves to the north side, where, as a keyholder, he could open a door of steel bars that opened into a narrow corridor—he often wondered how such a corridor could have met fire safety standards. His was the fifth and last cubby, and with a second key, he opened that door with a small frosted-glass window covered with a metal grate. There was a small metal desk with a brown linoleum surface stained with old ink and four drawers on each side. On the wall opposite the desk, there was a wooden bookcase where the occupant of the study could keep books properly signed out by the circulation department. Between the bookcase and the desk, there was scarcely enough room to move the chair provided. Thinness was an expected physical quality in Thornton faculty members. A desk lamp was plugged into the sole electric outlet on the wall just above the desk surface. The outlet offered one remaining socket into which Greg could plug his new portable Smith-Corona electric typewriter. It did not make much noise, and at any rate, there was rarely anyone present in the neighboring studies. The view from the only window would not be distracting. Beyond an expanse of tarred rooftops, Greg could see only the hills to the north. In the stillness, Greg realized that if he died there, his body might not be found for several weeks.

Working enthusiastically on decoding the symbolic significance of Baroque works, Greg found that time generally passed quite quickly in this monastic setting. The bells from the chapel that announced the ending and starting times for classes reached the cell faintly. There was an image of solitary study that came repeatedly to mind. It was from the famous letter of Machiavelli to Francesco Vettori, in which the author, essentially banished from Florence, describes how he passes his time.

"When evening comes," wrote Machiavelli, "I return to my home, and I go into my study; and on the threshold, I take off my everyday clothes, which are covered with mud and mire, and I put on regal and curial robes; and dressed in a more appropriate manner I enter into the ancient courts of ancient men and am welcomed by them kindly, and there I taste the food that alone is mine, and for which I was born; and there I am not ashamed to speak to them, to ask them the reasons for their actions; and they, in their humanity, answer me; and for four hours I feel no boredom, I dismiss every affliction, I no longer fear poverty nor do I tremble at the thought of death."

Greg felt so energized by this passage that he copied it out and attached it to the wall over the little desk. When he came through the locked doors and removed his jacket or parka, depending on the season, he would sit and read Machiavelli's words, which seemed to be written precisely for his situation. Although he did not put on regal robes, in his mind, he felt transported out of time. Machiavelli's words, like those of Vasari writing about the lives of artists, or Baldinucci's writing about Gianlorenzo Bernini, or Cellini writing about his own life, spoke to Greg in the immediate present, so much so that he felt closer to them than to most of the people around him—at least for the time when he was locked in his solitude. Imagining himself in Machiavelli's place also helped him forget, for a while, that he was not in Stockholm.

In that fall of 1977, thanks to the NEH fellowship, Greg no longer had classes, committee work, and office hours to fall back on for procrastination. His mind, ever seeking detours from the intimidating challenge ahead, behaved the way Paul Simon sang about in his new song, "Slip slidin' away." The nearer Greg got to his destination, the more he slipped sideways.

His particular detour or sideway concerned two important people in his life—two people he had never met but about whom he frequently had occasion to think—Anthony Blunt and Volker Baum. In all his work, both teaching and writing, Greg's principal guide was Anthony Blunt. At Brown, he fell in love with French Baroque architecture, painting, and sculpture thanks to *Art and Architecture in France, 1500-1700*, which was on reserve in the Rockefeller Library. For Christmas, during his last year of college, his mother gave him his own hardback copy. It was his last Christmas with her. Now that he was at Thornton, that copy was visibly well used, though all the pages were still there, some worn more than others. Without Blunt's critical catalog of Poussin's works and his freer, more essayistic *Nicolas Poussin* that appeared just before Greg's arrival at Yale, his dissertation would not have been possible—or at least, would have been quite different and much less complete.

A shared interest in Poussin and the influence of Blunt were two things that linked Gregory Byrne to his immediate predecessor at Thornton. It was a great good fortune that among the books that Ruth had left in Volker's office, and that Greg thus inherited, was a complete collection of every book Blunt had published up to 1972, even the single one that had nothing to do with early modernity, the recent essay on *Guernica*. One of the things that seems to have fascinated Baum was that Poussin was an expatriate. In Blunt's words, "By a curious freak, French painting of the seventeenth century produced its most remarkable and its most typical works not in Paris but in Rome, since it was in Rome that Poussin and Claude spent almost the whole of their active lives."

Having written his dissertation on the artist, Greg knew that the "Paris parenthesis," as it was sometimes called, was generally regarded as insignificant. It produced only one work that continued to draw the attention of art historians, *L'Institution de l'Eucharistie*, and that painting, commanded by Louis XIII for the royal chapel at Saint-Germain en Laye, was almost invariably mentioned as a neglected work, "*une œuvre méconnue.*" Strangely, Volker Baum, who followed Blunt closely in nearly everything, took precisely the opposite view about the "Paris parenthesis." Among Baum's unpublished papers was an essay without a title, but it might have become something like, simply, "Poussin in Paris" or "Why did Poussin leave Paris a second time?" It was written in black ink on yellow legal paper. Greg smiled when he realized he and Volker had the same writing habits. According to Ruth, Volker had worked on this just before the start of the spring quarter of 1972, shortly before his fateful trip to Rome.

It surprised Greg that Volker did not give much space to the royal commission for Saint-Germain. Yet the more he read, the more Greg understood why Volker might find it difficult to substantiate his argument enough to submit it for publication. Volker speculated that although Poussin had initially gone to Rome as a young man simply to paint, later, to supplement what he could earn from his art, he served as a well-paid spy for the French, specifically for Mazarin, the minister who replaced Richelieu as the power behind the throne at Richelieu's death in December 1642. Poussin lived in Rome from 1624 to 1640 and then returned to France in December of that year. The French monarchy invested lots of resources to get him back, part of a larger plan to counter Italian hegemony in the arts. Some things are well documented, but, suggested Volker, there may have been enticements and coercions that remained confidential. What is certain, he wrote, is that the superintendent of buildings, Sublet de Noyers, sent his cousins Roland Fréart de Chambray and Paul Fréart de Chantelou to negotiate personally with Poussin, promising him a magnificent title and a comfortable residence within the Tuileries Palace itself. What else did they promise? Or what would they have threatened if Poussin had failed to obey the royal summons?

Whatever they did, worked, and Poussin remained in Paris until the autumn of 1642, shortly before Richelieu died at the beginning of December and Mazarin ascended. Greg could see that all this was solid, not disputed, and for that reason, not worth a publication. Yet Baum then started to spin a web that purported to link Poussin and Mazarin to a series of incidents in both Rome and Paris in the following two decades. The last page, only half filled, was a list of names and dates, most with question marks next to them in the margin. At the end of the list, in Volker's hand but in pencil rather than ink, was written: "Need to check Vatican YR°78f: 1659." This idea that Poussin was a spy seemed to go nowhere. Did Volker leave the text unfinished because he realized it made no sense? Or was he waiting to read some document in the Vatican, hoping to find the missing link or at least a clue that would open some new path?

As Greg thought about Volker's mixture of art and diplomatic history, the patchwork of documented facts, a neglected painting by Poussin, and the interpretive leaps that implied a fantastical narrative, he suddenly thought of the first time he had seen Thornton Night—that weird eruption of primitive torchlight magic with Edward Constable Adams's evocation of a global network of people faithful to the *sacred night* of the bonfire. Why should he think of that night at this moment? It had nothing to do with Poussin. So why had that image popped into his head at that moment? Then, suddenly, he remembered the conversation with Clara Marsh. She had told him that Volker requested interlibrary loan materials concerning a baffling array of topics. She could not figure out what Volker was looking for. What stood out was that strange title, the one that sounded like the name of a dino-saur, *Stega-* something. It was *Steganographia*. But what was that? Thornton no longer had the microfilm, and so he would not be able to find out what Volker was looking for in that late medieval text. He knew this was a complete waste of time, and he would not bother Clara to get him a Latin manu-script that would take so much of his precious time that it would be professional suicide to get involved with it. The title of the book might be enough for now. Fifteen minutes in the Chandler reference room gave him what he needed. Steganography was simply a combination signifying "hidden writing." A little more poking around in an old *Encyclopaedia Britannica* yielded an indication of what Volker was thinking. Steganography was a technique of secret communication that differed from *coded* messages of the ordinary sort in that a steganographic message *would not look like a coded message.* If intercepted, it could appear as the most banal of missives, a poem, or a prayer, and the foe would not try to decipher it. Did Volker think Poussin's well-known correspondence from Rome contained secret messages for Mazarin? There was no time for this. It would have to wait.

Between his work on the book and puzzling over Volker's manuscript, Greg managed to procrastinate nicely. He had a set of fine analyses that, however, were not yet linked into a compelling, forward-driving book-length manuscript. Withdrawn as he had been from the world in his monas-tery-like cell in Chandler, now he felt the need for contact with other art historians to whom he could try to present an argument.

This is why, in March 1978, he accepted an invitation to give a talk at Cambridge University. The day he left Mayfield for Logan Airport, he did not actually have a fully written paper. What he took with him was a small box of slides, a folder containing the handouts for his talk, and a legal pad. He planned to write a lecture that fit all the quotes and the slides together. He counted on the hours in airports and on the plane to scribble out remarks that would be coherent and persuasive. By the time the coach from Heathrow arrived at the Parkside bus terminal in Cambridge, he had a respectable number of pages scrawled on the pad. He hoped that he could read them when he got up to speak.

Greg's ignorance of British life made everything at Cambridge exotic to him. Italy and Romania were rather ordinary in comparison to English pomp and circumstance. After his talk, Greg found himself sitting next to his host, the art historian Ian Darling, at the high table in Trinity. On one side was a young scholar of British colonial history, and on the other was a particle physicist. Though both knew a lot about art—Greg thought that in the States he would find few university colleagues so broadly informed—it was hard to put his lecture into a nutshell for them. Ian tried to spark their attention by mentioning that Greg's work was inspired by the research of a distinguished fellow of Trinity and, in fact, a member of the Royal Victorian Order, "our own Tony Blunt." This comment produced two widely divergent reactions. The historian seemed to find that "quite nice" and noted that Trinity was a small place but, at the same time, a whole world. The physicist, on the other hand, turned white and then grew red in the face. Ian asked if he was feeling quite well, to which the physicist, John, said, "We'll talk later."

Later came when they were having some port in the senior commons room. After some small talk, John lowered his voice and said, "Look, this thing about Blunt. It's not to get out. But in my field, we do work that we can't discuss. Most of all, we can't discuss it with anyone who has had anything to do with Blunt. That's all I'll say. Figure it out for yourselves," he told Ian and Greg, "and then don't say a word to anyone."

Greg walked with Ian out of the college to get some air before turning in for the night. Ian guided him out the porter's lodge and through King's to the Backs, then across the river and through the Paddocks, then through a couple of turns back towards the college. As they walked past, Ian pointed with amusement at the Thornton Building on the east side of the Cam.

"You Americans got a whole set of hand-me-down names, isn't that right? A whole continent with places to name."

Ian had not yet been to the States but knew a lot about U.S. geography and had read a novel, or something like a novel, by a French author who made much about how the same names kept appearing throughout the country. As they walked, Greg could not help thinking about what the physicist had said about Blunt.

"Are all physicists paranoid?" he asked Ian. "After all, what harm could Blunt do? Would he possibly even understand anything that a particle physicist carelessly mentioned during a meal?"

Greg was surprised that Ian did not immediately agree with him. Actually, Ian thought the insinuation that Blunt could be passing information to a foreign power was not far-fetched at all.

"You know, I've heard lots about Oxbridge men of Blunt's generation thinking that they had to help the Soviets fight against American hegemony. Trinity seems to have been—and maybe still is—a hotbed of this kind of activity. So, I wouldn't dismiss it out of hand. But then, Greg, you know more about Blunt than I do."

Tossing and turning later in bed, being still somewhat jet-lagged, Greg drifted in and out of sleep and dreams. Poussin, Blunt, Baum, Mazarin, and the Soviets all swirled together. Was Poussin a spy? Was Blunt a spy? If Blunt was a spy, why wouldn't he recognize Poussin's possible espionage during a century of high-stakes intrigue? But maybe *if* Blunt *was* a spy, he would shy away from writing about the topic….

30

The Reckoning

ONCE GREG RESUMED teaching in September 1978, everything passed so quickly that only his trusty Quo Vadis agenda kept him grounded with dates, class times, and submission deadlines. He mailed his book manuscript to the press in two copies, as required. Then he waited for the readers' reports, and three weeks after they arrived—mixed—he sent his comments on the readers' reports. The editor encouraged him to revise and resubmit, and so things went until the day when he carried the two copies of the revised MS to the Mayfield post office for priority delivery. By then, it was April. Would the revisions work? And if the press finally issued a contract, would Greg have it in time for the June 1, 1979 deadline? Would the college be flexible if the editorial decision came in positive, but after June 1?

Then, the phone call from the editor came on May 26. Penn State Press accepted his book, and the contract was going in the mail. Greg was shaking so hard that it was hard to put the phone receiver back on the hook. He sat down on the kitchen floor with his back pressed against the dishwasher and his legs stretched out. The tears just dribbled down his cheeks. Bogart came and lay across his thighs. They stayed there for quite a while in the quiet. Greg was not sure how long it was before he spoke, rubbing his cat's head and saying, "We did it, buddy. The two of us."

In the following days, after the celebratory drinks with his friends, Greg put together, with Jean's help, the required packets of copies of the book manuscript and his articles. There was also his personal statement and a list of students who might be willing to write letters concerning their experiences with him. All that went to Larry Dwight's secretary in the Dean's Office. Then, for the first time he could remember, Greg realized that he had nothing to do. Nothing. He felt a strange listlessness after seven years of running towards a goal always just over the horizon, sometimes running slowly, sometimes sprinting, sometimes missing the track and wandering into the brush. Now, there were months of waiting ahead of him.

He painted the front porch, put new mesh on most of the screens, pruned the trees around Ruth's house, drove to Montreal for a few days, swam in the outdoor pool near the Thornton field house, and invited friends over for dinner. The days went by, light, empty of obligation but not empty of care. It was still a kind of race, but a race where you stand still. You cannot run over the finish line. The finish line is not really a line but a gate. And you have to wait to see if the gate will open. Greg was now a character in a Kafka story.

In the fall of 1979, as usual, there came the surge of foliage seekers from south of Vermont, the flatlanders. Thanks to the home football games, Thornton Night, and the cars and busloads of tourists, the Mayfield Inn, as well as the larger hotels in Montpelier and Burlington, were booked for weeks. The highway department had closed the covered bridge over Beaver Creek to through traffic (it was feared that the picturesque old landmark would collapse under the load) except for locals who would otherwise have to drive fifteen miles around Mayfield to get to and from their homes. But this brought complaints from some of those same locals, who found tourists parking in front of their houses in order to be able to walk to the bridge to take their snapshots. Fortunately, outsiders were unaware of Otter Brook, and Greg could walk out his back door, cut through the back of the Shugarts' yard, and walk down into the small valley.

Among his cohort of fellow assistant professors—the ones whose probationary period like his had come to an end—panic reigned. They were all scared to death; it was only a question of intensity. Sally Hammond, in chemistry, told Greg that her migraines were so bad that she could hardly get through her classes. Ira Hasenstein, on the other hand, said he and his wife were looking to buy a larger house, but his wife Rose told Greg that their plan B was to move back to Pennsylvania. Preparing classes and grading papers kept Greg reasonably busy. Still, there was an odd freedom, a sense of being on holiday, because he no longer felt pressured to finish the book and write an additional article or two. The die was cast, the hands were dealt, the jury was out—all he could do was wait. He had never before watched so many films on Vermont Public Television.

The promotion and tenure committee—P & T—released its decisions on an unpredictable timetable. Instead of waiting until all the cases had been decided and then communicating the resulting decisions simultaneously to all the individuals concerned, week after week came news of someone being promoted and others being denied. The negative results always seemed to outnumber the successes. Of course, this was not public knowledge. As a personnel matter, it was confidential. Yet, within hours of the candidate being notified, virtually everyone in Mayfield knew. One would see the cars parked in front of some people's houses carrying bottles of bubbly to celebrate. In other cases, you would pass a colleague or a faculty spouse on the street or in the Mayfield Co-op, avoiding eye contact.

It was in the nails, screws, and tool section of Mayfield Hardware in mid-September that Greg heard about Sergio Frosoni. His was an especially sad case. Sergio had left a mid-level position with a Boston bank and, at the age of 32, had decided to go to Chicago to get a Ph.D. in economic history. So now, in his late forties, with a wife and three children, he would be looking for another place to teach Middle Eastern economic history. Two weeks later, one morning at Drew's, Judson Henry of the English department told Greg that Martha Wray had gotten tenure with a book on the Gothic novel. Judson did not seem especially happy at this turn of events. Savoring the buckwheat pancakes with Drew's extra dark maple syrup, Greg conjectured that Judson feared Martha's promotion would fill the ranks of associate professors in English and thus diminish Judson's own chances when he came up two years later. Beatrice phoned him with the news that Sally Hammond would no longer have to worry about migraines. She got her promotion in chemistry, but "I've heard it was close." Steve Churk got his promotion in German (God knows how), and would continue to draw fascinated spectators to the Thornton tennis courts, where they could marvel that such a tiny round man with short legs could be so speedy.

The foliage peaked in early October. Greg watched Bob Shugart raking up his leaves. Bob had his own method for disposing of fallen leaves. He spread out a tarp and then raked the leaves onto the tarp, gathering them into a large, sack-like bundle, which he dragged over to the edge of the slope down into Otter Brook. He let the leaves fall down into the woods and then began again. It was like the work of Sisyphus in reverse. Greg's solitary maple was now bare, but there was still no news for Greg. "Why was it taking so long?" he asked himself. Bogart could feel that Greg was tense. He brought the little spongy ball again and again, looking up eagerly for Greg to throw it into the living room or, even better, up the stairs.

Then, just after sundown, the phone rang. Greg grabbed the yellow wall phone, feeling sure that this would be that call. It was that twerp Terry, associate dean for the humanities.

"Greg, I'm glad to find you at home."

The tone said it all, as did the choice of words. Terry needed to convey gladness about something, and if finding Greg at home was the only thing to be glad about, it did not bode well.

"The committee was very impressed by your book manuscript and pleased that you have a contract at such a prestigious press. The outside readers all wrote thorough, thoughtful commentaries. The student letters, too, are very supportive. And few junior faculty members have given so generously of their time…"

The eulogy smelled of the incense at a high Mass for the departed. Greg immediately thought of the widespread fantasy of wishing to hear what people say about you after your demise.

"…So it is all the more difficult for me to have to convey the news that, in the end, we have had to decline to recommend tenure. Of course, you'll have a terminal year here while you look for a position worthy of someone of your caliber."

Greg took the cue to thank the dean for his call, forestalling further praise, condolences, and details of the paperwork that would be in his mailbox the following week.

Should he have a drink? That seemed a no-brainer, but he needed to explode, go outside, and run around. He would not scream. He was not a screamer; besides, he did not want all of Mayfield to be sniggering for weeks about *that screaming madman Byrne*. He needed fresh air and movement. Bogart looked at him with his concerned green eyes as if to say, "What you really need now is your cat."

He banged out of the back door, took his usual route through the Shugart's backyard to Otter Brook, and ran down the slope to the path along the stream. He ran the mile to Highway 21 in a burst of energy and rage, then turned around and ran back even faster, with an intensity he had never felt before. Then he sat on a granite boulder near a cluster of birches and a patch of bearberry and just listened to the brook babbling. It was still, with only some distant traffic and occasional brass band music from the football field on Montpelier Street. He did not think about the future. He was not worrying about what was to come. He remembered later howling, to the brook and the trees, "Seven fucking years!"

Then he went back up the hill towards his house.

Megan Shugart was coming up her driveway with her standard poodle, Daisy. She greeted him cheerfully, "Hi, Mr. Byrne! Did you have a good walk?"

She was an excellent cat sitter for Bogart. Tall and gangly, smart, fun to talk with about the books she was reading. It was Megan he had to thank for being able to identify the plants near Otter Brook. She could see that Greg was not in his usual chatty mood.

"Is everything OK?"

Only a few seconds later he regretted blurting out about bad news. After all, why bother a kid about things like that? But the words were out, and now it would be more impolite to run away.

"Is it about the tenure committee? Danny told me his dad is in a really bad mood, waiting for a decision."

Mayfield is a small town. Greg admitted it was the tenure committee and added that everything would work out in the long run.

"I'm sorry for Bogart," she said. Megan was smart. She knew. "This means you'll probably be moving away."

"Not for a year, yet," he said.

They stood there for a moment while Daisy sniffed his shoes. She, too, Greg understood, liked Otter Brook.

"I know you're a really good teacher," Megan said. "My dad brings home the *Yearly Thorn*. He's popular, but you're even more."

"Well, Megan," he said, "We both know that popularity isn't everything."

"Yes, but your students really should count. They really should."

31

Rota fortunae

R UTH WAS THE first person to hint to Greg that all was not lost. This happened so subtly that, at first, he did not realize it was a hint, perhaps even a "leak." On that October evening, it seemed to him only an expression of wishful thinking, as if she were offering him a sedative that could tide him over during the first moments of trauma while the open wound scabbed over and then became a scar.

On arrival, as was a habit when he visited Ruth, she asked him to pour them a glass of *sauvignon blanc* in her stemless conical glasses with bees in relief below the rim. They each had a sip, saying nothing much, and then she set about preparing a risotto.

"You know," she said, "these decisions have been overturned. It doesn't happen often, but there are a few examples."

"But there's no appeal process, Ruth. I've practically memorized the Faculty Handbook. Why should I make myself look even more ridiculous by going to see Larry Dwight and Hugh Terry to complain and beg?"

"You're right. There's nothing *you* can do, Greg, dear. But that doesn't mean that some people couldn't advocate on your behalf. You did learn that the decision was not unanimous. And Gino Cashman even let slip—perhaps it was not actually a slip—that the discussion in your case was unusually long."

"So I should just wait?"

"Yes. Wait, relax, enjoy the nice weather, your good students, and your friends, read some good books, and don't do anything at all."

And in the subsequent days he went numbly through his daily routine, even enjoying it much as before—the class discussions, the jokes with colleagues in the mailroom and at the photocopier, tossing Bogart's favorite toy and giving him treats when he brought it back for him to throw again. What hurt were the kindly reminders from people who meant well but who, in effect, reopened the slowly closing wound.

"Greg, they made a big mistake!"

"How obtuse can they be?"

"It's a real blow to the college!"

Then, that Tuesday, ten days after the bad news, came a phone call from Clare Higginbottom, the president's secretary.

"Mr. Byrne, President Chauncey would like to talk with you. If you are free tomorrow after your 3 o'clock class, could you come to Keller House? No, no preparation is necessary, and I really can't say what the president wishes to discuss."

This was the standard administrative playbook, he knew. All the power was in their hands, and the less he knew, the more vulnerable he would be. There was, in fact, and as they knew, no likelihood that he could ever guess what they were about to do. Had someone in the upper administration seen some vulnerability on *their* side that he might exploit, should he discover it? Were they trying to cover their ass with some "generous" gesture, like moving expenses to help him get as far from Mayfield as possible or a month or so of extra salary to cushion the blow? Such conjectures made less and less sense the more he pondered them. His case was open and shut. There were no complicating factors. It was not as if he had had maternity leave, or a spouse or child who had been ill, or an auto accident, or a house fire that might have destroyed his research documents. He had been given the agreed-upon time to produce the expected publications. He had taught the regular number of classes, and while he had directed the program in Florence twice, that was the sort of thing that many on the faculty and in the administration would view more as a perk than as a burden.

The following day, they wrapped up their class discussion of Bernini's Piazza Navona at 4:15. Greg realized his attention was flagging toward the end. He wondered what was in store in Keller House. How unpleasant was it going to be? How much bullshit along the lines of "I am personally very, very sorry, Greg. Thornton will miss you, but we know you have a *great* career ahead of you!"

It was drizzling and humid, and he felt himself sweating under his raincoat. He walked across the Green, turned at the administration building, and followed the ornate brick walkway toward the Victorian mansion, which housed the offices of the president, the provost, and the treasurer of Thornton College. Lowly faculty members almost never entered this space, and his only previous visit had been during the reception for the big donor to the Italian program.

Ms. Higginbottom's icily perfect welcome conveyed the effort it cost her to pretend that his presence mattered in any way.

"Mr. Byrne has arrived, Mr. President."

Chauncey's eruption through his office door was the first thing that really surprised Greg. He looked genuinely enthusiastic and eager to see him as he said, "Greg! I'm glad that you could get here so soon. There's some terrific news I want to share."

Greg felt his legs shiver. Either Chauncey was a spectacularly good actor—not impossible: college presidents are hired to perform in various spectacles—or something significant was going on.

"Come on in. By the way, I have read and reread the letters that came in about you, not just the letters from the outside evaluators, but the ones from your students, and I am really impressed."

Even though his reasonable self told him to keep his mouth shut at this point, the sting of the P & T decision was still so raw that Greg blurted out, "Apparently, the committee wasn't so 'impressed.'"

He smiled. "Well, I know how it must seem to you because you have not heard a full account of the discussion. But without violating the confidentiality of who said what, I can assure you that the committee had only positive things to say. Yes, yes, you will object that it is preposterous to say only 'positive things' and then recommend that you not be granted tenure. And it *is* preposterous in terms of the institution's best interest, but it is also the logical outcome of a set of budgeting mechanisms that we have been using for decades."

So far, Greg could not recognize any of the "terrific news" that Chauncey claimed to want to share. Yet this time, he just sat there quietly.

"Now, here is where I have been able to intervene. My aim is to reconcile the best interests of Thornton College as a place of learning and scholarship with the need to keep the department budgets in order. I could not have done it without the help of a benefactor, someone who wishes to remain anonymous. Let me explain what it means for you."

Greg realized that his heart was pounding, and he felt a wave of positive excitement.

"We both know that when you were first appointed as assistant professor, it was on a line from the Department of Art History. Fairly soon, the needs of other departments caused them to approach you for help—help that you generously provided, even though it required extra preparation for you. Fortunately, you speak Italian, and fortunately, your approach to the teaching of art leads to connections with the literature departments. A college—perhaps I shouldn't generalize too much, but at least Thornton—is like a federation of territories, and each territory has its own budget. If future historians were to look over our financial records, they would never be able to figure out what department Gregory Byrne belonged to. This is the dilemma the P & T confronted. On one hand, you are a valuable jack-of-all-trades, but on the other hand, you are an orphan."

He paused and then said, "I think it's time that I got us some champagne." He picked up his phone and said, "Clare, could you please bring in the Veuve-Clicquot and a couple of glasses."

"Well, Greg, the benefactor of whom I spoke, and who was a student of Volker Baum quite a while ago, has helped us establish a tenured chair to be known as the 'Volker and Ruth Baum Professor of Humanities.' I have already polled the board of trustees by phone, and I am pleased to tell you that we are offering you the appointment as the first Volker and Ruth Baum Professor—or, technically, for now, the 'Baum Associate Professor'—to be effective July 1, 1980."

Greg walked directly to Ruth's. Or rather floated. No sooner had he walked out of Keller House than he was in Okrent Lane. Finding himself in front of Ruth's, he was thankful that there had been no traffic on Park Street or that the drivers had avoided him, thinking he had started drinking early. The lights were on at her place, and since he did not see any cars outside, he figured that he probably would not be disturbing any visitors. It took her a moment to come to the door, wearing one of her painting smocks. As she opened the door, the smile on her face told him she already knew.

She just said, "Greg!" and gave him a big, long hug, pulling him into the hallway.

"You knew!" he said. "You knew all along!"

"Not really *all along*, because I was as shocked as you were by the P & T decision. But I did talk to some people who felt as I did, and then I heard about the solution."

"Are you the 'anonymous benefactor'?" he asked.

"Heavens, no! Do you know how much it costs to fund a chair? I do know who it is and that he is a devoted former student of Volker's, but I must not say any more. So don't waste your time trying to get it out of me. We need to celebrate!"

He had not even thought of celebrating. In fact, he hadn't even thought about what being the Baum Professor would entail. All that it meant to him was that he would continue his life at Thornton. Megan would still cat sit Bogart, and life would go on. But he knew that he should celebrate and with Ruth, most of all.

"Why don't we go to the Fragola? It won't be too busy on a Tuesday night."

And that's what they did, taking Ruth's car. They parked behind the Thornton National Bank. Caffè La Fragola was in the narrow, brick-paved alley, Birch Lane, between the bank and the Jewel cinema. It was small and filled quickly, but on arriving, they had the place to themselves. Then several tourists took a couple of tables, and the Hasensteins came in with their daughter, clearly in a festive mood. Ira must have gotten tenure, and they wouldn't need the plan B after all. They just greeted Ruth and Greg with a wave, but after they were seated, Ira and Rose looked around at Greg and his companion furtively and seemed to be talking about them. They must have wondered why Ruth and Greg looked so cheerful so soon after he had been denied tenure.

He did not try to probe Ruth any further about what happened behind the scenes. He felt subdued, still stunned. People had warned Greg about "post-tenure depression," and he could understand the concept. For six years, his horizon had been limited by this one decision. There was in his imagination nothing beyond. Perhaps he felt that to think beyond would tempt fate. What if it didn't happen? Or maybe he was just then flat-out exhausted and whip-lashed by the two extreme and contradictory outcomes.

Ruth was the one who led his thoughts towards the future.

"You need to think about yourself now, Greg. You've poured yourself into your work. You live alone. Since Anja, you haven't talked to me about anyone you are attracted to. I know that it ended with you being hurt, disappointed, and rejected, but don't forget about the good moments and how happy you were with her. You can be happy with someone else."

"Who am I going to meet here? I can't date students. And I won't get involved in the musical chairs scene that so many faculty couples are into."

"Greg, you need to show more initiative. From what I've seen, you wait until a woman shows an interest in you—in fact, more than an interest. From your own account of meeting Anja, she took over from the moment she met you in the Palazzo Capponi library. Isn't that right? It's time to risk being rejected. Yes, I know you have had a *big* rejection after a serious relationship, but I mean little rejections. The woman who declines your suggestion that you have a coffee, get together for a drink, go to a museum show together… The tiny, harmless little moments when you hear 'No thanks.' That's not going to ruin your day, is it?"

Fortune's wheel had indeed turned.

32

Chiaroscuro

NOW THAT GREG did not think obsessively about his situation, there was time to ruminate about other things. In the fall of 1979, while the suspense of the tenure decision utterly absorbed Greg, something momentous shook the art history world. And it concerned the most crucial figure in Greg's special field. Even outside the world of art historians, the shocking revelation of November 19, 1979, made headlines. The news came with typically British understatement, during Prime Minister's Questions in the Commons.

> *Mr. Leadbitter and Mr. Skinner: Asked the Prime Minister if she will make a statement on recent evidence concerning the actions of an individual, whose name has been supplied to her, in relation to the security of the United Kingdom.*
>
> *The Prime Minister: "The name which the hon. Member for Hartlepool (Mr. Leadbitter) has given me is that of Sir Anthony Blunt."*

Two days later, going beyond this gnomic sentence, Margaret Thatcher disclosed more details, which had become known to the queen and the security service MI5 *sixteen* years earlier. In April 1964, several years before Gregory Byrne had read a single word of Blunt's *Art and Architecture in France 1500-1700*, Blunt had confessed to spying for the Soviet Union while serving secretly in MI5 beginning in 1940. Greg, like art historians everywhere, now eagerly read the latest details as they trickled out during that winter. When Blunt was confronted with the evidence in 1964, he confessed, and it was reported on the condition that his treason be kept from the public. The monarchy and government agreed primarily because it was a scandal that would have sullied the intelligence service and the monarchy themselves. During all that time he remained "Sir Anthony" and benefitted from all the honors—the *honours*—as a fellow of Trinity College and a member of the British Academy. Now he lost these. He was no longer "Sir" Anthony Blunt. He was simply a disgraced old man, Tony Blunt.

As soon Greg read about this in the *Boston Globe,* he recalled the conversation at Trinity two years before. Even though Blunt's confession was classified as an "official secret," some people, like the physicist Greg had met after his lecture, must have been tipped off to be on their guard against people close to Blunt. Greg thought of Volker's unpublished speculations about Poussin's possible role as a secret agent for Mazarin in Rome. Blunt, Greg was sure, had never published anything that suggested such a role as a spy for the renowned painter. Could Blunt, consciously or unconsciously, have *avoided* this topic precisely because he did not wish his name to be connected to espionage in any way? Blunt wrote that Poussin maintained a steady correspondence with Chantelou, the king's (that is, Mazarin's) agent in negotiating with Poussin for his return to Paris. Then, when Poussin left Paris after two years, Blunt says that "the two friends continued to write to each other regularly, and this correspondence, of which luckily Chantelou kept the part which he received, gives us…most interesting details." How do we know that Chantelou kept *all* of what he received? What about steganography?

In this connection, thought Greg, it was interesting that Blunt's professional activities gave him many opportunities for journeys during which he could both carry out his apparent business and profit from the occasion to do other things. Many of these things involved behind-the-scenes favors for the monarchy.

Sometimes, Greg recognized that his modest career resembled that of his great role model. Both had been French majors as undergraduates, later became art historians, and had ample opportunities to travel for professional reasons in Europe. They sometimes did favors for their superiors and sometimes carried unwritten messages.

In describing Blunt's colorful life, the press frequently used terms like "dark," "in the shadows," "hidden," "contrasting," and "dramatic." However, these would probably not have occurred to the public at large before 1979. Few people who read his many books and articles about seventeenth-century art would have thought of him as having a dramatic life, with anything hidden or dark about it. His life seemed to dispose him to be, as he was, a major proponent of Poussin's clear, generally calm rationality, far, far away from the violent, dark tensions of Caravaggio. Now, the one-dimensional Blunt was gone, replaced by a genuinely Baroque persona. *Chiaroscuro*, the French *clair-obscur*, is the term for the sharp contrast between light and dark, a technique of amplification.

When the two values are juxtaposed without gradation, the light seems brighter, and the dark seems darker. Paradoxically, when a painter uses this sudden, intensive contrast, both the light and the dark can make things difficult to see. It is not for nothing, as Greg thought, that people refer to the "blinding light" of a winter day in Mayfield when the sun glares off the surface of the fallen snow. But in most of Poussin light is subtly distributed about the primary focus, while the dark fills the background, unlike the maelstrom of blaze and shadow of Caravaggio, La Tour, or even Rubins.

In 1972, eight years after he was already a confessed double agent and disgraced in the eyes of the monarch, Blunt published a review of the Georges de la Tour show at the Orangerie. Blunt had previously shown almost no interest in La Tour, as Greg knew from *Art and Architecture in France*. Now, however, the critic showed an acute sensitivity to the things that are hidden, writing that "La Tour is not simply a competent follower of Caravaggio, but an artist of great and individual talent" whose painting had "characteristics of calm grandeur, mystery, and silence that bring it close to the great masters of French classical art and literature of the seventeenth century. His paintings constantly evoke the *silence éternel* of Pascal and the *profonde Nuit* of Racine."

Blunt must have hoped that his own full identity could find its place in the *silence éternel*. The more he thought about it, the more Greg realized that all of his scholarly work centered on those silences—on cocking his ear, straining to hear the faint whispers of Baroque secrets. Was not the Thornton motto, after all, *Vox gaudentis in silentio*, the voice of someone finding pleasure in the silence?

33

Humanities

FOR GREG, THE Humanities Program consumed the 1980-81 Thornton year. In the spring of 1980, Charlie Wood took him to lunch at Peter Pagan's to celebrate Greg's promotion. As they waited for their food to arrive (Peter Pagan's was famous for its beef stew), Greg saw that Charlie had something pressing in mind.

"You know, Greg, having tenure brings responsibilities. Sure, you've got the weight of publishing your first book behind you, and your position here is totally secure. But the whole thing works because we do our part. The Humanities Program needs new blood. I've been directing it for six years—my God, where does the time go?—and I need a break. I've got a book to finish."

In an attempt to deflect Charlie from his task, Greg asked about the book, but Charlie would not be distracted from his goal.

"There are lots of reasons it should be you, not the least of which is your new title, the "Baum Professor of Humanities.""

"Sure, Charlie, sooner or later I'll take my turn, but for me, it's not as if finishing the book that cost me years of my life meant that I'm now *finished* and ready to be a one-book wonder like Churk, who spends his summer days on the golf course and then plays squash every day in the winter. Or like Emily Latouraine. Have you heard that she submitted the *same* article seven times to different journals—successfully!—simply by changing the title and the introductory paragraph?"

"Sure, Churk gets under my skin too, and Emily's become a joke—believe it or not, she used to be promising—but you're just not like them. There's no danger of that. Think of it this way. I've noticed that you, like me and like Larry Elliot and Wanda Andros, get some of the best new ideas and new questions for your research from your teaching. Directing the Humanities Program gives you a larger field for inspiration. It will stimulate your restless, curious mind even more. That's what it can do *for you*. But I'm also asking you to think what it can do for Thornton."

Their stew and garlic toast arrived, and there was a reprieve from Charlie's spiel.

Then Greg decided to get it over with by asking, "OK, Charlie, what's in it for Thornton?"

"Looking around at the probable alternatives, if you don't step up, the job will go to one of the eager but incompetent self-promoters, like Kenman or Wilson Potts. And do you know what the frosting on the cake is for them?"

Charlie leaned forward to hammer home the decisive point.

"Besides the slight course reduction—one fewer course every two years—it's the title, 'Director of Humanities.'

Think about it. *Director.* It sounds so goddamn power-ful, even though it's only a quirk of Thornton bureaucracy. Haven't you noticed? Each department has a 'chair,' but every program has a 'director.' I guess that no one ever thought that this would draw the bloodsuckers. To them, though, it sounds like *duce.* It brings out the despot in them."

For a while, Greg resisted Charlie's pitch, coming up with names of other people who might be persuaded to take the job. But Charlie returned to the image of Kenman in that role.

"Kenman already spends ninety percent of his energy promoting himself inside and outside the college. You've seen it! You know he even has his stationery, the envelopes with **KENMAN** printed vertically on the left side. And on his door in Densmore Hall, that plaque two feet high with **JUSTIN KENMAN, PHD. DIRECTOR OF THE STAR PROGRAM?** We both know about that bullshit! It doesn't matter if you know what the hell "STAR" means. To people on the outside, and even to our administration, it sounds impressive. In fact, the *less* you know about it, the *more* impressive it sounds!"

Greg finally gave in. Upon Charlie's recommendation, the Dean's Office sent his nomination to the Executive Committee of the Faculty, and it was a done deal. Greg took over on July 1 for the next three school years.

Much of the work was interesting. Best of all, from Greg's point of view, was the fact that all the students who wanted to do an interdisciplinary honors thesis in humanities had to come to discuss their plans with him, and once admitted to the honors division, Greg would follow their work, even though each student had two specialist advisors as well. There was not such a large number of students inclined to take on this extra challenge. So, the many hours Greg spent talking with them—both with those who inquired about doing the thesis and those who indeed followed through—all those conversations were varied, lively, and stimulating. Among those admitted was Chris Pugh, a German-speaking student with blond dreadlocks who considered himself a "white Rasta" and wrote about the history of ganja. And there was Erin Lynn, who wrote about nineteenth-century women cross-dressers. Paolo Silos came with his proposal to write about twins in Romantic novels and poetry. One student wanted to compare two recently released films about the Vietnam War, *The Deer Hunter* and *Apocalypse Now*. Were these the first signs of a reappraisal of the war? She planned to take into account critical reception as well as statistics about the box office.

Administering Humanities presented him with some challenges that ranged from the simply baffling to one that involved a complaint to the United Nations.

The simply baffling one resulted from the least pleasant routine chore of the directorship. The director was responsible for informing participating faculty members that the program steering committee had denied their teaching requests. Of course, it was fun to tell someone, especially a newer faculty member, that their course proposal had been accepted. But the explosions of anger from those passed over were so intense that the afternoon following the committee meeting was harrowing.

Greg particularly dreaded the call to Marta Martin. Her course on Latin American and African novels was among the most popular. She was regarded as a colorful excentric and also as a challenging person. She widely boasted that all the women in her family had been known as powerful *brujas* for generations. Several steering committee members argued that Marta should let someone else have a turn and that the courses should be rotated to ensure the most varied coverage possible. Others said that it would seem as if they were punishing Marta for her success if her course were passed over for a year. In the end, it was decided that it would be the best course of action to congratulate Marta and ask for her cooperation in generously allowing one of the newer faculty members to have a chance to teach the following year.

After telephoning all the other colleagues on his list, Greg braced himself for Marta. He knew her reputation for vindictiveness and had experienced first-hand how she could play mind games to reach her goal. When taken by surprise, she could explode in loud profanity.

She answered the phone, eager to hear the good news she expected.

"Marta, it's Greg. As you know, the steering committee met today. We were all impressed by the success of your course. It is, of course, the most popular course year after year. And this is great. But after much discussion, it was decided that we should postpone the next offering for a year and let someone else have a chance in that slot."

He held the phone away from his ear, already wincing from the anticipated blast.

There was silence. A long silence.

Then Marta asked, "So you're saying that I won't be able to teach my course next year?"

"Yes, Marta. That's right."

After a short pause, she said softly, "Thanks, Greg, for calling."

And that was that.

After hanging up, Greg wondered what had just happened. Was Marta now planning one of her little "indiscretions" of the sort he saw after her dust-up with Emily Latouraine? Marta had gone around saying how sorry she felt for Emily and saying that Emily's husband had told someone that his wife had been diagnosed with Parkinson's disease. She did not accuse Emily of anything and pretended to feel the most profound concern, but it was the sort of gratuitous mischief that Marta loved. And Emily was, in fact, perfectly healthy. Or did Marta plan something more serious, like saying that a student had complained of an unwanted sexual advance? Or did Marta really believe that she had magical powers and that she could mess up Greg's life in some other way?

Nothing happened in the following months, and as he waited for the ambush he feared was coming, he thought back to a bizarre thing that had happened a couple of years before, when Greg had taken advantage of the flexibility of the Thornton quarter system to take the winter term as his annual vacation, and then to teach in the summer quarter. He left his car with Wanda, asking her to drive it at least once weekly to keep the battery charged. On his return, Wanda told him of a strange experience involving Marta.

"I was leaving the Co-op, and Marta was coming out at the same time. She was lugging two heavy bags of groceries and asked me if I could give her a ride. You know how far she lives from the Co-op, and it was obviously almost impossible to get there without a car with those bags. So I said sure, and we walked out into the parking lot. When we approached your car, and she saw that I was heading towards it, she said, 'That's not your car! That's Greg Byrnes's car, isn't it?' So I explained that you had left it with me for the winter. And then she said, 'I prefer to walk.' It was weird. I pointed out how crazy it was for her to walk all that distance on icy sidewalks, but she just headed off as if she was afraid of your car."

The more Greg thought about that incident, the more convinced he became that Marta's strange behavior connected in some way with his call on the day of the steering committee meeting. Since that time, he had not discerned any counter-attack from her, despite her reputation for settling scores. Why had she been so mild, even meek, on the phone? Her fear of his car seemed crazy, yet Marta was known to be cunning and capable in everything she did. Unless, he thought, she really believed in *brujería*. In that case, perhaps she perceived him as a dangerous *brujo*.

The other Humanities incident that stood out was so bizarre that it even surpassed this hypothesis about sorcery. And in this case, the facts were, for the most part, out in the open and on the record.

A senior English major, Fritz Grumbach, wanted to do an honors thesis in Humanities on the Greek conception of heroism. He requested that Prof. Kenman be designated as his primary advisor, although he was neither a specialist in Classics nor Drama nor History. The required letters of recommendation came from Kenman and from an assistant professor, Henry Bulgar, who was widely known as "Kenman's shadow." The transcript submitted to attest to the minimum GPA for an honors thesis showed multiple A+ grades from Kenman, which barely compensated for the C and C+ grades in English. To complicate the situation still more, the proposed secondary advisor (also known as the second reader) was Xenia Crabapple, in Music, who was scheduled to be in Europe for the whole year, first as director of the Thornton program in London and then on leave for the following two quarters. The instructor of record for all the Humanities honors students was the program director, and therefore Gregory Byrne.

Greg read the skimpy and vague project proposal. It was clearly a non-starter. As required by the rules, he asked Elizabeth Wegner, the secretary of the Humanities program, to photocopy the application materials and get copies into the mailboxes of the program executive committee. The following week, to Greg's dismay, the application was accepted by a bare majority, just one more vote in favor than against. When he spoke to a few of those in favor, they just said that it was not worth the hassle of having to listen to the expected complaints from Fritz, who was well known to be a pushy student who always complained about his grades, and from Kenman, who frequently objected that people did not take him seriously.

After writing the acceptance letter to send to the student (with copies to the advisors), Greg did not give the matter a second thought. There were plenty of other things to do. When grading time approached, Greg reminded the four honors students of the deadline for submitting the thesis, which was all the more pressing in that they were all scheduled to graduate. Greg received three of the four, not including Grumbach's, on the specified date. He also sent an urgent note to Grumbach, with a copy sent to Kenman through campus mail. As for Xenia, no one knew where she was, but it was certainly not Mayfield. Two days later, a handwritten note from Kenman appeared in Greg's box.

"This is the best honors thesis I have ever read! Its subject is heroism and it is heroic! Fritz is brilliant! Off the charts. I give him an A+."

This hyperbole from Kenman was unsurprising, but Greg wondered what he would find in the thesis. Not having heard from Grumbach, he sent the student another note through campus mail, asking him to come to see him.

Grumbach did show up toward the end of Greg's office hours, smelling strongly of alcohol. It was 11:30 a.m., and the conversation was not cordial.

"I gave the thesis to Justin. I don't have to give it to you."

"I am the instructor of the thesis course, and therefore, I have to see the work that I am grading."

"You don't trust Professor Kenman? Who are you? Some little functionary? I don't have to put up with this diddly stuff."

Greg had Elizabeth Wegner contact Kenman for the thesis and try to get a phone number from the Music department for Xenia. A few hours later, Kenman telephoned.

"Greg, why are you persecuting me? I have zillions of things to do. I'll send you the paper when I have a moment. I still need to write the comments."

Greg replied that he would like to have the thesis now. Why didn't Kenman have his secretary make a copy and send it ASAP? Then, the comments could follow.

"Sure, I'll see about that."

Two days later, when the grades for graduating students were due, Greg needed to file a grade. There was the A+ from Kenman, no word from Xenia (had she even seen the thesis?), and no thesis in the Humanities office.

Greg opted for a solution that he found far from satisfying. He looked at Grumbach's transcript, where he could see that his average GPA was C+, and decided there was no reason to think the student had done anything other than his average work. If anything, Greg reasoned, he might not have written a thesis at all. In that case, the grade of C+ would be an exceptionally blatant case of grade inflation. The burden was on Kenman, Xenia, and the student.

When the students got their grade reports from the registrar's office, the phone calls came from Kenman and

Grumbach. Obviously, still nothing from Xenia. Kenman complained of "disrespect for a colleague," and the student said it was a matter of honor. He would now *never* let Greg or anyone else in the Humanities program see his paper, which he described as the "best work I have ever done."

But then things became really weird. As Greg knew, Grumbach was an international student from Switzerland. However, Greg was unaware of the extent of his wealthy and well-connected family. Only two days after the official grade reports were released, Greg received a phone call from Tim Douglas, the new associate dean for Humanities.

"Greg, it's Tim. It is not a term that I use in teaching my students about the Pre-Socratics, but the phenomenon we have before us could best be termed a 'shitstorm.' Chauncey just called me to ask what in heaven's name is going on with this Grumbach guy. Apparently, not only did Grumbach hand-deliver an angry letter to his office, but Grumbach's father also sent a fax to the chair of the trustees. Up to that point it was the sort of thing that happens just before graduation. There's always some little shit who gets upset about not graduating or not making *cum laude* or some such thing. But this time…this time it's like a fantasy horror film. Grumbach sent Chauncey copies of letters he wrote to…You'll never guess, but I'll let you try."

This game did not appeal to Greg, but to get it over with, he said, "The president of the United States."

"Oh, Greg, you are not thinking *big* enough! You're not just dealing with one country here. Grumbach is from Switzerland."

"OK, to the prime minister or chancellor or whatever they have in Switzerland."

"No, much bigger!"

"I give up," said Greg. "Tell me."

"He wrote to the Secretary General of the United Nations, *plus* the president of the AFL-CIO."

"Jesus! What has organized labor got to do with this?"

"Well, it turns out that the AFL-CIO guy is somehow related to Grumbach's family. As for the United Nations, Grumbach complains that he's being discriminated against on the basis of his nationality."

"Much ado about nothing," said Greg. "And when I say 'nothing,' I mean Grumbach's paper. We have no assurance that it even exists."

"Chauncey wants me to do something about it, and I'm going to meet with the kid. I have an idea about how this is going to work out. I think you'll be fine with the solution. Stay calm. Go out and enjoy the nice weather, and I'll keep you updated as things evolve."

Going out to enjoy the weather did not suit Greg's mood. He was too annoyed and in too much suspense about the outcome of whatever Tim was planning. So he walked home, gave Bogart a special treat of canned tuna, and drove to Burlington to do errands.

As he sat having a late supper, the phone in the kitchen rang. Somehow, the most important calls arrived on that phone. It was Tim.

"I finally got you? Where have you been all afternoon? No, I don't really need to know, but I've been trying to reach you. Everything is settled. Grumbach agreed to accept the C+."

"How did you do that? That seems incredible! He was adamant that he would not accept anything less than A."

"Well," said Tim, "I gave him the option of getting a fresh reading. We'd agree on an unbiased person to read the thesis without having seen any other comments. I had in mind Wilson Potts, in my department, who's written on heroism. Then Grumbach asked if the new reader would have to see the thesis."

"He actually asked that?" said Greg. "Isn't that a dead giveaway?"

"That's exactly what I thought. So I asked him how soon he could get us the copy, pointing out that if he planned to graduate next week, we would need to get it to Prof. Potts tomorrow by noon."

"So Grumbach said he couldn't get us a 'clean copy' that fast. So, I proposed that we get the copy that Kenman saw. He countered that Kenman's copy would be marked up and wouldn't offer a completely fresh reading. He asked if the new reader, instead of reading the thesis, could talk with Kenman or Justin, as he said. I said that a 'reading' is a 'reading,' and if Kenman's copy was marked up, the only bias would be in Grumbach's favor, since he raved about it being 'fantastic work.' At that point, there was a fairly long pause. I just waited to see what he would propose. And all of a sudden he stood up, said 'Fuck it! Fuck the piece of shit! I'll take the goddamn grade!' And he walked out of the office and slammed the door."

"So it is pretty clear that Kenman doesn't have the thesis any more than I do," said Greg.

"That's what it looks like to me," agreed Tim. "And by the way, make sure you make explicit the rule requiring the student to give a copy of the thesis to the instructor of record. It seems obvious to all of us in academia, but maybe a judge wouldn't see it that way. You should also add the specification that the instructor of record—the director—will have the last say on the grade."

34

Therapy

I

T WAS A Thursday during the January thaw of 1981
when Greg drove over the bridge across the Winooski
to Wardsville for his first appointment. Dr. Hicks had
been recommended by his primary care physician, who said
that even though the psychiatrist would be more expensive
than a psychologist or social worker, Greg's Thornton insurance would cover a portion of the first ten visits. She thought
that his problem was mild and would be resolved within that
time. Although the mounds of gritty plowed snow were high
along Bank Street, the road itself was free of ice and glistened
black with meltwater. At Green Street, he turned left and felt
a sudden loss of control as he hit a patch of ice. Fortunately,
there was no traffic, and he managed to get back onto the
right lane, driving slowly to distinguish number 34. The
receptionist had told him it would be the only yellow house
on Green Street. "Easy to remember: yellow on Green."

Greg pulled into the small parking lot, made smaller by

the encroaching banks of plowed snow. The practice was in an old clapboard house converted into professional offices. Dr. Hicks had no associates, and the receptionist worked both for him and for the investment advisor whose office was in the space on the other side of the ground-floor corridor. Greg was relieved that there was no one else in the waiting room.

The tall, thin psychiatrist, wearing a grey tweed sportscoat and a dark green turtleneck, came out to shake his hand.

"Gregory—or would you prefer that I call you Dr. Byrne?"

"Greg will be fine."

"Come on in."

Greg had not known what to expect. He had heard about the Freudian couch but now found himself sitting in an easy chair facing the doctor sitting opposite him.

"So, Greg, tell me what brings you to me?"

Greg began by explaining that it was hard to explain and then realized that that made no sense. As he paused, Dr. Hicks smiled and said that it usually was.

"But one day, you said to yourself, 'I need to get some help.' What was going through your mind when you came to that decision? Something made you pick up the telephone and call Dr. Saunders, who referred you."

"I felt trapped," said Greg. "Trapped and bored and burned out. I guess it's what people mean when they say they're depressed."

"The term 'depressed' covers a lot of territory and has a lot of symptoms. Loss of appetite, difficulty sleeping or too much sleeping, persistent anxiety, hopelessness…many things."

There was a silence—a long pause. Greg soon learned that that was what happened in this place. It was up to him to talk.

"Hopelessness. If I have to choose one word, that would be it."

Saying that word was like taking the stopper out of a tank. Suddenly, everything flowed, and he could not stop. Getting tenure, and then what? Living in Mayfield and never being able to get away from work, even in the supermarket, even in the gym…

"Well, Greg, our time is up for today. Is next week at the same time good for you? You can go out this other door."

In the following three weeks, the gush continued, but now Dr. Hicks interrupted from time to time, orienting Greg's tale, sometimes in ways that Greg found disconcerting. Why, for instance, did the psychiatrist want to hear about Greg's publications? About his travels? About Volker Baum?

The next session, their fifth, had to be rescheduled because of a heavy snowfall that shut down almost everything. However, it could not stop the fraternities from building the ice sculptures that were the signature of the annual Thor-Fest, the Viking-themed winter carnival that had been a Thornton tradition since 1932. Although classes were canceled, and roads were impassible to motor vehicles (except for snowmobiles), many administrators managed to get to their offices on cross-country skis.

Two weeks after the Thor-Fest, there was a feeling of a real thaw coming as Greg pulled into the parking lot for the rescheduled appointment. It was quite different from those that preceded. This time Dr. Hicks did most of the talking.

"Greg, you weave together a set of fascinating narratives. It does not surprise me that your research and publications all concern narrative in some way—stories in paintings, sculptures depicting a dramatic moment, stories about the lives of artists. And then, too, you often have stories about your students and colleagues. And yet, I have a feeling that you are avoiding the most important stories, the ones about Gregory Byrne."

Greg immediately objected that he had told lots of stories about himself. He said he felt that the more he talked, the more he realized how self-centered he was.

"Of course, Greg. We are all 'self-centered.' I can only see through my eyes and hear with my ears, and that's true for you. But your narrative, overall, is about a man carried along by fate. Extraordinary things happen to you and around you. I'm not denying that you are active. Indeed, you seem to be on a micro level, exceptionally active and busy all the time: papers, articles, book projects, foreign programs, committees, classes, fighting the good fight in college politics, mastering the minutia of administration. My God, it's exhausting to listen to you! I'm amazed that you can even spare an hour each week to come to see me. But what has Gregory Byrne *decided* about his life?"

Silence. Greg sat there stunned by this way of summarizing what he had been saying for weeks.

"One thing that often happens in psychotherapy is that the patient tries to seduce the therapist. Sometimes, that seduction is sexual, but other times, it takes the form of trying to get the therapist to be mesmerized by the web of illusions that make up the patient's own account of her or his life, illusions that have not been conducive to happiness. Your storytelling is the most multifaceted, cultured, and sophisticated I have ever seen. And I've been in practice for twenty-eight years."

"Now, perhaps you have noticed that I am not inclined toward the prevalent Freudian way of packaging people's neuroses. But here, I find it irresistible to mention a few salient points, or rather people, in what you have told me. Volker Baum and Ruth Baum are all over, from start to finish. Heck, you even have taken their name—or rather, because everything essential about you is deeply passive—it has been *conferred* upon you. On your business card that you gave me, I read "Gregory Byrne, Volker and Ruth Baum Associate Professor of the Humanities. You present yourself, essentially, as Gregory Byrne-Baum."

Greg felt a strong urge to shout, "Bullshit!" But the word didn't come out. He realized he only made a gasping sound.

"So what would old Sigmund say? He would note that you have avoided telling me anything about your actual mother and father, except that your mother died when you were still a student and that you are estranged from your father because he disapproved of your choice of a career. And then, you come to Thornton, and you find—guess what?— you have a father figure, conveniently deceased so that you can take his place. And you have a mother figure, one who plays the role well. You have given this Oedipal narrative an appropriately 'Byrnean' twist in that you did not have to kill your father; he was already dead. Once again, you did not do it. It just *happened* to you."

Greg sat there, feeling a creeping chill throughout his body and a slight feeling of nausea. He had a strong sense of *déjà vu*.

"The story is embellished by a hall-of-mirrors effect. The Volker figure (it almost sounds like 'father figure') leads to another father figure, whom you share (so that Volker is both father and brother), this Anthony Blunt, who turns out in real life to be a spy, so that he is the bad father who takes the symbolic place of your own estranged father, whom you have written out of your life. And the mother figure is reflected in another significant person in your story, Anja. She is your age and, therefore, a more believable sexual and amorous partner, but as you described your encounter, she is the one who took charge and wrapped you with care and guidance when you felt yourself an 'orphan' in that Institute in Florence. And then, it would be interesting to know if anyone has ever suggested to you that you might be 'paranoid.' That would be something I'd expect with your level of passivity. It's not that you are psychically passive. Your mind seems quite active in collecting, stocking scraps of the life around you that you find puzzling. This is characteristic of paranoia—a high level of story-making activity. And then you try to stretch the scraps and twist them and hook them together like a braided rug to make some larger pattern. Perhaps that inclination is what powers your long-standing interest in visual art. So you strive actively to find pattern (and succeed repeatedly) while in terms of your most intimate and important relationships, you drift along passively—feeling sorry for yourself."

But that's all we have time for today. Think about what I've said, and we can follow from there next week."

Greg left the office and sat in his car in the parking lot for a while. The psychiatrist had dropped a bomb on his mental museum. He felt stunned. His mind went back to the day in May 1972 when he first heard of the position at Thornton. He could understand the mention of paranoia. If he had been more religious, he might have spoken of "the hand of God." But he had always considered himself the opposite kind of person. When he heard, time after time, the banal assertion, "Everything happens for a reason," he was always tempted to say, "You can invent a reason for everything."

By the following week, Greg was ready to engage the psychiatrist with objections. Not that he wanted to fight back. After all, the purpose was to find a way out of his situation, and he had no ideas of his own about how to better his life. But he needed to find out from Dr. Hicks how that interpretation was going to get him unstuck. And that's the question he now asked.

"It looks to me, Greg, that the answer is obvious. Some people might even say (with exasperation) that you paid a shrink to tell you something that your common sense could have shown you. You need to take more initiatives to break away from this pattern. You feel trapped at Thornton. Don't wait for someone to write with a job announcement or an invitation to interview. Put yourself out there. Find something. Get away from here! And if there are no professorships, there must be positions in museums, foundations, or fine arts publishing. You're an intelligent man. Have faith in your abilities. Take a leap of faith!" Greg immediately recalled Irene's advice to go "bungee jumping."

In the course of this conversation, Greg felt increasingly positive and hopeful. It had not been a waste of time to come. However, it was a real stretch to see Anja as a mother figure. She was a warm and helpful person, but it was not his fault that they had broken up. She was the one who left him, he pointed out.

"That's your way of telling the story, Greg. And maybe you are right. I wasn't there. I haven't read all the letters you say the two of you exchanged, but I have a feeling that Anja may have felt you didn't make enough effort, that you weren't reliable or committed or enthusiastic enough."

That was their last session. The rest of the work—the rest of his life—was up to Greg now.

35

The Empty House

AT FIRST, ON that Friday in March 1981, Greg thought it might be just a stomach "bug." Bogart's usually robust appetite abated. He would sometimes not finish the canned food that Greg put in his bowl, even when Greg started serving smaller portions. Then, he stopped altogether. He drank lots of water but no food, wet or dry. On that Friday, Greg knew he needed to call the vet. Alcott Snow's assistant said that the doctor would be back on Monday and suggested a veterinary practice in Burlington that could take urgent cases. Greg got a Saturday afternoon appointment and got his small furry companion into his travel box. That was usually a chore. Greg had always had to sneak the box from its storage place into a place closer to Bogart—the kitchen or Greg's study, for instance—and then snatch the dozing cat and whisk him into the box before he could react. Bogart made alarmingly little resistance this time, though, remaining inert in Greg's arms even after seeing the box. As they drove north on I-89, Bogart was frighteningly quiet.

The veterinary clinic on St. Paul Steet was in a building that must have been a primary school once, repurposed as space for a number of small businesses. Besides the veterinary practice, there was the Salon de Nails, a loan office, a tobacco shop, and a vacant space. The stench of some cleaning product hung in the air. Greg carried Bogart into the clinic and immediately had doubts. There was something neglected about the waiting area where two other pets, one a large dog and the other a young cat, were waiting with their owners. Despite his misgivings, Greg tried to persuade himself that his bad feeling was irrational. He was worried, he reasoned, and so he tended to be spooked by little things. The vet was surely competent, but her assistant was just too busy to clean up the waiting room.

The wait was long. He forgot to bring something to read. The tattered hunting and golf magazines did not hold his attention, and the other people waiting did not seem interested in talking. But a little redheaded girl shyly showed Greg her pet stuffed toy lizard. The man who was assisting the vet finally called Greg's name. The examining room looked even dirtier than the waiting room, and now he wished he had not brought Bogart here. Greg took his lethargic cat out of the carrier and put him on the raised examining table. There was a small animal scale on the counter for weighing cats, and Greg assumed that Bogart would be weighed, but the vet did not do that. She looked at Bogart's mouth, then pushed on his abdomen. That snapped the cat out of his lethargy, and he made a muted meow of protest. Then the vet said, "It's a stomach thing that's going around among cats here. I'll give you some antibiotics. It should clear up in two days. You can go back out into the waiting room, and I'll have Devon come out with the pills and your invoice. You can pay with a check."

And that was that. The vet left the examining room by another door, and Greg put Bogart back in his carrier. They were soon back on the highway towards Mayfield, and he just hoped that the vet was right, but he did not have a good feeling. Back at home, Greg got the first pill down Bogart's throat. It was shortly after five. He would have to set an alarm for 1 AM for the next dose, and then it would be easier to administer the 9 AM one. Bogart drank a lot of water after taking the pill but, not surprisingly, did not yet show any change in his appetite.

On Sunday, Greg walked to Westman's drug store to get the *New York Times*. He alternately read the newspaper and reviewed his notes for Monday's class. Bogart dozed next to the new Vermont Castings wood stove. Greg was worried but took comfort in having his companion next to him on the sofa. There, he could watch the cat's slow breathing and reach out from time to time to stroke its back, avoiding the sensitive abdomen. Perhaps the medication was just slow to take effect.

By the evening, though, Greg was frantic. Although Bogart did not whimper or complain, he was eating nothing, and the medication had no noticeable effect. The thought that Alcott Snow would be back in his office the next day was a comfort, but he was a popular vet. Would he have any time to see the very sick kitty?

At eight o'clock on Monday, Greg got Alcott Snow's office on the phone. There *was* an opening, at 2 PM. That was exactly the starting time of Greg's AH 1 course, and in all these years, he never canceled a class for sickness. His priority was clear: it was a life or death matter for Bogart. He would call the office to cancel class. Time crawled through the morning. Greg was in a state of extreme anxiety mixed with occasional spasms of hope. Most of all, he was cursing the loss of time. This was the fourth day. Bogart was surely weakened by the lack of food. And would the disease have progressed irreversibly?

To console him, there was Bogart himself. Despite his lethargy, he seemed to sense that Greg needed him. He pressed his warm little body up against Greg, and several times he looked into Greg's eyes and then touched his cheek with his paw.

Finally, they were at the office. Bogart allowed Dr. Snow to lift him out of the carrier and then lay sleepily on the cat scale. He had lost a quarter of his weight since his annual examination six months before. His heartbeat was fast, and he had a slight fever. When his abdomen was touched, he shrieked in pain.

The vet went into exquisite detail to enumerate the many possible explanations for the symptoms. The emergency vet in Burlington had clearly done no good at all. "Apparently, the practice has changed hands. I'll need to find somewhere else to send patients when I'm not available," said Dr. Snow. "But at least she did no harm except to waste some time. Is it an obstruction? Or is it a tumor? Or is it irritable bowel syndrome? We need an X-ray to start and then probably a biopsy."

Greg was not happy to have to go back to Burlington for the x-ray at a larger veterinary practice, but he was grateful, at least, that they were willing to fit Bogart into their schedule on an emergency basis. The technician stayed late, and Greg left with the x-rays at 7:15. Dr. Snow would see them the next day. The technician could not say anything about the results. He just took pictures. But as Greg sat in the parking lot, holding the large plastic sheets up to the windshield to get enough light to see anything, he saw a large lump in what he knew must be Bogart's abdomen.

At noon, he returned to Dr. Snow's clinic with Bogart in his carrier. Greg was now desperate. It had been so long since Bogart had eaten. He had dropped off the images that morning with the secretary, and as he arrived, he hoped that the vet would have had some time to look at them.

But when he entered the examination room, Greg saw the look on Dr. Snow's face.

"Greg, it's certainly a tumor—a large one. We can do a biopsy if you wish, but I do not recommend it. If the tumor is malignant, at this point there will be no hope. If the tumor is benign, we could remove it, but the operation itself will be so destructive that the cat will probably not survive. I think that it is time to say goodbye."

They were silent for a long while.

"So, really, there's no choice?" asked Greg. "Either way, I lose Bogart and either way I make him suffer."

"Either way, we lose Bogart. But if we put him to sleep, it will be painless, I promise you."

"Painless for him," said Greg.

"Yes, painless for him."

Bogart lay on the table, drowsy but looking at Greg. The two of them just stared into one another's eyes until the injection sent the cat into a peaceful sleep. Greg kept his hand on Bogart's little furry chest, feeling the heartbeat. And then came a second injection. And Greg's fingers felt the small beating heart slow and stop.

Greg returned home with Bogart in his carrier. He called Ruth with the news. She suggested that they bury Bogart in her garden. Greg knew at once what to do. He went to his bedroom and opened the drawer with his sweaters. He took out an old, much-worn green pullover. On the sleeves were holes and other signs of a cat's nibbling. It had been Bogart's favorite sweater. He loved the texture, and Greg had the idea that when Bogart licked, chewed, and sucked on it, he was somehow recalling how he related to his cat mama.

Greg wrapped the small remains in the sweater and then went to the cellar, where he found an old wooden wine crate. He put the body in the crate. He wished he had something to put over the top, but perhaps Ruth would have something.

Then he drove to Okrent Lane and put Bogart to bed for the last time, in the dark, loamy soil of Ruth's garden.

Toward midnight, Greg returned home to a silent, empty house. Bogart had accompanied him through all those years of suspense and anguish as Greg struggled to establish himself at Thornton. They had been brothers in arms. Bogart had been there when Greg returned from Florence, with him in Boston, on the desk as Greg wrote, and had made the house on Welldon Street come alive. And now Greg felt a desolate, throbbing loneliness in the silence.

36

So Full of Life

EASTER IN MAYFIELD was not a flowery feast, except for the indoor flowers or the ones people bought at Mayfield Blooms to give their hosts. On April 11, 1982, there was still frost on the ground, though no snow except in the shade of the evergreen trees. Ruth had an indoor garden next to her studio, and that is where Greg joined Ruth, Larry, Moira Elliot, and (a surprise!) his former student Carla Ledyard, who had come up to Mayfield from Boston "on a whim," she said. She and Ruth knew one another from church and she was staying with Ruth. Greg had brought bread, as agreed, two loaves of sourdough made with a starter that Moira had given him several years before. The years were passing now so quickly that it was hard to keep track.

"Soon, we'll be celebrating your first decade at Thornton," said Larry.

"It was about this time of year that I first heard about the opening and sent in my application," said Greg.

"We're all so happy you did, Greg dear," said Ruth. "I cannot even imagine Thornton without you."

"I certainly can't," said Carla. "You were my favorite teacher ever."

"Well, we have all made *our* Thornton what it is, and other people have *their* Thornton, made up out of all the courses they took, the friends they made or failed to make, and the moment they came and left."

"That's our Greg," said Moira. "Waxing philosophical!"

"I heard you buried Bogart here," said Carla. "Could I see where?"

Greg and Carla went out into the garden and found Bogart's spot. Even though spring had not yet begun in earnest, they could see that the mock orange Ruth had planted next to the cat's resting place had made it through the winter.

"It's hard to believe that it was a year ago that I lost him."

During the meal, they talked about lots of things, including Greg's new responsibilities in his tenured position. Larry asked about Carla's experiences moving up the curatorial hierarchy at the MFA in Boston. Now, she had assistants working under her supervision. All the offices had new IBM personal computers. She predicted that all the department offices at Thornton, and perhaps each faculty member, would soon be using them. "There's a screen, like on a television, and a keyboard, like a typewriter. We find it useful for storing information about our collections, but unfortunately, there is no way to display images in color." She sometimes missed the quiet days in Mayfield.

The meal was cheerful, warm, and friendly.

Carla was leaving the following morning to return to Boston, and she made Greg promise to call her in advance before his next trip. Greg went home feeling happier than he had in a long time, even though his house still felt deserted.

On Easter Monday, there were no courses. It was another sunny day, and Greg spent the morning getting the screens out of the garage to hose and brush. By the time they were clean enough, he was soaked. That was enough work for the day. The window screens would go up on the following Saturday. After a shower, he spent the rest of the day reading an Italian novel, *A ciascuno il suo*, a gift from Larry and Moira. It was a relaxed, cozy weekend.

On Tuesday, he returned to work and reviewed his notes and readings for a new course, a seminar on Rococo, which met late Wednesday afternoon.

At 11, the phone rang. Afterwards, Greg recalled a sense of foreboding and recalled that he had hesitated to pick up the receiver. But did he really? Or was that his way of projecting backward all the darkness that followed in his life?

He heard Moira's voice. She sounded frantic—Moira, ever the most serene.

"Greg, I'm calling with horrible news. It's Ruth. They're taking her in an ambulance to Burlington. At the local hospital, they said there was nothing they could do. I knew that you would want to know. To the emergency department on Colchester Avenue. Larry and I are leaving now. We'll talk more later."

Greg's hands were trembling as he put the phone down. He had just seen Ruth, not even two full days before. So full of life! He had a class to go to, but he could not do it. Even if he stayed and showed up in Wellman Hall, his mind would be elsewhere. He phoned Olivia, who had replaced Jean in the department office, to say that he would have to cancel his class for the day because of a personal emergency.

He got shoes on, grabbed his old leather jacket, and drove out Main Street to I-89. Even though he thought he was going slowly, he realized that the flashing blue lights on the State Police cruiser behind him were for him. He pulled over to the shoulder and waited with his motor off. The officer—a policewoman—came from her cruiser behind him and asked him if he knew he was going 80 miles per hour in a 65-mile-per-hour zone. She asked for his driver's license and the registration. Greg gave her the documents and started to say that he was driving to the hospital.

"Save that for the judge, Mr. Byrne. You don't look sick to me."

"It's not me, officer," he replied. "It's a friend in the emergency room."

He realized his words would not have any weight as he tried to choke back his tears. But they came anyway.

"I'm sorry," the officer said. "It must be a very good friend."

She handed him back his documents and then said, "Look, I can't let you go 80, but you follow me. I'll have my lights on, and when we exit the ramp at South Burlington, we'll be able to get through the intersections faster."

He followed the cruiser all the way to the emergency room turnoff. The cruiser's lights went off, and it left. There was a special parking area marked "Emergency Room Parking only." Greg parked there, went to the intake desk, and asked for Ruth Baum.

"Are you family?" asked the woman at the desk.

"Yes," said Greg.

"Ms. Baum is in the critical unit. Go over there to your right, down that corridor, and follow the red line."

Moira and Larry were in the crowded waiting area with its bleak lighting and hard plastic chairs. Moira had clearly been crying, and Larry was pale and shaken. Seeing that Greg was joining the Elliots, a young man yielded his chair to Greg.

Moira explained that Ruth's neighbor, Mary-Elizabeth Herndon, had called with the news. Mary-Elizabeth had seen the rescue squad and the police car pull into Ruth's driveway. The policeman was pounding on the front door, and she knew it must be an emergency, so she ran over with the spare key that she had. Mary-Elizabeth went in with the rescue squad, and they found Ruth lying on the floor in the kitchen with the telephone receiver dangling near her. She was alive but unconscious. The policeman said that Ruth had dialed the emergency number, but when the dispatcher answered, she heard the caller making some noises but could not make out words. They quickly traced the call and sent assistance. At the Mayfield emergency room, they took one look and sent the ambulance to Burlington. That was all Moira knew.

They waited for a while. It must have been close to an hour. Then a nurse in green scrubs came out and asked, "Someone here with Ruth Baum?"

Moira, Larry, and Greg leaped up.

"She's still unconscious. The doctors say it won't last long, but if you want to be near her, come now."

They crowded into the space next to Ruth's bed. Curtains separated it from the beds on both sides, and there were monitors on a rolling stand and a pole with an IV drip bag with a line to Ruth's left arm. Her eyes were open and moved a little but were not focused on anything.

A "vascular accident" was what the doctor called it. Ruth stopped breathing at 4:26, two days after Easter.

In the following weeks, Greg managed to get through his classes. The students could see that he depended on them to keep discussion going. They rose to the occasion since they knew he was in distress for some reason. A paralegal called from the Thibodeau law firm to say that they held Ruth's will and that they were calling because he was named as executor. They asked him to come to obtain the will. He could decide whether he wished them to assist him or instead to find another attorney.

The will was a short document. After naming Gregory Byrne as executor, the will left him Ruth's house and all its contents (with exceptions to be specified in subsequent paragraphs) along with a substantial sum of money for the future upkeep and repair of the house during his lifetime. If he should wish to relinquish the property, or upon his death, the house would become the property of Thornton College for the purpose of housing visiting lecturers or invited faculty. Under the category of exceptions came all portraits of people still alive. All identifiable models should be given the option to take possession of their portrait or portraits.

The summer of 1982 was a melancholy one. During many hot days, Greg and a couple of students he hired to help him went through Ruth's possessions and determined what was to be given to a charity, what to be sold, and what to throw away. Greg made sure that all papers and most of the books were packed carefully in bankers' boxes and stored in the large attic. He would go through them another time. He advertised the house for rent to faculty or students with good references, noting that the studio area and the attic were not part of the rental.

In August, he welcomed a British couple who would be visiting for 1982-83. He showed them how everything worked and gave them the keys.

No longer would he spend evenings on Okrent Lane.

37

Tabled

WITH RUTH'S DEATH in April, Greg had lost two companions in the space of a year. As the fall term of 1982 began, he could not flee from the emptiness of his own house to Ruth's warm, always welcoming home. With those two dear beings gone, there were too many others, less benevolent, who surrounded him like watchers. Mayfield was a panopticon. Florence, Paris, and even New Haven shone in his memory as places of release and euphoric anonymity.

One person with whom he shared some of these thoughts, Charlie Woodruff, told him that he empathized deeply. That he and his wife also felt that Mayfield was like a *Lager*. They had spent a sabbatical year in Rome fifteen years before, and on returning, they had both fallen into a deep depression. It took more than two years to rise above the gloom. Greg asked why they had not gone away more often. He was a distinguished historian. Charlie must have had, Greg was sure, other sabbaticals, more grants, invitations to be visiting professor. Charlie's answer was chilling. It even seemed insane.

"When we returned from Rome, we decided never to leave Mayfield again. As long as we're here, life is in some ways bearable. But we know we could never again survive the shock of reentry."

Worries about work and other satisfactions seeped into Greg's life to fill the void—trivial things now loomed absurdly in his days. In his now obsessive fixation on the quotidian low-grade hostilities of the college, Greg realized that he was now filling his emotional void with an addiction. If he continued, he would never do anything else. He would become like Frank Kellenberger and his joy would not come from teaching, not come from publishing, not come from discussions of ideas or paintings.

For years, he had found his bearings in a highly factionalized department. He had even become a master at controlling essential decisions. Early on he realized that investing time to understand *Robert's Rules* would someday pay off. He observed virtuoso examples of policy warfare on the faculty executive committee. Few people in his own department bothered to learn those tedious technicalities. Greg, however, knew what you could amend and what not. What votes took precedence over others. What was a friendly amendment and what not. How to insist on the agenda and how to deviate from it. When you could speak and when not. At first, before his third-year review, people just thought of him as a technician, a resource they could call upon. Later, even before he came up for tenure, many began to be somewhat intimidated. Greg could recall the turning point. There was a motion that he particularly disliked, but he realized that a simple frontal attack would not work. He was sure that he would lose a plain up-or-down vote. Carefully avoiding any strongly negative comments on the motion, he suggested that they improve it. He moved an amendment, taking care that it filled all the requirements of amendments. It passed. And then he mentioned one other thing that they could do, and he moved another amendment that passed. There was one last thing that he brought forth. It only involved removing one word in the final sentence of the motion. That passed. Then he called for the question on the motion as amended. It was only at that point that the colleague who had put the matter on the agenda and made the original motion realized what had happened. Just before the vote (and out of order), he exclaimed with great surprise, "Wait! There's nothing left!"

And he was right.

But still, that was nothing compared to the situation Greg now faced. There was a move afoot to weaken the requirements for the art history major. Fewer courses in the department were to be required. Students could have courses taken in other departments counted. The changes for the minor were even worse. A minor in "Art History" would now require only a light dusting of knowledge—not even a frosting, not even a patina, hardly even a coating, just a couple of squirts, a spritz of art terminology and, *voilà*, "Minor in Art History" would appear on the transcript.

From years of experience, he knew how to count the votes in advance. There were certain "hard" factions and certain soft alliances, and then the lukewarm colleagues, the undecided, and the ones who blew in the wind. It was important to prepare the meeting in the course of casual conversations, during lunches and over coffees. This time, he knew that some people, even on "his" side, would go along with the proposal. He was desperate. He was in despair.

On the day of the meeting, he almost didn't show up. Since it was going to pass, let them do it without him. In future years, he could say, "Don't blame me. I warned you." But he had never shirked a department meeting. And so he walked into the room, ready to bow his head, be one of the few to vote "no," and then go have a drink.

But then, as he sat there, something unheard of came into his mind. It would be his masterpiece. Suppose he decided to be *in favor* of the proposal? Suppose he decided to be *much more in favor* than the people who had invented that…that piece of shit?

His mood brightened. He sat there cheerfully waiting for Jay Curran to call the meeting to order. Opposite him in the seminar room on the north side of Thornton Hall were most members of the enemy faction. Most of "his" people and a few drifters were on his side of the table.

When Jay started the meeting, Greg called for the orders of the day. That was totally unnecessary because there was no indication that they were about to deviate from the agenda, but it would spook people. It would make them think that he was ready to play hardball. Once the agenda was then formally announced, he raised his hand.

"I move to accept the proposal to revise the requirements for the major and for the minor in Art History. And, if my motion is seconded, I request the privilege of being the first to speak."

Everyone—everyone—looked as if they had not heard properly.

Jay turned to him and asked, "Greg, did you move to *accept* the proposal?"

"Yes, I did."

There was a pause, and then Jay asked if anyone wished to second the amendment. Kenman said simply, "Second."

The floor was now Greg's, and he pulled out all the stops. He admitted that he had been telling people he had reservations about the proposal and that he had, in fact, been adamantly opposed. Everyone he had discussed the matter with knew that he thought it was one of the worst ideas that had come along. But having thought more about it, he realized that this was a creative idea and that it gave the department enormous advantages going forward. He thanked Kenman for his initiative in putting this together and for thinking in such detail about these complex changes. And he pledged to work hard to implement them.

He knew that he had never spoken with more enthusiasm or with more cheerfulness. People clearly felt the energy in his words.

It was eerily still. No one spoke against the motion. And no one else spoke in favor of the motion. He had the impression that they all wondered what he was up to. He surmised that some of them thought he had detected something in the text that he would be able to exploit when the occasion came. Others didn't know what to think.

Then Emily Latouraine raised her hand and said, "I move to table the motion."

After a brief pause, Jay asked, "To table *sine die*?"

She said, "Yes."

And every single one, except Greg, voted to table.

It never came off the table. The whole proposal exists now only the files of the Thornton College Department of Art.

Of course, he was happy. He was proud of himself. He had never played it better.

That evening, he decided that he would leave Thornton.

That he would devote himself to art history. That he would burn his copy of *Robert's Rules*. That he would say goodbye to Otter Creek and Main Street Mayfield. That he would become a different, and better, person.

38

"Et in Arcadia ego…"

H E SAT IN the cool shade of Ruth's studio. The faint scent—the beloved scent—of her painting still lingered, as did Greg. Now, in the last year of the twentieth century, it was so many years, so many *decades*, since he first arrived as a young man so tender and unformed that it now seemed to him that he had been a child.

From outside, he heard Anja calling Agata and Markus. They were playing with their kittens, Bogart Junior—called simply Junior—and Sunshine. Anja would be driving them with some of their Mayfield friends out to the pond. For years, this summer sojourn had been something to look forward to, just as much, really, as their Christmases in Malmö, but quite different. In Sweden, they could see their grandparents and practice their Swedish. And instead of the pond, they had the sea—but no swimming. They rarely went to Sweden in the summer. Anja would have liked to travel back there more often in the milder season. But she understood

Greg's need to see about the house—about Ruth's house, now his. At least, that was the practical reason or the pretext for coming. At a deeper level, Greg wished to keep in touch with the place where he spent those intense, anxious, joyous, angry, happy, peaceful, suspenseful days. That medley of feelings that returned to him now in an attenuated, nostalgic way.

One decisive event that Greg and Anja celebrated every June was the chance meeting that had brought them back together. In 1990, they were both at a conference precisely in the same place where they had first seen one another when, on that fall day in 1977, Greg had walked into the Kunsthistorisches Institut. Greg was in Florence, six years after leaving Thornton, to chair a session that he and Carla Ledyard had organized on programmatic mural series. It turned out that after heaping scorn on the Puvis de Chavannes murals in the Boston Public Library, she had decided it was a good idea to bring some attention to that neglected painter. The Boston MFA chose not to do the retrospective she was hoping for, but with Greg's encouragement, she sought out some scholars who would contribute to a collective volume (her first) about Puvis. The roundtable in Florence would be the first public tryout for the project.

When the final program arrived in his mail, Greg saw Anja's name. His immediate reaction was to try to avoid the scene altogether—someone else could chair the session, after all. But he had promised Carla to support her in this project, and he finally decided that he was a grown-up, Anja was a grown-up, and everyone would be polite and calm.

When Anja and Greg reconnected at the conference back in Florence, the magic was not gone. Even though they had not written—how hard that was to believe!—they rediscovered that they were still soulmates. They found that in their minds, they had continued to "write" letters that they never sent. Their wedding was in Malmö, with a honeymoon in Stockholm, where Greg never got to live while Anja was a student. He never got to share that crowded apartment, but Jude and Ping were at their wedding.

For Anja and Agata and Markus the summers in Mayfield meant something quite different than they did for him. It was always for them only summer and a holiday. They had none of the memories…and they never felt like ghosts. But Greg was generally a happy ghost.

In his essay "Of practice," Montaigne taught about the sweetness of dying. We cannot learn to die, he pointed out; that is, we cannot practice doing it until we know how to do it right. We do not need to because it is the one single thing that all humans can do flawlessly. No one had ever failed to die. Montaigne fell from his horse and appeared, to those accompanying him, to be dead. In his semi-conscious state, he felt his soul readying itself to leave his body. It did not leave on that occasion, but he felt—he believed—how easy and even sweet that moment would be.

Had Greg outdone Montaigne? Had he managed to practice dying? He sometimes thought that leaving Thornton had been a kind of death or at least an exercise, a practice. When the moving van arrived to take all his belongings from Welldon Street in the summer of 1984, he thought he was going to die. He felt the vomit rising but managed to control it. The nausea subsided. He remembered thinking: "What have I done? How can I depart from here?"

To leave, that was possible. To return, however, was not. Not really. Which of them was the ghost, the *revenant*, the fetch? Was it the young Gregory Byrne? Or the middle-aged man who, strangely, had the same name?

How could one answer that question? Ghosts are mostly invisible. Rarely do people see them, and at such moments, they are called "apparitions." When Greg walked into Thornton Hall or into Chandler Library or into Drew's or into Perkins Center, *no one saw him*. They did not say, "Hi, Greg!" They did not say "Good morning Mr. Byrne!" They did not even say, "Oh, it's you."

It was the places that consoled this invisible Greg. The Topos was still there, and with it came the memory of the day when Bogart had found him. And Main Street was still there. One summer, Greg noticed that Mayfield had begun installing teak benches on the wider parts of the sidewalk. They had little metal plaques with the names of people to whose memories they were dedicated. One day Greg noticed such a bench near the entrance to Drew's. The plaque was inscribed with the name of someone he remembered from a committee. The man was a gruff economist. He and Greg always seemed to be on the opposite side of issues, but sometimes they had lunch together. Mugg Clement. Teak is a durable wood, but it does not last forever. Greg supposed that some year in the future, this bench would be removed and would be replaced with another with a different name on it. The current bench would have served its purpose. It was destined to last about as long as there were people to remember Mugg.

In the summer of 1997, on returning to Vermont, Greg learned that Thornton Hall was scheduled for "renovation." That was what it was called. However, when Greg learned about the plans, he understood that the building would be gutted. Only the shell would remain to preserve, for the faithful alumni, the illusion that Thornton was eternal, preserving their student days in a bucolic, timeless world. That summer, Greg made a last visit to the fourth floor, where he still found the Art History office. Everything looked a bit shabby and worn. Apparently, it was not worth repairing things that would soon be blasted and bulldozed out of existence. He had to explain to the secretary who he was. She then let him browse the faculty mailboxes, where he found that there was only one current member of the department who had been there in his day, a young man who had arrived during Greg's last year. That man was away for the summer, however. But Greg saw the names of Wanda, Jay Curran, Bill Farrington, and several others on a list next to the mailbox used for emeriti. The secretary said that none of them lived near Mayfield and that their mail was forwarded to them. Greg learned that Douglas Sykes had moved to a retirement community in the South. Kenman had died several years before. And Larry Elliot had died, though Moira lived in a nursing home near her daughter in Colorado. When he asked if he could see his old corner office, the secretary told him that she could open the door for him to look, but for reasons of faculty privacy, she could not let him enter.

The office looked radically different. From the photographs on the wall, it was clear that the occupant focused on contemporary twenty-first-century visual art, extending to tattoos and other body modifications. Standing in the doorway under the watchful eye of the secretary, Greg could make out some titles on the bookshelves. Graffiti, digital art, 3D printing, and re-use, were among the words that caught his attention. The view from the window, however, remained timeless. From the threshold where he stood, he could barely see the peak of the roof of the tourist information cabin rolled out for the summer and fall seasons. He thanked the secretary for letting him look, and he walked down to the ground floor and peeked into the meeting room where he had had his great "triumph," that moment when he knew he must leave Thornton. At that great remove in time the event seemed to him high comedy. He left the building knowing that he would not be able to bear seeing the interior in some new configuration.

During the summers, Greg tended to Ruth's garden, especially Bogart's resting place. After surviving many harsh Vermont winters, the original mock orange next to the grave had lived its life, and Greg had planted a new one. Ruth's garden nymph stood nearby during the summer to watch over Bogart, but Greg always took the statue inside before driving south.

Like the shepherds, Greg had lived in Arcadia. Like them, he had tried to comprehend its mysteries. Had there really been any mysteries to comprehend? Or was it all the product of an angst-ridden, overactive, immature imagination?

One day Greg learned that after all these years Brother Damian was still alive, back in his Benedictine monastery. Greg got in touch, and, amazingly, Damian responded.

> *Dear Yale friend,*
>
> *I may well be the complete antithesis now, of the viral, insane person I was at Yale…*
>
> *Thanks be to God!*
>
> *I have since picked up additional degrees in civil engineering and architecture.*
>
> *All in hopes of doing something of the slightest value before I pass.*
>
> *But to no avail.*
>
> *Ad multos annos!*